The Moment I Saw You

Lisa Samson

HARVEST HOUSE PUBLISHERS
Eugene, Oregon 97402

Cover design by Paz Design Group, Salem, Oregon

THE MOMENT I SAW YOU

Copyright © 1998 by L.E. Samson
Published by Harvest House Publishers
Eugene, Oregon 97402

Library of Congress Cataloging-in-Publication Data

Samson, Lisa, 1964–
    The moment I saw you / Lisa Samson.
       p.   cm.
    ISBN 1-56507-759-8
    I. Title.
PS3569.A46673M66   1998
813'.54—dc21

                             97-33298
                                CIP

Printed in the United States of America.

98 99 00 01 02 /BC/ 10 9 8 7 6 5 4 3 2 1

∽

*To Bill & Arlene Samson,
whose love and
encouragement made
my career possible.*

*Thanks for being such
great in-laws
& thank you for Will,
the Love of my life.*

∽

Acknowledgments

Many thanks, first and foremost, to Carolyn McCready of Harvest House. Your belief in me as a writer, and your friendship to me as a woman, mean the world.

To Betty Fletcher—thanks a million.

To Anne Severance—you taught me so much. I enjoyed every minute. Thanks for being so much fun to work with. May the Lord make His face shine upon you.

Lori & Jeff—thanks for reading the rough stuff.

Will, Tyler, Jakey & Gwynneth—you are my world.

Praise to the Father, Son, and Holy Ghost.

One

*H*ere it is, Ms. St. John—a check for thirty million dollars."

"What?" Natalie watched in disbelief as the lawyer across the table held up a slip of paper. His Brooks Brothers suit was a testimony to his exorbitant fees.

She stood instinctually and frowned over at her own attorney who had shot to his feet beside her. "Andy, what's going on here?"

Andrew Gatto shrugged, running a hand through his mop of curly black hair. "Don't know, Natalie. But I could wager a guess." He eyed Wagner knowingly, man to man.

She snapped back to face the attorney and the check. "We agreed on forty million, Mr. Wagner. I find it hard to believe there was a misunderstanding."

Wagner stood to meet her level gaze. He straightened his Burberry tie with a smug grin.

"No misunderstanding, Ms. St. John. Everything else we discussed remains the same. But my client feels that thirty million is more than enough for PluraNet. It's thirty . . . or it's no sale." He turned the check around and laid it on the table between them.

"This isn't the deal I came for." Tone clipped. Expression masked.

"It's more than fair. And since it is the only deal I'm authorized to make, I suggest you take it or leave it."

"Then we have nothing further to discuss." Natalie closed her briefcase with two crisp clicks and pushed in her chair. "You know PluraNet is worth at least forty million. I'll get a fair deal. But it looks like it will have to be from someone other than you, Mr. Wagner. Come on, Andrew," she muttered. "Let's get out of here before I do or say something we'll both regret."

"Right." Andrew shuffled some papers, stuffed them into a portfolio, and followed her to the door.

Wagner moved to bar their retreat. "Let's not be hasty." He attempted a chuckle.

"No way, Wagner. You're not getting off that easy." Natalie walked around him. "You've heard all we have to say." She grasped the knob firmly. "Time is wasting, and I've got a company to sell."

"My client may be willing to negotiate—"

She whipped around to face the overstuffed, well-manicured attorney. "Look, I make it a point not to be rude, but I've had it with you and your client. We took PluraNet off the market because *your client* agreed to pay forty million dollars. We shook hands on it. And where I come from, that means something."

"Come, now, Ms. St. John," Wagner began condescendingly as Natalie plunged her hand into the large pocket of her trench coat, "you and I both know PluraNet isn't worth that much money."

She shoved a copy of The *Wall Street Journal* under his nose. "MeteorNet was sold yesterday. Fifty million. Two-thirds the number of subscribers we have. Your client could have walked away with the deal of the century." She paused, and retrieved the paper. "Let me make one thing clear: PluraNet is for sale again. And if you want to take advantage of the most technically advanced ISP in D.C., you're going to have to cough up another five million."

Wagner drew in his breath, obviously as indignant as Natalie, though not nearly as cool. "You'll never sell it for that!"

She smiled. "Mr. Wagner, you tell your client something for me. We're all headed to the prom; it's up to him to decide if he wants to take the queen." She tugged open the boardroom door, sailed past the receptionist and into the brightly lit hallway.

"Wait!" Wagner yelled, hurrying after her as she pushed the elevator button. "I can have a check for forty million within five minutes."

Natalie had never been so disgusted in her life. "You could give it to me now, Wagner. It's right there in your portfolio." She jammed the down button one more time. "But I've changed my mind. I'm upping the ante. Forty-five million—or I go back on the market. Your client has until 8 A.M. tomorrow to give me an answer. At 8:01, I'll officially be up for sale."

Wagner's face turned ashen. "You're serious?"

"You'd better believe it. These are the nineties. I'd think you would have learned by now not to mess with someone simply because she's a woman." The elevator doors opened.

Thomas Wagner was still shaking his head as the doors slid slowly shut.

"Eight o'clock, sharp!" Natalie said loudly just before the space between them was severed. "You tell him that."

～⁓

Natalie burst through the door of the office building and into the spring rain. "What a jerk! I don't usually go in for name-calling, but this guy—"

Andy looked over at his client, his old friend, the love of his life. He'd promised himself that one day he'd tell her. But for now, he allowed himself the pure pleasure of staring at her fine profile— the long, straight nose; the small mouth; the wavy, auburn hair pulled back by a tortoise-shell clip; the brilliant green eyes, feline in their shape and forthrightness. "Hey, if the shoe fits—"

"You said it!" She stopped, turned on her heel, and looked at Andy. "Do you think they'll call my bluff?"

He scratched his scalp. "No way. You'll get a call at eight o'clock tomorrow morning, and not a second earlier. And it wasn't a bluff. If MeteorNet went for that much, PluraNet can easily go for forty-five. You should've asked for more."

"Nah. It wasn't about the money."

Andy chuckled. "I like to see stuff like that happen to guys like him. The creep."

"If only all lawyers were as nice as you, Andy." She sighed. "Well, now we'll just have to wait for the call—*if* they call."

"They'll call. But, hey, it's only 11:30. Whattaya say we have an early lunch? My treat."

"Fine. But nothing fancy. I'm not in the mood."

"Whatever melts your butter." Andy hailed a taxi and soon they were inching toward the capitol area. Typical Washington day. Typical Washington traffic. Irritated pedestrians leaned out from the concrete curbs, scrutinizing the street for a break in the flow. The exhaust fumes and the gray drizzle rendered them more weary-looking than usual. "The Blue Mirror okay with you?"

"Mmm. I love The Blue Mirror. Meatloaf, mashed potatoes, and hot sandwiches with gravy. And the pies!"

"That sweet tooth is gonna get you in trouble one-a-these days." His New Jersey accent was particularly thick just then as he patted his ample midsection. "I hate people who can eat whatever they want and never gain a pound."

"Me, too," Natalie said, ignoring Andy's fake leer as she retrieved her cellular phone from her briefcase and called her office. "Hi, Gail, what's up? Any messages?"

In fascination, Andy watched her changing expressions, listened to every word. *Natalie.* Was there anyone else like her in the world? He'd known the answer to that question years ago when they'd met in the cafeteria during the second week of their freshman year at M.I.T.

Natalie opened her laptop computer, pulled up her organizer. Her fingers pounded the keyboard with rapid strokes. "Okay . . . okay . . . okay . . . oh, no . . . yeah, that's fine . . . no, not tomorrow night, I'm busy . . . okay . . . hmmm—" she looked up and thought for a moment—"tell him I'll think it over . . . thanks, Gail! I'll be in by 1:30." There was a pause before she added, "Well, then, you just tell Mr. Gates to bug off!"

Andy looked horrified. "Gates? *Bill* Gates? You just told your assistant to tell Bill Gates what?! As your lawyer, I highly recommend that—"

Natalie burst into laughter. "Of course, I didn't! She'd already hung up."

Relieved, Andy loosened his tie as Natalie snapped her phone shut and eyed the screen. "That's one thing I won't miss," she said, "all the calls. I hate talking on the phone."

"The Blue Mirror!" the cabbie piped up as he pulled up to the curb. Andy paid the driver, then scribbled the figure in a small spiral-bound notebook.

On the way into the restaurant, Natalie chuckled. "I saw the meter and how much you tipped that guy. I'll be watching for my next statement from you."

Andy feigned shock. "Would I do that to you? Come on, Nat, we've known each other since we were eighteen."

"Which is exactly why I don't trust you a bit, Andrew Salvatore Gatto!"

He broke into a grin, sliding his lips over his teeth. "I was a mess back then, wasn't I?"

"You weren't called Heathcliff for nothing. And I'm not talking Emily Brontë, either."

They were seated by a petulant young hostess with clothes a bit too nice for her salary level, and without much deliberation over the menu, they both ordered the special. Pot roast, potatoes, carrots, and "lots of gravy," Natalie told the waitress.

"Any way you like it, Ms. St. John." The older woman shoved her pencil back to rest on top of her ear and shuffled away on thick legs cocooned by support hose.

Andy raised his eyebrows again. "I'd forgotten you were a regular here."

"Just call me a sucker for home-style food."

"These days, if it can't be heated up in a microwave. . . . " Andy took a sip of his iced tea. "Now for the 24,000-dollar question."

"It's the 64,000-dollar question, Andy."

He waved a hand. "Whatever. The question is, what are you gonna do now? This ISP is your life!"

"That's the problem. Hooking people up to the Internet is all well and good, and I've enjoyed being a service provider, I really have. It's just time to move on."

"Why? I thought you were in love with D.C."

Natalie sighed. "I'm just tired, Andy. Is that okay? Maybe I want a change of scenery."

"Change of scenery? You? Come on, Natalie, you deal with the best of 'em. What kinda scenery are you yearning for?"

She traced the rim of her coffee cup with her index finger and looked through the window at the snarled traffic, the stressed-out faces of the Washingtonians on their way to stressful jobs. "Mountains, grass, oaks, elms. Flowers in big border gardens. Victorian houses. Mailboxes that aren't stuck to the wall by the front door. Windows not blackened by exhaust . . . windows you can leave open all day, even when you're not home. . . ."

"But look at you! Donna Karan suit, Coach shoes, bag, *and* briefcase. Silk scarf (nice touch, might I add?). Gold jewelry—the real stuff. Highlighted hair and—"

"Hey, you! This is my natural color!" She held out a lock of curly hair, and he watched as she released it to spring back into place.

He felt a little sheepish. "Sorry, Nat. But you get what I'm saying? Personally, I think you should consider traveling awhile. See Europe, China, you know, some exotic place like that."

"Maybe. But right now there's my mother to consider, remember."

"Oh, yeah . . . your mom." He followed her gaze out the window, then spoke a little more gently. "What about . . . *afterward?* We're right back to the 84,000-dollar question—"

"That's *64,*000 dollars, Andy," she corrected him idly.

He waved away her reply. "Whatever. I wanta know what you're going to do with the rest of your life."

"I'm really not sure. But you'll be the first to know as soon as I find out."

Andy shook his head in exasperation, but he knew Nat. She wouldn't say one word until she was good and ready. The hostess appeared just then with a cordless phone. "Ms. St. John? Phone call for you."

"Rats," she mouthed to Andy, then chimed brightly, "Natalie St. John!" She took a sip of water. "Well, of course I understand, Bob. . . . But it's terribly short notice . . . no, no, I don't have other plans, but that isn't the—" Apparently the caller interrupted her, and she rolled her eyes at Andy. "Oh, all right. I'll go. But you owe me one, Senator!" Andy could hear the rumbling baritone laugh reverberating through the upper end of the receiver as Natalie punched the power button.

"Bob Vaughn," she began, with a wry twist of her mouth. "Wants me to go with him to a fund-raiser tonight at the Hyatt."

"Which charity this time? Might be good for business."

"I'm *selling* my business, remember? And the fund-raiser's for pediatric AIDS research."

"Pretty safe cause." Andy couldn't resist a stab of sarcasm.

Natalie rested her chin in her hand and glared at him, her eyes green and glittering.

"What?" Andy asked defensively. "What did I say?"

"That statement you just made is one of the main reasons I want to get out of this town."

~

By seven o'clock that evening the rain had stopped. Natalie regarded herself critically in front of the full-length mirror. It had been a hectic day at PluraNet. Scrambling home, she had only time to snare her hair into a quick, tousled updo. Uttering a prayer of thanks that her favorite evening dress was back from the dry cleaner, Natalie slipped the simple sheath over her slender hips. Classically cut, the heavy silk dress had been serving her well since college, though the luscious, ebony fabric was now set off by diamond earrings and a choker.

"Make-up!" she remembered with consternation, sat down at her dressing table and hastily applied concealer, mascara, blush, and deep red lipstick. Ready at last, she frowned at her reflection, bending over to give her gray cat, Delilah, a few affectionate strokes.

Then she stood up, snatched her hand-beaded purse and wrap from the bed, and with a click of the light switch, started for the stairs. Bob Vaughn expected punctuality, even when someone else was doing him the favor. Besides, the sooner she hit the road, the sooner she could put another boring Washington affair behind her. On the way down, a familiar odor stopped her in her tracks.

Murphy's Oil Soap.

The pungent smell enticed Natalie into the freshly cleaned kitchen, her favorite room in the house. Mrs. Bellows, the cleaning lady, had definitely been there earlier. Her tracks were evident: spotless counters, degreased stove, shining tiles, floors that afforded you your reflection if you cared to bend down that far, sparkling appliances. Despite Andy's casual remark about microwaves, Natalie knew how to cook. She'd learned to prepare a full dinner by the age of twelve—and not because she wanted to. It's what came of being the only child in a single-parent family. Of sharing a house with an exhausted working mother, too tired to move by the end of the day.

On the other hand, there was a certain advantage to such know-how. By the time she entered M.I.T., she could throw a full-scale dinner party, entertaining friends with homemade gumbo, pasta, or chili. That old saying, "The way to a man's heart—" Worked every time. Whether she wanted it to. . . .

Or not.

Through the back door and down the brick path, the sound of her high heels clicked in the darkness. She opened the low door of her racing green Jaguar, slid behind the wheel, and shut herself into the car. The tan rag top was definitely going down on the way home, she decided, knowing her British heritage would get the better of her on such a cool, clear evening. She shoved the stick into first gear and roared out of her driveway. Bob had offered to pick her up, but she had politely declined, preferring to exit the evening on her own terms.

"This is the last time I ever attend a formal function in the name of business, friendship, or anything else," she firmly resolved on her way to the black-tie fund-raiser. "From now on, I'll just send a check!"

But it was more than dressing up and applying three times the amount of make-up she normally used that frustrated Natalie. It was the motive driving these evenings. Andy's statement had been so telling. "A safe cause." These days in Washington, it was almost impossible to follow your conscience. She was tired of being tagged "a narrow-minded right-winger." Tired of apologizing for the fact that she believed abortion was murder. Tired of keeping her mouth shut. Tired of all the games and the posturing. The capitol attitude seemed to filter through most Washington offices, including her own, whether they were run by the government or not. Definitely time to go.

Turning into the underground parking garage (Natalie didn't trust valets), she donned her Washington smile and uttered a silent prayer that at eight o'clock the next morning, the phone would ring and she could put all this behind her.

Senator Bob Vaughn, at forty-five, was aging with the grace of an angry rhino. He greeted her in the lobby. "You look fantastic," he murmured into her ear as they walked into the ballroom together. She recoiled inwardly at the touch of his hand on the small of her back, the way he gazed at her body with a familiarity that wasn't his to assume. The evening went downhill from there.

It was after 11 P.M. by the time Natalie emerged from the underground parking garage, exhausted from thwarting the senator's advances, her jaw aching from the permanent smile.

The top of the car whirred down with the push of a button, but instead of feeling carefree, young and full of adventure, Natalie was numb with dread as the tires took to the road. I-95.

North.

She wasn't going home. A much more important task lay at hand.

Sudden tears blurred her vision, the tail lights of the other cars now red halos before her aching eyes. Instinct kicked in, and she drove as through a heavy downpour. Automatic responses. The memory of the drive just a feeling.

She almost missed the turn.

~⌒~

Machines clicked and beeped, hungry for more medication. The monitors, blipping with slow points of sound, described the patient's heart rate, told that the wasting body was yet living, if only barely. The room was alive with the sounds of dying. In the bed, the patient's thin frame barely supported the covers. The hands, spare and curled, were tucked close to the narrow body. They held nothing. Hadn't for weeks.

Natalie stared, eyes dry now. For some reason she could never cry when she was here at the hospital. She wanted to see each lift of the chest, hear each shallow breath, feel the hope that God might still answer her prayers.

Heal her, please. Heal my mother.

In her chair, she leaned forward, resting her forearms on the bed rail in front of her, wondering why the nurses bothered to click the cold metal barricades into position.

"She probably won't regain consciousness again," came a voice from behind her, warm with sympathy, tinged with a distant sadness. "I'm sorry."

"How much longer?"

Dr. Fauber, a good man and a fine oncologist, shook his head and pulled up the other chair. "Not much, I'm afraid." With a weary hand, he rubbed his reddened eyes beneath the thick lenses of his wire-rimmed glasses. "You'd better notify anyone who might want to say their last good-bye."

"There's no one else—only me."

"What about your father? Wouldn't he want to be here?"

"He left us when I was seven. I haven't heard from him in years."

"I'm sorry about that, too."

She shrugged. "Don't be. I got over it a long time ago."

"Any other relatives?"

"No. Mom was an only child. Like me."

Dr. Fauber sat with her as Natalie's eyes glazed over and she entered another dimension, silently willing her dying mother not to give up, to stay a little longer.

When his pager vibrated, he squeezed her shoulder and left quietly. Natalie didn't hear his departure. That's the way it had been every night for the past week. For she really wasn't here in the room at all; she was dreaming of better times.

Remembering Janet St. John when she had been young, healthy, and beautiful. When the perpetually sad expression would melt into happiness at the sight of her daughter. She remembered sitting on the stool behind the counter of Janet's dress shop, staring with pride at the tall woman who was adored by all her customers.

But mostly Natalie was remembering the evenings, when the hues of day danced closely with the night, and the crimson sky was becalmed by the softer pink of the windblown clouds. They never missed the sunsets. It was then they would talk of God, the Father who never abandoned His own.

"Please, Mom," she whispered. "I need you. Please . . . don't *you* leave me, too."

But there was no response. And the sun had set long ago.

Two

~~~

Frowning, Natalie clicked off the TV. Even one of her favorite old movies hadn't been able to bully away the heaviness in her chest. The funeral was over, everyone was gone, and she was alone. She had endured it all with a tenuous smile, greeting the well-meaning friends and the others who came out of duty. When Andy had suggested they discuss the terms of the will, she'd gently told him, "Tomorrow, And. Tomorrow."

Over the back of the mahogany hall chair was Natalie's coat, where she had slung it earlier. On the floor beside it—and resting on every other conceivable surface in the spacious living room of the townhouse—were potted plants, reminding her of her mother's funeral every time they caught her eye. Giving live plants rather than cut flowers had always seemed a strange sentiment, another way of saying "life goes on." But to Natalie, they were grim tokens of a life that would never be remotely what it was before.

"I chose this little vine because I knew it wouldn't die, dear," sang out one elderly lady, a loyal customer of her mother's dress shop, surely not intending to be cruel.... *it wouldn't die, dear.* She might as well have added, "like your mother did."

All the faces swam before her, hands thrusting out an offering, begging a response. Take these flowers, Natalie, maybe they'll make you feel better. Here's a pound cake. A casserole.... And yet another houseplant to bring the whole thing down to jolting reality. Surrounding you with a refrigerator full of grief and a hothouse jungle of sadness just in case you take a moment to forget you'll

16

never see your mom again, never hold the familiar hand or kiss the lips that had praised and reprimanded too many times to recall.

"Thank you, Mrs. Peters. Thank you, Phyllis. Thank you, Don, Rick, and Mr. Bell."

Callous. It all seemed so unwittingly callous.

Natalie raked her fingers through her disheveled hair. Janet St. John had loved the wind, and the day she was buried had been one of the windiest in recent weeks. Mashing their little black hats on their heads, grabbing their black shawls under their throats, the mourners had attempted to voice their sentiments, but it was pretty obvious that all they could really think of was their hair. And the words were, sometimes thankfully, lost in the rush of air.

Well, of course, her death was not unexpected, was it? Really a blessing. Think of all the suffering the poor dear had to face at the end. It's better this way, hmm?

The poor dear. The poor dear.

Better this way.

Natalie stroked the gray tabby cat, lazing contentedly in her lap. "What now, Delilah?" The faithful pet purred a little louder and freely shared her warmth, which was exactly what Natalie needed just then.

When the mantel clock chimed six, she shuffled wearily into the kitchen to fix herself a pot of tea.

The phone rang. She ignored the old-fashioned ring, hoping whoever it was would think she hadn't returned yet from the funeral. Three rings. Four. She counted as she poured water into the kettle. Five. The gas burner fired to life. Six. Out came the pot from the cupboard. Seven . . .

"What?!" Natalie blurted into the receiver.

"It's me, Natalie. Andy."

"Oh." Her body sagged with relief. "I was afraid it might be one of the ladies from the Junior League."

"Nope. Definitely not a member. And with no plans to join!"

In spite of her utter fatigue, she chuckled and began rummaging through one of the cupboards. Andrew Gatto could relieve her tension like no other person alive. Now, if she could just locate the honey, she might be on the road to an evening that wasn't quite as bad as she had suspected. It was evident he was in his kitchen, as well, judging by the rattles and clanks in the background.

"How are you doing?" he was asking. "You okay?"

"I think so. I realized I hadn't eaten anything since the packets of saltines I fished out of my coat pocket this morning. I'm making myself a pot of tea."

"Well, although everyone says it's best to get on with your life, it isn't that easy, is it?"

"You said it."

"I know your mom was sick for a while, Nat, but that's not much comfort tonight."

Natalie couldn't help but smile. "You know, Andy, you're the first person who's said that. If I hear, 'at least you had time to prepare,' one more time, I'm going to scream. Time to prepare only means more time to grieve beforehand."

"Tell me about it."

"Oh, Andy, you understand all too well, don't you?" she said, recalling that Andy's father had died their sophomore year at M.I.T. Leukemia.

"Yeah, wish I didn't. But if I can give you half as much comfort now as you gave me then, I guess somethin' good's come out of it. Hey, you said you were hungry. Whattabout comin' over here? Ma's makin' a pot of sauce for rigatoni."

"I wondered what that racket was in the background. As much as I appreciate the offer, I think I need to be alone right now. I've got some work to catch up—"

"Natalie! You're not working tonight, are you?"

"Work makes me feel better, And. It always has, you know that."

"Okay. I'm not going to argue with you. I'll bring over some sauce tomorrow. You know Ma—always makes enough to feed the entire neighborhood."

"Only if I can trade it for a couple of these casseroles," she hedged.

"Deal. Listen, Nat, you take care of yourself. Call me if you need anything—anything at all, y'hear?"

She sighed into the phone. "You've always been my good friend, haven't you?"

"Always will be," he assured her. "Hey, *Thoroughly Modern Milly* is on tonight. Isn't that one of your favorite old movies?"

"Uh-huh. Thanks for reminding me and . . . good night, Andy."

"'Nite, Nat."

The line went dead and she was once again detached from the outside world. Great. She hoped to keep it that way. Just to make sure, she gently placed the receiver on the phone table, leaving Delilah to bat playfully at the springy cord.

With the delicate teapot now full and hot, a plate of consolatory cookies baked by a lady from her mother's garden club, and a cream pitcher loaded onto a tray, Natalie plodded up the steps to her bedroom. The design on the stair runner, tacked down by brass dowels, seemed to jump up at her alarmingly in a bizarre juxtaposition of black hands and spiders. She made it to the top before they could keep her there forever, trapped between her belongings upstairs and the houseplants on the floor down below.

The shining walnut grandfather clock in the hallway bonged seven times. At the thermostat outside her bedroom door, she turned up the heat.

Once inside, Natalie stripped off her ever-useful black dress and pantyhose and pulled on her fuzzy green robe and a pair of gray rag wool socks. A dismal March had been tamed by a clear, cool April, and although the days were generally sunny and warmer, the evenings were still chilly.

Into the spare room she trudged, flipped on her computer, and went to work on her final recommendations to the new executives at PluraNet. She had decided, in the limousine on the way to the cemetery, that there would be no going back. The future lay before her like a perfectly ripened pear.

But as the pressure of her flying fingers jarred the keyboard, all she could contemplate was the past. One where no gloomy houseplants covered the floor, no hastily concocted casseroles congested the refrigerator, and no store-bought cookies—arranged on a tray to look homemade—sat in unappetizing splendor on the polished surface of her dining room table.

Eight hours before, her mother's body had descended into the earth, and there was no one left to care what happened to her, one way or the other. Who would send casseroles and houseplants when *she* passed away? No one but good ol' Andy—if he was still around. Not unless things changed drastically.

Still, one simple bouquet of cut daisies stood out in her mind from the rest. From some people she had never met. The card had read: "These were always her favorites." Signed: "The staff at Pleasant Valley Inn." Natalie had already pressed one of the cheerful blossoms between the pages of her Bible.

Pleasant Valley Inn. Oh, yes. She remembered now. Her mother's favorite personal retreat. Janet St. John had spent at least three weeks a year at the quaint, somewhat exclusive inn, an activity she had always kept to herself, usually choosing to visit there when Natalie was at her busiest.

"Oh, Mom," she whispered, remembering a woman who had never been truly happy, who'd done everything out of a sense of obligation or guilt. A woman who had never stopped trying to atone for a marriage that had ended in divorce. Not that Natalie had ever blamed her. After all, George St. John, a geologist teaching at Georgetown and a dashing Englishman, had deserted them for one of his pretty young students. If the divorce was anyone's fault, it was her *dad's,* not her mom's.

And now Janet was gone. Taken at the age of forty-eight by breast cancer.

She and her mother had had their good times together. Lots of them. Traveling . . . the beach . . . shopping . . . wearing big hats and reading together on lawn chairs . . . eating at greasy spoon diners . . . strolling through model houses on Sunday afternoons. But even in the most lighthearted of moments, there was an underlying sadness to the tall, graceful woman with the chestnut hair and the impeccable style. Her wistful smile bespoke a private tragedy, a never-forgotten pain. Natalie grieved her unhappiness almost more than her death.

Still, Janet St. John had been a good mother, and Natalie's sorrow was pure. No mixed emotions. No secret relief that she was gone.

The proposal was written. Natalie pressed *enter* and a few seconds later the laser printer whirred to life and birthed a sheet of paper supporting her inky words. No great fonts or snappy formatting. Just *Courier New* and an extra space between paragraphs.

She slid the pages into a thin plastic binder, tucked it in a pocket of her briefcase, and stood to her feet. The yellow walls faded to a warm, dark gray as she flipped off the light, then hoisted the tray.

It was only 7:30, but through the study doorway, her duvet enticed her with its downy softness, promising an oblivion like no other. Sleep. A drug for the drugless with dreams for those who have lost theirs somewhere along the way.

A new life.

That's what she needed now that the transition period at PluraNet had come to a close, now that Mother had finally yielded to the horrible disease that had tortured her for three long years.

Natalie tugged off her socks and rolled down the comforter, easing her tired body onto the feather mattress. And reaching over to her nightstand, she picked up a book entitled *Love's Undying Mystery*, by Jeanine Beaumont. Natalie's smile was small and sad as her fingers flittered over the embossed cover. Just where her favorite author would take her tonight was still a mystery, but she was ready to be *anywhere* but the lonely bed she had never once shared with anyone.

Now transported into Victorian London, she was soon picnicking in St. James Park, eavesdropping on Lord David Swansea and the stunning French actress Jacqueline François, who were arguing over "what happened last night."

But the journey didn't last long. Fatigue from the sad events of the day crowded her mind, and she put down her book. From the bedside table, Janet's Bible beckoned. Tucked into the pages at Psalm 23, her mother's favorite passage, was a brochure. It was tattered and worn, as if Janet's fingers had sought it frequently during her stay at the hospital, her eyes feasting on the lovely pictures of gardens and grottos, her heart comforted by sweet memories.

Another place, another time. At Pleasant Valley Inn, you will experience life the way it should be.

Why not?

Natalie had nothing else planned for tomorrow. The decision was made, and she clicked off the light, hoping that somehow her mother might be watching.

Harrisonburg, Virginia

The voices from an old movie filtered out onto the small screened-in porch. Alex stared into the darkness of his back yard, thinking. Every so often he smiled when a familiar line from *Thoroughly Modern Millie* seeped through his thoughts and into his consciousness. He knew the movie almost by heart anyway.

"So sad to be all alone in the world," the faux Chinese villainess clucked to the unsuspecting Millie, played by Julie Andrews.

Ah, but not for long, eh, Mil? Alex thought, grinning a crooked grin.

Hearing the phone ring, he swung himself out of the hammock and ducked back inside, reaching for the receiver. "Hello?"

"Alex?"

"James!" His brother, calling from his home near Denver. "Good to hear from you. How did the deal go?"

"I took your advice, but she didn't bite. In fact, it ended up costing me another five million bucks. Tough cookie."

"You still got yourself a good deal, if what I read in the *Wall Street Journal* is correct."

"I really think Andrews screwed it up. I told him to offer thirty-five million, like you said, but he dropped it to thirty. From what he said, she was irate."

"Well, it never hurts to try. So, you're forty-five million dollars less liquid. Mum is going to think you're ready for the poor house."

"Not our mother," James said with a twist in his inflection. "It'll be Grandmum who makes a fuss. She still believes she's the head of the family, you know."

"And she is, really. All you do with your inheritance is invest the money. You've forsaken all the other . . . benefits, shall we say?"

"Easy for you to say, little brother."

"I wouldn't be in your shoes for all your money, James. Actually, I'm relieved that I'm the youngest and not expected to wheel and deal. I much prefer my books and my lectures."

"Yes, well, it's not medieval times anymore, is it? You should know that better than anyone, *Professor* Elbert. But what about your manuscript? Is it coming along well?"

"As ever."

"And what about the mysterious Miss Graham?" James chuckled, waiting for a response and hearing nothing. "Good grief, man, what's so special about your love life that you can't confide in your older brother?"

"Felicia moved away a year ago, James. That's all there is to it. I've found it to be a good rule not to indulge myself in long-distance relationships. They never seem to work out."

"Anyone else worth talking about these days?"

"No one. I'm much too busy."

"Why you don't pick one of those lush little fruits you call students, who sit in your classroom staring at you all day, is beyond me. With those pretty-boy looks and that upper-crust British accent, I'll bet you're the hit of the campus, old chap. In fact, rumor has it that the gals are standing in line to get into your classes, whether they give a fig about medieval history or not!"

"That's absurd. I wouldn't jeopardize my position at James Madison with that kind of nonsense. Besides, you know what crushes on the teacher are like. One day she'd fall in love with either another man or a career, and old Professor Elbert would be nothing but a dusty memory." He changed the subject. "What's going on with you and the environment? Spiked any trees lately?"

James let out a stiff chuckle. "You know me."

"I do. And if I didn't love you, brother, I declare I'd have nothing to do with you!"

"Ah, well, there you have it. Blood is thicker than everything else. Take comfort in the fact that the feeling is mutual! Someone who wastes his life on church and the like is beyond my comprehension."

"We'll just leave it at that then. Truth be told, we both know how the other one feels all too well. You know I'll always—"

"—pray for me," James finished. "Yes, I know. I called Mum and gave her the news about PluraNet, then arranged her hook-up to the Internet through UK Online last week. Send her an E-mail when you come out of the Dark Ages long enough to invest in a computer." He hooted into the phone.

Alex didn't let that bother him. "Oh, I can always use the one at the library. Meanwhile, I'm perfectly satisfied with my old portable typewriter. Suits my needs just fine."

"Better run. Neve is waiting for me out in the car."

"Any plans for a wedding yet?" Alex asked with a trace of sarcasm. But James had already hung up.

Alex poured himself a glass of chocolate milk, grabbed a couple of cookies, and sat down to watch the rest of the movie.

Three

*P*leasant Valley, Virginia, boasted a population of five thousand souls. Tucked into the landscape not far from the Shenandoah River, the town enjoyed the fruits of tourism. Most of the residents swam in calm financial straits, Natalie had learned. And the sound economy was further boosted by silver-haired, be-sneakered retirees, who congregated on the village green and frequented the many interesting little shops lining the shady streets.

Tooling down East Main, Natalie had to admit the brochure had not been a bunch of hype, after all. Coming here *was* like stepping back into another time.

Picket fences pointed freshly painted fingers at the turquoise, springtime sky. Small dogs yipped excitedly in the well-cared-for yards, where the owners clipped bushes and pulled weeds, or rustled their newspapers as they turned pages from their perches on their decks. At every turn, the azaleas' fiery blossoms burst delightfully through the dark green foliage of yew and holly.

Natalie pulled her car into the local IGA. A little brass bell slammed against the smudgy glass when she pushed on the door and entered.

"Hi!" she called to the cashier. "Got any maps of the area?"

"Sure." With a nubby finger sporting sparkly blue polish on its nail, the young woman indicated a rack near the door. "Right there."

Natalie walked over, her leather riding boots softly echoing on the linoleum. "Any houses for sale around here?"

The cashier shook her head. "Not really. They go fast. But," she lowered her voice, leaning forward in a posture of confidentiality, "there's something else goin' up for sale."

Natalie approached and cocked an ear. "What is it?" she whispered back, guessing she'd stumbled onto one of the town gossips.

"The inn."

"Pleasant Valley Inn?"

"No other. Old Elva Jacks—she was the owner, you know—passed on a couple'a months ago. It's being offered privately, but so far—not a nibble. There's a real estate place just down the street a little ways. You might want to ask in there about houses."

"Thanks." Natalie quickly made for the door. "I'd better get on the road."

"Hey! What's your name?" the girl yelled after her, but Natalie was already scooting behind the wheel of her car.

She drove off the parking lot and cruised slowly down Main, admiring the shop windows. Pulling into the small parking lot of the Pleasant Valley Inn, smack in the middle of town, she exhaled a puff of relief. She'd escaped without confiding a thing.

Natalie climbed out, feeling a quiet sort of wonder as she viewed the inn for the first time. Painted a soft yellow with green and white trim, the large Victorian mansion was quirky in every sense of the word. A large, glassed-in sunporch poked its head out of the left side, while wrapping itself lovingly around the front and right side of the house was a sprawling verandah approached by great stone steps. Highly polished double doors with engraved glass panels welcomed guests. Above all this first-floor busyness, turrets, gables, and garrets decorated the roofline like the icing on a wedding cake. Four brick chimneys jutted skyward. Standing sentinel on the front lawn were two large sugar maples flanking the brick walkway that led up to the front of the house.

Imagining the place at sunset, silhouetted against a sky holding all the promise of tomorrow, Natalie fell in love. Home. She'd come home. She didn't know how or even why, but somehow she sensed her mother had paved the way.

Spotting a gardener kneeling beneath a small Japanese maple, Natalie walked over. He immediately stood to his feet. "Can I help you, young lady?" He was a tall, lanky man, with large hands and smoky brown hair, his smile as sweetly lopsided as Jimmy Stewart's.

"Got any rooms available?" Natalie asked, positive that this guy must have broken a lot of hearts in his day.

He removed his cap and scratched his head. "Yep. Most likely we do. Go on in and ask for Lu."

Natalie thanked him and stepped toward the house. Just as she reached the double doors, one of them was thrown open by a plump woman wearing a long batik jumper and dangling silver earrings. Her paddlelike feet swam in a pair of dark brown Birkenstocks.

"Would you be Lu?"

"Lucinda Luckadoo, at your service." The woman beamed a broad smile; her teeth, looking like a perfect row of shoepeg corn, were small and yellowed with age. A pair of bright blue eyes practically disappeared into the folds of her face. "Housekeeper, cashier, and general runner-of-things these days. You come right in."

She ushered Natalie to the back of the entrance hall where a small hotel-style counter and keyboxes, polished to a high sheen, were planted in the corner. "River view or street view?"

"Street view, please."

"Oh, more of a people-person than the outdoorsy type."

"Definitely."

"Name?" The woman was suddenly all business as she plucked the black pen from its holder and slid on a pair of mother-of-pearl, half-eye reading glasses that hung around her neck on a chain strewn with gaudy, glass beads.

Feeling a twinge of guilt, but determined not to give herself away—not yet anyway—she offered her first and middle names only: "Natalie Gray."

"Hmm. Nice." The cashier-cum-housekeeper scrawled it down in an old-fashioned ledger—no computer, Natalie made a mental note—then turned to pluck a key from one of the boxes. "Room 12. Up the stairs, turn right, then right again. Last room on your right."

"Right."

Lu squinted momentarily and broke into a laugh. "Yep, you're a people-person, all right." She handed over the key.

"I'll get my bags."

"Don't bother." Lu waved a hand and took off her glasses, setting them carefully to rest on her large bosom. "Oren'll get 'em. Oren's my husband. Does whatever needs doin'. And I'm the one who says what needs doin' around here now."

"Are you the owner?" Natalie purposely queried.

"Heavens, no! That was Elva Jacks. She died a few months back." Lu leaned forward in that way that seemed characteristic of these small-town folks. "Don't know anyone who'd like to buy an inn, do you?"

Natalie laughed warmly. "You never know."

"I keep telling that slick, city lawyer he should put a 'For Sale' sign right there by that old dogwood, but he won't listen to me." She strained underneath the counter with a grunt and pulled out a schedule. "Breakfast between eight and nine—comes with the room. The dining room don't start servin' until six, and you'd better make a reservation come mornin'. We only reserve so many spots for the overnight guests."

"Is the food that good?"

"Our chef graduated from the Cordon Bleu in Paris." Her ample chest swelled with visible pride.

"Then put me down on that list right now. I haven't had a decent meal in four days!"

"Been busy?"

"You could call it that." Their eyes met, and something sparked between them. Something warm and solid.

Lu's voice softened. "You look tired. You an executive type?"

"I was. But I just sold my company and actually—well, I'm not sure what to do next."

The woman squinted through her bifocals. "As I told you, we're for sale and despite what you say, you don't look like the indecisive type to me."

"I've never been before. It's just that—" Natalie looked into the piercing blue eyes and decided to trust her new friend. "I think I'm supposed to wait right now . . . for God's timing. Oh . . . you must think I'm some kind of nut."

Lu put her arm through Natalie's and led her to the stairs. "I think no such thing, darlin'. You're a Christian, aren't you?"

"Since I was nineteen."

"I could tell. There was just that—" She struggled to come up with the word.

"I know exactly what you mean." Natalie laughed. "It's like we have radar or something."

Just then, a hulking pyramid-shaped figure obstructed the ribbons of late morning light streaming through the open front door. It was Oren with the suitcases. "I reached in and popped the trunk. Hope you don't mind, ma'am. What's this about radar?"

"Oren was in the Air Force during the Korean War," Lu whispered an explanation, "but don't ask him nothin' about it." Louder now, "Ms. Gray here is a believer, honey. Isn't that somethin'?"

"Sure is. To tell ya the truth, Miss Gray—" He set down the suitcases and rubbed his back a little— "if you hadn't been a'ready, I reckon you soon woulda been. My wife here loves to tell the old story. Has a lot of converts, too."

"Not in Tika's case," Lu reminded him. "She wants nothin' to do with 'religion.'"

"Who's Tika?" Natalie asked, immediately curious.

"She's the chef I was telling you about. The best there is south of D. C. and north of Atlanta, folks say," Lu announced proudly. "Far as I'm concerned, the best there is—period."

"Then the prospect of dinner sounds even more intriguing."

Lu crossed her arms over her ample bosom and turned to Oren. "Come on, now, mister, get a move on. I'm sure Ms. Gray wants to get to her room. And you standin' there lollygaggin'!"

Oren shrugged and rolled one eye—something Natalie had never seen before—then reloaded the baggage into his wiry arms, and followed Natalie up the steps. "She's a tartar, that one," he said with a wry smile. "But I guess that's one of the reasons I fell for her. Lu's one to get things done."

Natalie turned the quaint skeleton key in the lock and shouldered open the swollen door. "Then she and I should get along just fine."

"You stayin' for a while, Miss Gray?"

"Not too long this time. I have a cat back home."

His light blue eyes brightened. "That so? I like cats myself. They're the only animal I know that really appreciates a good flower bed without eatin' so much as a leaf! And speakin' of flower beds, I've got to skedaddle. There's a mound of mulch out back, just waitin' to be spread."

"Isn't it a little early for mulching?"

"I take it you're not a gardener."

Natalie shook her head. "No, sir. But hopefully I soon will be."

"Then you'll find out that gardening is a year-round enjoyment. Come December, I'm already sorting my bulbs. I sort and sort, and sort some more. And when the spring catalogues come from the nurseries, I'm shut away for days. Lu says it makes up for the fact that I've never been a TV sports hound."

"I love gardens. My mother always had lots of flowers. But daisies were her favorite." She shot him a sidelong look.

"Only knew one lady that liked flowers as much as me. Used to come here a lot and just sit in my gardens. She liked daisies, too." Oren's pickled face puckered up with genuine sadness. "But she won't be comin' back no more."

"Oh? Why not?"

He removed his cap respectfully, twisting it in the scratched, brown hands. "She's dead, Miss Gray. No more flowers for Janet St. John."

Feeling the sudden, blue wash of grief, Natalie hurried into her room to cry alone.

Four

Three days later Andy sat across from Natalie at the huge farmhouse table in his kitchen. The mellow wood surface had been scrubbed and scarred, yet loved, for over a hundred years: first in Genoa, Italy; next, in Pompton Plains, New Jersey; and finally, in Potomac, Maryland. His old house on River Road had required a complete overhaul when he'd bought it four years previously. The sprawling chateau-style mansion, sitting uncomfortably in the unmowed grass, had been in sad need of repair, but when he'd sauntered through the heavy double doors for the first time, Andy knew it was home.

The kitchen was the first room to be redone, no expense spared. And his mom had loved it so much that she'd shipped the table down a week later—all her other belongings quickly following.

Andy didn't mind.

In fact, living alone had lost its allure long ago. He'd come to the conclusion way back in college that Natalie would never fall for a garden-variety New Jersey boy with a thick accent and bitten-to-the-quick fingernails. And if he couldn't marry Nat, well, he wouldn't marry anyone. Sure, it probably looked to everyone else that he was a Mama's boy. But who cared? For one thing, she was a fabulous cook.

An earthenware bowl of his mom's spicy red sauce now sat on the table between Natalie and Andy. They dipped crusty bread into the sauce, wolfing down as much as possible before she returned from her bridge club meeting and fussed at them for spoiling their dinner.

"So, what did you think about that Pleasant Valley place?" Andy wondered aloud, hoping for a negative report.

"I loved it."

"Oh." He hadn't felt much worse when he'd lost his first case.

Natalie patted his hand, understanding. "The little town is so quaint, positively charming. Unfortunately, there's nothing on the market—no house anyway—that really suits me. Mostly small ranchers on the outskirts of town." Andy raised an eyebrow, and Natalie hurried to justify the remark, "Not that I think I'm too good for a rancher, mind you. I just wanted something old."

He held up his hands. "Hey, you don't hafta apologize to me. If I had *your* bucks, I wouldn't be livin' in a rancher, that's for sure. Although, I must say, I grew up that way, and it's a belief of mine that some very nice people live in ranchers."

"You'd better believe it," Natalie agreed. "When my father was still with us, we lived in this little rancher near the Beltway. It was the happiest place I ever remember. But I'm no big-time millionaire. The I.R.S. took care of that."

"So, you markin' that place off your list or something?"

"Well . . . not exactly." He loved it when she wrinkled her nose that way. "I was going to save the news for later . . . for a more majestic setting."

"What news?" he asked, feeling suddenly that he already knew. "And what could be more majestic than my kitchen, for Pete's sake—restaurant stove, walk-in refrigerator, and copper pots hanging over our heads?" Andy tore off another hunk of bread, which never made it to his mouth. "What is it?" His voice issued forth in an overly inquisitive honk.

Drat the woman.

"I've decided to buy the inn. We close in a few days. I move next week."

"What about your house?"

"For sale, as of nine o'clock this morning."

He curled his lips. "Don't you think you should've talked this over with me, Natalie? I *am* your lawyer, after all."

"Yes, and I'll need you there when I sign the papers."

Natalie rose from her chair and came around to his side of the table. She took his hands and pulled him to his feet. "Be happy for me, Andy. I really think I just made the best decision of my life. I'm going to be an innkeeper!"

Andy stared at her for a moment, not trusting his voice.

"Say something, Andy."

He let out a long breath. How could he begrudge her one trace of happiness? Even if it did seem a little wacky. An innkeeper, of all things. "You'll do great, Natalie. You'll put that little town on the map."

She hugged him tightly, and he held on, relishing in the feel of her closeness. "Thanks, Andy. Thanks for being my friend for so long."

"Sure, Nat. It's always been us. You know that."

"And it always will be." She kissed him on the cheek, and he grew dizzy with the subtle scent of her perfume. Something expensive. "You're the best friend I've ever had."

Then they were eating more bread and sauce, talking and dreaming of what the inn could become. And before Mama Gatto had placed the antipasto on the table, Andy was fully immersed in Natalie's newfound vision.

Three minutes after she left, he was on the phone to Elva Jacks's lawyer, a husky-voiced woman named Lori Chester.

Harrisonburg, Virginia

Alex Elbert's brow creased beneath the weight of serious consternation. One day, he vowed, he'd rip that telephone out of the wall. The shrill ring. Its greedy ways. His office mate called it "the almighty instrument," and he had to agree. When it beckoned, everything else might just as well disappear.

He picked up the receiver and growled, "Yeah?" He wasn't normally this curt, but when he was writing, interruptions made him grumpy.

It was his editor. "Alexander! I just got wind of your new contract. Congratulations. What's the deadline?"

"January fifteenth."

"Glorious, darling! Let's just hope you'll still need me with this one."

Alex couldn't help but grin. He and Celine had worked together for ten years. She always improved his manuscripts dramatically, no matter what time period he was writing about. "What do *you* think?"

She suddenly became all business, and he could picture her there in her tiny New York office, wearing graduated faux pearls and a leopard-skin suit. "Now, Alexander, don't forget to get away this time. Last time you swore you could finish up the project from home, and we ended up going a month over deadline. You know you do much better in a quiet, unfamiliar atmosphere where you can't procrastinate by making pot after pot of that dreadful tea."

"Lots of people like tea, not just the English," he reminded her.

"Well, lots of people go swimming in sub-freezing water on Polar Bear Day, or whatever it's called, but that doesn't mean it's *good* for them. All that caffeine. You really should drink more water, Alexander."

Alex had to laugh. Celine was such a mother hen. "You're my editor, not my doctor. And while we're dishing out advice, I'd advise you to *eat* a little more. You're going to blow away with the next spring storm."

"You know the old saying about being rich and thin. Well, I'm not rich, so I might as well be thin. Gotta run, darling. Do what I say. Find a little out-of-the-way place, and write, write, write!"

"It's only May, Celine."

"Just do it, Alexander."

The phone clicked in his ear. He shook his head, a bit bemused at the way she always hung up so abruptly, and laid the receiver back on its cradle.

Sitting back down at his dining room table, he stretched his fingers and proceeded to bang out another paragraph on his Royal manual typewriter. 1945 vintage. A good year. Too bad they didn't make 'em like that anymore.

⁓

"This is so right," Natalie said to Delilah, who meowed from her carrier. "And it's a decision I'm not going to regret. Hello, there," she called to an old man sitting in a rocker on the front porch. She had met him briefly on her first visit to the inn, and he was no friendlier today than before.

Silas Q. Wethington grunted a reply, his gaze aimed straight ahead. The cat on his lap, Merriwether, she'd learned, barely lifted her ancient head at their approach. Delilah strained against the bars of the carrier door, but Merriwether merely shuttered her golden eyes and nodded off to sleep, thus proclaiming herself the queen.

"That cat in there ain't gonna give mine no trouble, is it?"

Natalie shook her head. "I don't think so, Mr. Wethington." She set down the blue plastic container and straightened herself to her full height. "I'm Natalie St. John, and let's just hope this place isn't too small for the both of these furballs."

"Hmph! I'm not worried. I pay for my room up front—first day of every month. Ain't never stayed a day that wasn't paid for. I'm a valued fixture 'round here." He staked his claim. "Didn't I see you last week?" The words were clearly an accusation.

Natalie remembered what Lu had told her about the eccentric denizen of the porch, the Rambo of the rockers. "So you're a permanent resident?"

"Cheaper than a nursin' home . . . and I've got no kids, so I wasn't about to go committin' m'self. My brother lives over in Manassas, you know."

"No, I didn't know."

"Course you didn't. We just met."

"Formally, that is," she reminded him.

"All right, all right. If you've got to go and get particular. You remind me of my sister, Deadora," he muttered under his breath.

Natalie eyed the portly old fellow wrapped tighter than left-overs in a navy blue wind breaker. The red cap was a perfect match for his long cheeks and small, almost feminine nose. And there were more lines on his face than in his wicker rocker, which had yet to tilt even once. He was an old person's old person and a cur-mudgeon's curmudgeon. But his hazel eyes, watery and bleached pale by time, offset his tangy disposition.

"You've got nice eyes, sir," she declared, and without waiting for a reply, she breezed past him on her way into her inn.

"And you've got a snappy tongue, miss."

Natalie, feeling free for the first time in years, chuckled. "You'd better get used to it, sir. I'm the new owner of this place."

⁓

"So . . . she's coming today." Tamika Monroe leaned back against the stainless steel counter. "Here. Just made it fresh." She held out a cup of black coffee.

"Thanks, Tika, love." Lu took the cup gratefully and plopped herself down at the small metal table the staff used for meals.

Looking over her domain, cleaner than an operating room, Tika nodded. "Well, Lu. The kitchen's spotless, the pots are pol-ished, the floor's been scrubbed. We've got nothing to do but wait for the new owner to come in."

Lu sprang to her feet, her cheeks flushed with agitation. "You really don't think we should be out front to welcome her?"

Tika shook her head, her waist-long, skinny braids flagellating her sides. "We got here first, Lu. Ms. St. John is the newcomer, not us."

"I don't know," she moaned. "Our fate is in that woman's hands. What's to become of the lot of us is anyone's guess, I'll warrant."

Tika reached for the coffeepot. "Oh, an African-American can find work practically anywhere in D.C. There are restaurants that keep in touch with me on a regular basis."

"Oh, yeah?" Lu gratefully accepted the refill Tika offered and settled back down in her chair. "You never told me that before."

"No reason to. Never needed to think about leaving."

Lu's head jerked up in surprise. "You're thinking about leaving?"

"Not necessarily. It's up to the new owner."

"I suppose." Lu sighed.

Tika could have cut out her tongue with a carving knife when she read the doubt and pain in her friend's eyes. "I wouldn't worry, Lu. There's plenty of work out there for someone with all your experience."

"That's easy for *you* to say. Let's face it, Tika—" Lu wiped a bead of perspiration away with her hankie—"I'm just a glorified cleaning lady. And what about Oren? We're *old*. You're young and skinny and . . . trained. Highly trained."

"I just like working with food, Lu."

"You don't *eat* any of it. Neither does Oren. So . . . who finishes up the last slice of blackberry pie or peach gateau? Me, that's who. And now I'm overweight and unemployable," she moaned.

Tika could see Lu was working herself into one of her rare funks. She turned away from her friend's envious glance at her youthful, trim figure, but refused to feel guilty. The weight was genetic; all the Monroes were skinny—only the Lord knew how, since they were all good cooks. As for being young and employable . . . well, she was justifiably proud of all the hard work she'd done, beating the odds and achieving a goal unprecedented in her family. "You'll be okay, Lu. She's not going to let you go. If anyone is booted out, it'll be me. Elva was always telling me that she paid me more than I was worth."

"That was Elva, for you. But she never sent you packing, did she? Besides, Ms. St. John would be crazy to let *you* go. Folks can't seem to get enough of your French cuisine, and if they get tired of that, why then, your black-eyed peas and corn bread are a little taste of heaven. The dining room is booked for weeks in advance."

Just then Oren shuffled into the kitchen by the side door, his arms laden with bearded irises. "She just pulled up. I'll quick take some flowers to her new quarters."

"Natalie St. John?" Lu was transfigured into a bustling whirlwind, stacking the dishes that had earlier held their morning coffee cake, then the saucers, then the coffee cups. She whipped out a rag and wiped the surface of the table with five grandiose swirls of the checkered dishtowel.

Then she ran for the small bathroom, which doubled as a broom closet, and pulled a push broom from its wall clip, much in the same manner a warrior would grab his spear. "Did you see what she looks like?"

Oren's eyes sparkled with thinly veiled mischief as his wife pushed the crumbs out of the door, her wide derriere swaying with each movement, the tie-dyed gauze jumper whirling around her broad calves. "Not really. Just her car—a dark green Jag."

Tika grinned. "The mysterious Natalie St. John."

But Lu wasn't so easily placated. "Oh, Oren!" She slammed the broom back into place and closed the closet door. "Why didn't you go talk to her?"

"Well, she must be inside by now, or she might be still talkin' on the porch with old Silas." He shrugged, laying the flowers on a portion of counter space over Tika's protest.

Oren paid her no mind and began sorting the blossoms. "If you're all that keen on findin' her, Lu, you just go on and do it yourself. You know gabbin' isn't my sort of thing."

"Oh, Oren!" Lu huffed, and pushed herself hard against the chair back, her middle vibrating with the impact. "Aren't you the least bit curious?"

"Never had to be, Lu. Not with you around. Come to think of it, though, I did see the back of her head."

"Why didn't you say so?" the women replied together in exasperation.

"Well . . . is she pretty?" Tika pressed.

"Yeah, guess so. Had lots of those—" he waggled his fingers around his head—"curls, and well—great day, Lu, I don't know! I guess you'd say she's pretty. Looked like the back of a grown-up Shirley Temple to me."

"Is she an agreeable sort?" Tika asked, reaching behind her into a fruit bowl to pull off a grape.

"Now how am I supposed to know that from looking at the back of her head?" Oren twisted the faucet and began trimming the stems under the stream of clear, warm water. "You women!" he muttered with disgust. "Come on, Lu, get me the vases. I got to get the table arrangements done early today."

Lu's hands went on her roomy hips. "Why?"

"Reba's goin' to be on 'Oprah.' I've got to be done by five."

Lu threw up her hands, but hastened to oblige.

Tika clicked her tongue as she straightened the crisp white sleeves of her tunic. "Oren, Oren, Oren. Not much good if you can't supply us with a little gossip. Guess I'll go out to the smoke-house and cut down the pheasants for tonight's entrée."

"Does that mean I don't get my cuppa tea?" he complained.

"Not until you learn how to give out with more news than that!" To punctuate her retort, Tika pushed on the door with more than her usual vigor.

"Ouch!"

atalie had forgotten just how much it hurt to be hit in the nose. That peculiar, thick pain rammed through her head, and she buried her face in her hands with a startled outcry. Stars swam beneath her lids.

"Oh, no!" someone yelled. And the sound of footsteps pattering across the tile floor drew nearer.

"Are you all right?" came a motherly voice, and Natalie felt an arm go around her waist as she tottered on her feet.

"Let's get her to a chair." This one was decidedly male, and Natalie felt reassured as the man, whose name she'd learned was Oren, led her to the table.

Incapable of saying anything, Natalie listened with detached amusement as the people gathered around her whispered in quick bursts. "What have you *done*?" She recognized the voice of the woman she'd met that first day.

"What do you mean—what have *I* done? I didn't even know she was out there!" This voice was new to Natalie—slightly Southern, accented with an unusual foreign flavor—French?

"Well, you managed to get us all off on the right foot, Tika!" Lu's again. Tinged with sarcasm. "At least you can get yourself a job in D. C.!"

Oren's knowing chuckle. "Look, girls, she's beginning to come around."

When Natalie finally took her hands down and looked up, the stars were gone, but she had a spectacular nosebleed. If it wouldn't have hurt so badly, she would have had to laugh at the trio of faces peering down at her. One was the rich hue of chocolate melting on the stove; one, like crackled toffee; the third, the rosy shade of strawberries and milk.

The worry lines on the face of Lu Luckadoo relaxed into relief. "It's you!" she proclaimed. "It's Natalie Gray! What are *you* doing back here?"

"What?" Tika stood, looking from Oren to Lu and back again. "This isn't Natalie St. John?"

"No, it's Natalie *Gray*," Lu insisted, continuing as if Natalie were deaf and dumb and incapable of speaking for herself. "She stayed with us last week."

Natalie blinked with embarrassment. Better to end the charade right now. "My *middle* name is Gray. I really am Natalie St. John."

"Why didn't you tell us?" Lu cried.

"What a way to greet my new employer." Tika grimaced, handing her a tea towel to staunch the flow of blood.

"I can't believe it's you, Natalie!" Lu exclaimed, and began to shoo the others away. "You all tend to your business. I'll take care of Ms. St. John. You just relax, now darlin'," Lu soothed, dabbing at the tender flesh. "I'll try not to get any blood on your beautiful suit."

"Looks like a Vera Wang to me," Tika called as she picked up the knife, ready to try again for that pheasant.

"Uh-uh," Natalie mumbled through her swollen nose.

"Whoa. Big city businesswoman. They told us the new owner sold her business, that she's a real hardball player." Tika was clearly impressed.

Natalie grew uncomfortable. "I only sold it to get away from the rat race."

"Still, I'm sure you know all about managing things. And, believe me—" the tall black woman laughed—"I don't usually go around banging doors into people. I feel awful about that."

"Guess my timing was off. Ooh!" Natalie winced as she tried to stand and her face caught the sun's rays through the kitchen window. "Did a searchlight just go on, or is it just me?"

Lu's kindly expression was sympathetic, but for some reason twice as cautious now. "You're going to have quite a headache. Oren!" she yelled, inducing another wince from Nat. "While you're there at the sink, run some cool water over a washrag, will you?" He brought it over. "There now," Her touch was gentle as she placed the compress on Natalie's nose. "You'll be all right. Now why didn't you tell us you were going to buy the inn?"

"Would you have treated me like a regular customer? Like a person instead of an employer?"

Lu, hands on hips, smiled broadly. "You're right. You're exactly right."

"I would've done the same thing," Tika declared, then added with a twinkle in her eye, "Feeling better . . . boss?"

"Yes, thank you. And before anyone says another word, please call me Nat."

~⌒◞

Lu hummed to herself all the way to Ms. St. John's quarters—a spacious suite overlooking the east garden. Lu might not be as young as Tika, but she'd known just what to do for a bloody nose!

Catching a glimpse of herself in the hall mirror, she wished she had a dollar for every time she'd been told she was the type who could be really beautiful "if you'd just lose a little weight." Defensively, she patted at her hair—the colors of gray tweed, Oren would say. She wore it pulled back into a loose bun, to go with her loose dresses and her loose shoes. Too busy to fuss much with her looks, she kind of liked her wide mouth—just right to express her opinions.

And she always had one.

But she *didn't* like her nose. It drooped a bit at the nostrils and tended to get bright red at the tip when she was embarrassed.

Which wasn't often.

The long, narrow ears sagged beneath the weight of silver earrings, and the holes that had been put there by her sister when Lu was twelve looked like vertical slits. Still looking at herself in the mirror, Lu realized that years of bearing handcrafted earrings had taken their toll. She couldn't have cared less.

Hurrying on, she knocked at her new employer's door, then pushed it open without waiting for a reply. "Brought you a cup of hot chocolate. Tika made it special. See here, a real vanilla bean for stirring. Do you like your rooms?"

"I'm going to love it here. I've always wanted a house with high ceilings and tall windows. And the sunroom off the bedroom will be perfect."

After having rested for half an hour, it was obvious that the new owner was feeling much better. Still, purple circles had begun to form under her eyes. "I must look frightful," she apologized to Lu, gratefully taking the cup from her. "I guess I started off with a bang, huh?" She took a sip. "Oh yum, this is really good. I've never tasted anything like this before. What's in it?"

"It's one of Tika's secret recipes. She's got lots of 'em."

"Well, there's no mistaking the fact that she studied in France."

"She's a gem, she is," Lu went on loyally. "Tika's had offers from everywhere."

There was a moment of silence. "Do you think she might leave?"

Lu shrugged. "Not if she's got good reason to stick around." She'd best speak up for her friend while she had the chance. "Tika is well paid and has always been given free reign of the menu. She's also a stickler for high-quality ingredients."

"Hmm. Sounds temperamental to me."

"Only when she feels hemmed in. But I'll tell you this—" Lu felt her double chin waggle in her enthusiasm—"you give her all the elbow room she needs, and you'll keep Tika Monroe right here in Pleasant Valley."

"Well, as the old saying goes, 'If it ain't broke, don't fix it.' She won't have any interference from me." The new owner of the inn narrowed her gaze. "But what about you and Oren? Have you two made a decision?"

Lu crossed her arms and held up her chins proudly, the tip of her nose ruby red. "I suppose that's up to you," she said tightly. "But as Old Silas tells anyone who'll listen, the Pleasant Valley Inn is cheaper than a rest home." She fiddled with the glasses hanging around her neck like a pendant. "Oren and me, well, we're still plenty able to do our duties. We're hard workers, both born and bred on a farm. Not afraid of a little toil."

Natalie set her cup down and looked frankly at the woman. There were plenty of older people in D.C. who found themselves without a job just as their career should have been winding down to an affluent hum. No place to go, no one to want them. *Downsizing.* Natalie hated that term.

"Well, Lu, from what I've seen of the house and grounds, I'd have to agree. Not a speck of dust anywhere. And Oren's flowers speak for themselves." She pulled the vase of irises closer and inhaled their fragrance.

Lu straightened her shoulders. "Got nothing to be ashamed of. We do good work. All of us."

"How long have you been together—as a staff, that is?"

"Oren and I have been here twenty years—Tika, the last ten. Fact is, we've got things down to a gnat's eyebrow—runnin' this place, I mean."

"In other words," Natalie said, her eyes twinkling into Lu's, "mind my own business."

The tiny nose looked more like a cherry tomato than before. "No, it simply means 'rest assured.'"

"That's good to hear. Everything's going to be all right, Lu. The four of us—we'll make quite a team."

There was a definite easing of the tension crackling in the room. "Well, I don't see any reason why not."

"By the way, Lu, thank you for the daisies you and Oren sent for Mother's funeral. They meant more to me than all of the others combined."

"She liked our flowers, your mother. Mrs. Jacks, the old owner, she was pretty stingy about how many stems to put in the guest room vases. But Oren, he always packed Janet's nice and full. He's a simple man, my Oren, but if he can make someone smile who doesn't do much smilin', then he'll do whatever it takes. Your mother was special to us, in her quiet way."

"You were special to her, too." Natalie let out a long sigh. "I don't know how I missed it—my hectic schedule, I suppose—but I know now that she loved coming here."

"That she did. She'd sit in the garden for hours, wearing one of her big hats, not really doing anything but listening to the birds and watching the flowers bloom. We all liked her."

When Natalie's eyes filled with tears, she felt Lu's soft touch on her arm. "Such a fresh happening. You might want to take a couple of weeks to do nothing, darlin'. We can run the place and take care of you until you find your sea legs again."

Natalie took another sip of cocoa. "As true as that may be, and as tempting as it may sound, I think I'm just going to tag along here for the next week or so, watch what everyone is doing."

"Fine. We'll pretend you're a guest and then you'll know what it's like."

"I've already been that route, remember? I don't want to be pampered. I want you to put me to work. I'm here to learn all there is to know."

"You *sure* about that, Ms. St. John . . . uh, Natalie?"

"I'm absolutely positive. And please, Lu, my *friends* call me *Nat*."

~

"This is without a doubt the most disgusting thing I've ever done!" Natalie muttered to herself two days later as she snaked on her belly beneath the house. There were bound to be spiders the size of bed pillows under there, and maybe a pirate skeleton or two, she thought, suddenly remembering all the nightmares she had ever had as a child. The lattice work to her left winked in the light of her flash that did precious little to illuminate the gloomy underside of the ancient edifice.

"Just a little further!" Lu hollered, bending down from the waist to peer into the crawlspace. "Shine your flashlight to the left, and you'll see a brick jutting out from the foundation of the fireplace."

Natalie did as she was told. "I see it!"

"Okay, bang it some with your fist. Is it coming loose?"

"I think so!"

"Pull it out."

"Okay. Got it."

"Now reach inside. . . ."

Natalie grimaced, remembering the scene from *Indiana Jones and the Temple of Doom,* where the adventuresome archeologist had to put his hand through a small opening into a room full of huge centipedes and scorpion-like creatures. *Not now, Natalie, don't think about that now!*

"Feel anything?"

"Not yet." *Thank the Lord!*

"Stick your arm further in."

Natalie took a deep breath, and plunged deeper. She felt her fingers brush something cool and metallic. "I found it!"

"Good! Can you get a grip on it?"

"Yep. Here we go. Okay, I've got it. I'm coming back out."

"Better hurry—you don't have much time," Lu informed her as Natalie reversed herself, her sneakered feet emerging first from under the house.

"What do you mean I don't have much time?" she asked as she stood and brushed all the various nastiness out of her hair and off her clothes.

"The first dinner guest arrives in less than an hour and, unless you want to hibernate in your room all evening, you're going to need to get cleaned up. Besides, you just never know what might be hiding under a house as old as this one."

"Well, I'm certainly glad you didn't mention all that before I went underground, or I would have had even more of the creeps than I did. Why would Mrs. Jacks keep this box under there anyway?"

"Wanted to be sure nothing was stolen, I suppose."

"No gold in here. It's not heavy enough."

In the mudroom behind the kitchen, they shucked off their sweaters. "Here," said Lu, taking Nat's pullover from her. "Tomorrow's washday. I'll put this in with the other things."

"Thanks." She set the box on top of the washer and eyed it carefully. "You know, this box wasn't really *that* difficult to get to. If I had something of value, I certainly wouldn't put it where anyone could find it."

"Not many would try. Far as I know, you're the only person except Mrs. Jacks that ever did. The rest of us have no real stake in the claim—not enough to warrant climbing around like a squirrel, anyways."

They stared at the newly gathered treasure, now moved to the kitchen counter. It appeared to be the shape of a file box, actually. Once it had probably been a shade of terminal gray, but somewhere along the line someone had painted it bright red and tried to decorate it with swirls and childish flowers. Natalie was reminded of the bright decorations of the Pennsylvania Dutch. Had Mrs. Jacks's own hand executed the amateurish, yet endearing design upon the surface of what obviously held something very special?

Tika was too busy to bother with their find. She was doing some kind of whirling Mazurka from one pot to the next, then to the refrigerator, then back to the stove and over to the ovens. After four nights at the inn, Natalie had come to expect this familiar ritual. A passion for food. Fresh ingredients in heaps on the great wooden work table, and Tika, a whirl of dark brown and white amid the colorful displays of edibles.

"What did she keep in here?" Natalie asked, staring with consternation at the lock. No key to be found, of course. She shook the box, but nothing clunked around inside.

"Just papers and things, I guess. Every year around tax time, she'd go crawling under the house and pull out that box."

Nat drew her brows together in a frown. "Hmm. I hope there's nothing I'm going to need."

"Don't worry about it. You can always take it to a locksmith."

"Maybe I'll do that soon. I'm really curious to poke my nose into the life of Elva Jacks." Natalie smiled, ignoring the little stab of guilt issuing from her conscience.

"Most mysterious person *I've* ever known. But you probably realized that the moment you stepped into your room."

"Yes. I'm going to have to do some serious redecorating in there. Black is definitely not my choice for a bedroom. Although I've got to say, thinking about Mother, the color matched my mood."

"But not for long," Tika spoke up. "It's not good for you. Grandpop says the dead are dead, and it's best to keep them that way."

"You're right. It's just hard to let go. Next week I'll call a decorator and a contractor. I want to replace those windows on the sunporch. I'm going to install some baseboard heating as well. Make it a year-round room. I need the sun."

"Sounds like your head's already whirling with good ideas. It will be interesting to see what it'll be like after you get around to it." Lu was strangely silent for a moment. "There's one suggestion I've been wanting to make for years, but with Mrs. Jacks, you never wanted to overstep your place."

Natalie was still eyeing that lock. "Feel free to speak your mind with me, Lu."

The woman drew herself up, her bosom more prominent than usual. "All right then, I will. Our guest rooms are numbered 1-12. But I think we should give them names instead. In fact, I've always thought it would be right nice to name them after flowers—maybe Daisy, Rose, Violet—"

"Heliotrope!" Tika shouted, proving she'd been hearing every word of the conversation all along.

Natalie nodded. "Good idea. I'll leave it up to you and Oren to decide, Lu. And now on with this box. I can't wait to see what an old woman like Elva Jacks kept stashed away. Maybe a chisel and hammer will do the job."

Just then the phone rang. Since Natalie was nearby, she reached for the receiver from long habit. "You want to reserve a room for . . . *when?*" she asked, eyes wide, the other two lifting their eyebrows at her inflection. "Well this is only May, of course, but I don't see why we couldn't book you for December." She looked toward Lu, who gave her the nod.

"Your name?" Natalie scribbled the information on the pad near the phone. "Address, phone number, and the exact dates of your stay, please." She remembered that much from having observed Lu at the registration desk. "The *entire* month of December?"

Pause. She searched the faces of her colleagues. They merely shrugged, still baffled.

"You want a quiet room to do some writing?" The gears clicked into place. "I have just the spot. All right, Professor Elbert, I'll put you down . . . and thank you for calling, sir. Goodbye."

Lu crossed her arms and chuckled. "Now, if *that's* not the most advance reservation we've ever taken."

Natalie smiled dreamily.

"What is it, Nat?" Tika asked, glancing up from the bowl of salad she was tossing.

"That voice. British accent. Smooth, yet nutty, with a slight rasp."

Tika chuckled. "Sounds like my recipe for Raspberry Walnut dressing."

"In any case, I think I'm going to enjoy meeting Professor Alexander Elbert. Although, with my luck, he's probably a hundred years old! Now, let's get on with opening this box."

Lu looked startled. "Oh, I forgot! Marsha can't make it in tonight. She said that storm they've been talking about all day on the radio has already started there. She lives on a hill—and, well, if there's even a hint of bad weather—winter *or* summer—Marsha calls in and begs off. Have you ever hosted a dining room before, Nat?"

"No. But how hard can that be?"

Lu shrugged. "Wouldn't know. I've never done it myself. Marsha's a real pro, though. And she looks great in a black sheath dress."

"Oh, by all means the most important prerequisite in a hostess!" snorted Tika, a staunch feminist.

"Anyway, Mrs. Jacks always did the honors when Marsha called in."

"Hmm. I'm surprised the woman kept her on. Elva Jacks sounded like a tough operator."

"Oh, she was. She was also completely superstitious. And the thought of Marsha's demise on her hands and all the bad luck *that* would have brought was too much for her."

Thinking she might have to make some staff changes sooner than she'd intended, Natalie rose to her feet. "I'd better go find something to wear."

"Did you bring anything dressy?" Lu asked. "Friday evening is our most formal time. The string quartet is in the parlor setting up now."

Natalie burst into laughter. "So it's dressy you want? My dear, Lu, you just wait and see!"

She was still smiling to herself as she made her way through the hall to her rooms. Good thing she hadn't discarded it long ago. That old black dress would come in handy once again.

Six

It was a relief to wash away the dust of the crawl space in the warm spray of the shower. The singing of the pipes, or "groaning," as Lu called it, "sounds as if the ghost of Elva Jacks is still whisking around through the plumbing somewhere. Not that I believe in that kind of thing, mind you!" Natalie didn't, either, of course. But she had to grin at the thought.

Slipping on the faithful old standby, she turned to check her hem in the cheval glass—an antique that had witnessed many a young woman primping in her elaborate ballgown as she tilted the full-length mirror this way and that. Tonight the effect was less than cheerful. "If any more black is added to my surroundings, I'm going to be tempted to buy that funeral parlor across the street!" Natalie announced to no one in particular.

Using a long chiffon scarf to tie back her wayward auburn curls, she let the ends of the soft fabric trail down to her knees. A three-strand pearl choker and tiny drop earrings were just the accessories to add the final touch of old-style sophistication—the aura for which Pleasant Valley Inn was noted.

In her preoccupation on the way to the dining room, Natalie practically collided with Lu who was taking a dinner tray up to Mr. Wethington. "Old Silas Q. not joining us tonight?" Natalie asked, adjusting her pearls.

"Never does on Fridays and Saturdays. Claims the ambiance is much too fancy for a retired builder like himself. Says if we want him in the future, we should think about hiring on a bluegrass band."

51

Natalie laughed and made her way to the foyer. A bluegrass band—not a bad idea. Although tonight, the gentle sounds of several stringed instruments being tuned was soothing. Surely there were more than harps in heaven.

Heaven. She quickly squelched *that* thought and breezed into the dining room.

The two-person wait staff was busy setting the eight tables that would soon be filled with guests. White damask cloths, heavy silver cutlery, and fine white Sevres china lent a sumptuous atmosphere to the subtly papered room. The padded chairs were slipcovered with champagne-colored brocade and by each place was a tiny silver bud vase, tonight holding a miniature orchid grown in Oren's greenhouse behind the toolshed.

And candles, of course. Everywhere. Several, in heavy silver candlesticks, on each table. On either end of the room, two mantels, banked in fresh greenery, held more candles—silver, gold and white. *How festive,* Natalie mused.

On the hall table was the dining room's leather-bound reservation book. Natalie herself had jotted down several reservations over the past few days. Not for tonight, of course. These would have called in a while ago. Many were weekend guests.

One entry caught her eye. A great sprawling name, written in Lu's great sprawling handwriting.

Reverend and Mrs. Tyler D. Higgenbotham, 6:00 P.M.

Natalie had arrived on Monday and now it was Friday, and she hadn't even begun to think about where she would attend church. Actually, she hadn't done much thinking about the *Reason* for church, either. *One of my footprint times,* she thought, knowing that right now the Lord was carrying her. Her hardest moments were late at night, when she was alone in that mausoleum of a room. And what had made it worse was that "the geologist"—she could never think of him as "Dad"—had never once called to express his condolences that his ex-wife—the mother of his only child—had died. *Well, the only child he admitted to,* she fumed inwardly.

She gazed, unseeing, at the flickering candles.

"Excuse me? Miss?"

She was yanked from her thoughts by a cheerful, boyish-looking man—early thirties, she guessed—and a woman who was visibly pregnant. "My wife and I have reservations for six. 'Higgenbotham.' I'm afraid we're a little early."

"Oh, yes, Reverend Higgenbotham." She was expecting anything but this young, freshly scrubbed pair. "Would you like to wait in the parlor by the fireplace and listen to the music? Your table should be ready in just a few minutes."

She showed them into the cozy room, the musicians' offering now pleasantly melodious with the strains of Cole Porter's "I Get a Kick Out of You." The couple's eyes sparkled as Natalie directed them to the sofa table where a large punch bowl was brimming with one of Tika's special brews—a citrus concoction with lots of pineapple garnish, scalloped rings of it floating on the surface. Hot and cold hors d'oeuvres, as well, enticed guests to linger awhile.

The Reverend and his wife filled their plates and took a seat on an uncomfortable-looking Victorian couch, seemingly oblivious to the none-too-downy upholstery.

Natalie jotted herself another mental note: *Get comfortable couches for the parlor.* She loved old things as much as the next person, but antique couches were better left in museums to be admired or in dentists' offices, where the patients weren't expected to relax anyway.

Back she traveled to the dining room, lighting a few final candles and making sure each linen napkin was properly folded. She felt a tap on her shoulder. "Excuse me, Miss?"

Turning, she recognized the young minister. "Yes, Reverend Higgenbotham?"

"Please call me Tyler. We're regulars here—Erin and I. Once a month for the past four years. Where's Marsha?"

"The weather forecaster is calling for a storm tonight, and she was afraid to drive in."

"I see." He seemed amused. "Well, we live right down the street—not far from our church. We've served at Trinity Presbyterian for about five years now."

"*I'm* a Presbyterian. I just moved in on Monday, and I was wondering where I would go to church this Sunday."

He grinned encouragingly. "Come on down! Worship service at nine, classes at ten. Sunday night is more casual, if you're into that kind of thing. Not so 'churchy.' Lots of people prefer that service."

"Leaves the morning free for a round of golf, huh?"

He looked somewhat embarrassed, but not at all apologetic. "Maybe. Paul never said what time we were supposed to gather though, did he? But I've gotten off the topic, and Erin will wonder where I am. This is our anniversary . . . and I thought maybe Tika could do something a little special—" He dropped his voice and reached for his back pocket. "I'd be glad to pay any extra—"

"Nonsense! We'll do our best to make sure tonight is a memorable one for both of you."

"Thanks. By the way, I didn't get your name."

"Natalie St. John. The new owner."

He lifted his eyebrows in surprise. "Well, in that case, welcome to Pleasant Valley. Erin and I live down behind the church in the manse. I'm not just a Sunday-morning pastor, and Erin, well, she thinks of it as her ministry, too. If you need anything, just call."

"I will. See you in church. And . . . Happy Anniversary!"

With an airy wave of his hand, the young pastor returned to his wife, and Natalie was left to ponder her old church and how much she was going to miss it.

Fourth Presbyterian had been a dynamic place to worship. Stirring sermons. Beautiful music. She'd never experienced a single lackluster Sunday the entire time she'd been a member. It might take some getting used to—a small-town church—but Natalie wasn't choosy. If the Bible was being preached as the Word of God and folks loved the Lord, well, she could be content anywhere.

The next group arrived. A party of six, and there was no more time for reminiscing.

After that, the evening progressed quickly. Most of the guests had dined at the inn before and all welcomed Natalie warmly.

Saturday night was a replay of Friday, but Sunday morning finally arrived and Natalie, dressed in an ivory linen skirt, blue blazer, tailored cream blouse, and navy pumps, was out of the door by 8:45. She decided to walk the three blocks to the church.

"See you in a bit," she called to old Silas as he sat in his rocker.

He grunted in reply, and when she returned ninety minutes later, he was asleep—or pretending to be—and couldn't have noticed her shining eyes or how refreshed she was, both inside and out.

Later on in the morning, as she helped Tika chop some vegetables for a frittata, she hummed a tune.

"Hey Nattie, what song is that?" the chef wanted to know. "Pretty tune."

"'Jesus, Name Above All Names.'"

"You must be a Christian."

"Yes. You?"

Tika shook her head. "My grandparents are in church every time the doors are open. And Grandmom—that woman can definitely pray! I remember hearing her and thinking I was in the presence of the Almighty Himself. Once I went to France, though—" she shrugged—"well, I realized there were lots of different ways to know God."

"And what's yours, Tika?" Natalie cast the tall woman a curious glance.

"I . . . haven't made up my mind. Besides, I'm pretty happy with the way things are."

Natalie smiled. "Well, I don't deny that you seem to be. You have the most beautiful smile, the most *genuine* smile I've ever seen. But someday . . . if you ever need to talk . . . I'll be here for you."

"Yeah." There was a long sigh. "You've got something . . . never mind." Tika shut down and whirled back to the stove, saying over her shoulder, "Why don't you get started peeling the jicama, and I'll pull out the sauté pan."

When the last guest had left, the inn was practically empty. Natalie was about to turn on *Sunday Afternoon Theatre's* showing of *Arsenic and Old Lace* when the phone rang.

Lu got there first. "It's for you, Nat!" she called from the kitchen.

Natalie hurried down the hall to find Lu holding the phone in one hand, the swinging door in the other. "A member of the weaker sex," she whispered.

"You're as bad as Tika! I'll take it in my room."

A minute later she picked up the receiver. "Natalie St. John."

"Hey, Nat, now that you're not a high-powered executive, you know you can just say 'hello' like ordinary mortals."

"Andy! It's great to hear your voice. Long time, no see. What's up?"

"Just thought I'd call. Ma is playing canasta with a few of her old girlfriends, and I was just sitting here watching some TV. I saw a Cary Grant movie in the listings, and thought I'd let you know in case you'd missed it."

"You're a gem, And. As a matter of fact, I had just turned on the TV in the parlor."

"The parlor, huh? You're getting way too fancy for a poor schmoe like me!"

"Andrew Gatto, you know better than that."

"Well, guess I'd better let you go. Wouldn't want you to miss the first scene."

"You know me and old movies, don't you? What can I say?"

"Absolutely nothing, kid. I've got you pegged. All tough businesswoman on the outside, squishy romantic on the inside. By the way, did you see that Jeanine Beaumont's latest debated at number three on the *New York Times* bestseller list?"

"Really? Hope that means she'll be turning out more books in the future."

"You know, Nat, you puzzle me."

"Why is that?"

"You love old movies, read romance novels, and have all that—hair. Romantic kind of hair. Yet you've never really had a boyfriend the whole time I've known you. I can't for the life of me figure out why!"

"I've gone out with *lots* of guys, Andy."

"That wasn't what I meant, and you know it."

She looked down at her nails. The direction this conversation was taking was beginning to get on her nerves. "Oh, I don't know. The right guy has just never come along, I guess."

"Will he ever?"

Natalie shrugged, eyeing herself in her bureau mirror. "Probably not, Andy. If there's one thing I learned a very long time ago, it's that men can't be trusted."

"Hey, that's not nice. When have *I* ever let you down?"

She gave a little laugh. "Oh, you don't count, Andy. You're my best friend." Hoping to change the subject, she launched into neutral territory. "How was church today?"

"Great. Another fantastic sermon."

"Did you go to the singles' Sunday school class?"

"Yep, and guess what? Remember Peggy and Bill?"

"The two who used to make eyes across the room at each other?"

"Uh-huh. She's the blonde with the curly perm, and he works for the defense department. Well, they're engaged."

"Really?" Natalie was surprised, then wondered why. Wouldn't most of her old gang be pairing off one of these days?

"Yep, and the entire class is invited to the wedding next month. They're having a big barbecue out at Great Falls."

Why did Natalie suddenly feel like a square peg in a round hole? Life—even Andy—seemed to be going on quite well without her.

"Well, listen," he was saying, "Ma just came home and I hear her clanking around in the kitchen. Gotta go."

"Sure. Give your mom my best."

They hung up, Natalie thinking she couldn't remember when she had felt so depressed. Suddenly *Arsenic and Old Lace* didn't hold any appeal whatsoever. She decided to take a nap instead.

Seven

May exploded in a riot of lush greens and vibrant color. Blue lobelia, white petunias, and red geraniums cascaded from the window boxes, and—thanks to Oren's spadework—the border gardens stopped many a passing motorist. With all the gardening activity outside and the redecorating inside, there was barely time to breathe.

Despite all that, Natalie had fallen in with an active crowd at Trinity Presbyterian, making some new friends and generally enjoying life away from the big city.

Then, suddenly it was June. Not the bridal June of organdy and lace, soft breezes and gentle rains, but muggy and unseasonably warm. It didn't matter how one dressed, stepping outside was like being in a sauna at the health spa. Natalie was even more grateful for the high ceilings, but decided to install air conditioning so the summer guests could find plenty of comfort along with all the nostalgia and charm.

After that, things simmered down to a more leisurely pace as the temperature moderated and summer progressed, with the staff doing the lion's share of the day-to-day operation of the inn.

In fact, Natalie was bored.

"*Well*—" Renee Alcott, one of her newfound friends, rested her forearms on the table and leaned forward in a gesture of confidentiality. "I didn't know Mrs. Jacks all that well, but honey, from what I've heard, she was quite an eccentric."

A vivacious woman, more lovable than a stuffed bear, Renee was the unofficial chairman of Trinity's unofficial social committee.

The slightly overweight blonde had a knack for meeting people, planning events, and lining up volunteers—willing or unwilling—which was why Natalie had met her for lunch on the patio at Fussy's Place.

"But then we're not here to discuss the life and times of poor old Elva," Renee corrected herself with a smile of chagrin. "There's the Boston Creme Pie sale to plan for the church, and we thought you'd be ideal to—"

"Hold it." Natalie halted her with an uplifted hand. "Is it profitable?" The bottom line, please. Something she insisted on knowing if she was going to commit to another fund-raiser. With that, she buttered a slice of homemade brown bread and bit down into the still-warm goodness.

Renee shrugged her broad shoulders, her shoulder-length, hot-rollered curls bouncing in a very late-70s manner. She was one of those people who had never quite made it past high school. Renee knew what each of her classmates was doing and where they were doing it. Natalie had learned that Renee sent out a newsletter every year and planned her class reunions. And when the crowd returned for each get-together, their comment, "Renee, you haven't changed a *bit!*" was probably not completely a compliment. Blue eye shadow, winged bangs, and dresses made out of Visa, "The Freedom Fabric," were still major elements of Renee Alcott's wardrobe, when she wasn't wearing clothes her mother, a weekend crafter, made for her. Today it was a denim and lace vest, hand-painted, over a long denim skirt with wooden sheep—posing as buttons—lined up down the front. Painted sneakers anchored the craft fair ensemble. Janet St. John would have fainted in horror at such a get-up.

"Probably not," Renee was saying. "Not in the business sense, you know, if you count all the man hours. But it's a tradition, Nat. And it's all done by volunteers. Some of these ladies have been baking pies for fifty years—and the proceeds *do* go into the Deacon's Fund."

"Well, that's certainly a worthy cause. So what do you want me to do? I may have lived the corporate life, but I do know my way around an oven."

"That's the spirit!" Renee bubbled. She'd been the head cheerleader in high school as well, although her husband Tommy's letter jacket from his basketball days had ceased to fit after the birth of their first child eighteen years before. And it was a good thing, or she'd probably still be wearing it, Natalie suspected. "We'd love your help on the day we set up. But I was hoping . . . maybe . . . you could design some handouts for around town . . . you know, on your computer. You did such a great job for the rummage sale that we're already getting donations." She wound down, adding, "I know it isn't much notice—"

Natalie waved away her apology. "No problem. You can count on me to help out."

"The committee will reimburse you for any expenses, of course." Renee's eyes lit up, and Natalie could just see her mentally ticking off another name from her list before moving on to fresh meat.

"Forget it. The Lord is keeping score, not me." No one in Pleasant Valley knew Natalie's financial status, and she wasn't about to begin with the church busybody—or at least the one person who kept tabs on everybody in—and out of—town.

"Good deal." Renee reached into her totebag and pulled out a drawing. "Here's what I had in mind."

It was actually not bad, design-wise, Natalie noted with relief. "This will be fine to start with. I may have to make a few small changes, though, for layout purposes."

"Okay. I'll have to sign off on it anyway before we send it to the printer." Renee had also been the editor of the high school yearbook. Natalie took no offense.

So it was settled. She was actually looking forward to the project. Even found it a bit amusing—quite a change from running a multi-million-dollar ISP.

"We'll need the brochure by the day after tomorrow—just in case changes need to be made, you know. But I'm sure you're very busy at the inn, and I hate to put such a close deadline on you."

"Not at all. I work best under pressure. Actually, Renee, my staff is so capable that I've begun to feel like a spare appendage. I thought I'd be buying something to keep me busy!"

"Well, it's a wonderful place, although the dining room is a bit expensive for Tommy and me—raising three kids and all. But it's the nicest place in town."

Natalie sipped on her iced tea. "When is your anniversary?" she asked nonchalantly.

"In October."

"Why don't you and Tommy plan to stay at the inn that weekend? Room and meals on the house."

"Oh, really, Natalie, you don't have to do that."

"Look at it this way. You know everyone around here, Renee. The revenue such advertising would generate would be more than worth the expenditure."

Renee threw back her head and laughed heartily. "Well, I'm warning you—Tommy can eat a heap, you know."

"Good. I like a healthy appetite in a man. When I get back, I'll put you down. You mark your calendar."

"I'll do that. I'll even line up a baby-sitter while I'm at it."

Lunch was served. Chicken salad and crusty French bread for Natalie, and a Reuben for Renee. It was during coffee afterwards that the subject of Mrs. Jacks came up again.

"So you say she was a little eccentric," Natalie probed, stirring sugar into her Kenya roast.

"Never wore anything but black." Renee added whipped milk to her cappuccino. "And it wasn't just because she liked the color, either. She was definitely in mourning—I don't know why . . . or who. Wasn't a church-goer, though, so I didn't have a whole lot of contact with her."

Natalie rested her chin in her hand. "As far as the staff knows, she had no living relatives. I have no idea what happened to the money I paid for the inn—it was all handled through her solicitors.

The lawyers took care of everything from the minute she died. 'Practically before the body was cold,' or so Lu says."

"That sounds like Lu."

They sat and sipped their coffee, watching a group of third-graders make their way from the YMCA to the bank for a field trip. She wondered if they were so accustomed to the quaint town that they failed to notice the pristine streets and the cheerful Victorians. Almost every one of them, however, waved to Renee, who called to them by name. Natalie wasn't at all surprised when she was informed later that Renee was the president of the PTA.

"What about *Mr.* Jacks?" Natalie asked, once the little parade had ended.

"Died before she came to town," Renee replied, digging into her bag for an Avon lipstick. "She was a widow as far back as anyone can remember. But, I don't think she grew up here . . . she had a Northern accent—New England or something. Said 'cawn frittahs' instead of 'corn fritters.'"

Natalie opened her mouth to speak. Then thought it over.

The box. Should she tell Renee about the box?

She decided to take a chance, spilling the entire story.

"There was no key—that's the problem," she finished up. "For some reason I haven't been able to bring myself to break the lock or call in a locksmith. Don't ask me why. All I know is the box was so important to her, she'd crawl under the house every year around March to drag it out, then put it back the next day. Oren said on the night between, her light would be on until dawn."

"How did you find out about it?"

"Are you kidding me? The third day after I arrived, Lu talked me into going under there to fish it out. Imagine how disappointed she was when it wouldn't open!"

"She was definitely one of a kind—that Elva Jacks, I mean. No one really knew her. And sad to say, I don't rightly believe anyone *wanted* to. Tyler called on her a lot, for the church, you know—but there was never any response."

"In her pictures she looks so dignified. Almost regal."

"Yeah. I always thought of her as sort of a misplaced Park Avenue lady. Tall and stately. Her clothes were really expensive-looking and fashionable for around here. I can't imagine her crawling under the house for anything."

"Did you ever have a conversation with her?"

"Just once. She came in to buy a couple of Boston Creme pies one Easter. I tried to chit-chat, like I do. She was cordial enough, but a little standoffish."

"Didn't she have *any* friends?"

After this third degree, Renee arched a brow. "Hey, if you really want to find out about Mrs. Jacks, why don't you contact her lawyers? She must have been on close terms with them at one time or another."

Now *that* might be a plan. One Natalie quickly rejected. "Oh, I wouldn't want anyone to think I was snooping. All I'm interested in is knowing more about the woman who built such a fabulous reputation for my inn."

The waitress came just then, check in hand. Natalie and Renee paid and left separately, promising to stay in touch about the church flyer.

On the drive back home, top down on the Jaguar, Natalie made mental notes of all the flowers she wanted to see growing around the inn. French lilacs, davidiana, clematis, and blazing purple liatris. Oren would love it. Mrs. Jacks had never allowed him to "be English about the gardens," as he put it. Natalie decided to give him a budget and tell him to go for it.

Already, red and pink climbing roses were started by the four corners of the porch, and the impatiens were thriving in the shade of the oaks out front. The ferns, cascading between the columns, were a delicate touch, though Silas Q. had already registered a complaint that they obstructed his view of the funeral home across the street. But Natalie had taken care of that as well. To pacify him, she'd bought him a brand-new wicker rocker. He hadn't used it yet. Hadn't given so much as a blink when she told him she'd bought it especially with him in mind.

But it wouldn't be long now, she figured—if she knew men. On second thought, who said she knew *anything* about men?

Not willing to give much time to such a worrisome thought, she shrugged. Entering the inn and calling out a greeting to whomever was within listening distance, Natalie jogged back to her quarters.

Her room, now painted a bright white, was a welcome change from funereal black. Her Battenburg comforter, new lace curtains, and lots of pillows from her old bedroom in Georgetown had further transformed the place. The Sisal rug on the floor was scratchy and felt good beneath her toes, and now that Elva Jacks's antique furniture was cleaned up, the effect was quite pleasing, evoking a New England seaside cottage feel with the periwinkle blue touches and the ceiling tinted the same cool hue.

Pulling the tasseled cord to activate the ceiling fan overhead, she slanted a look at the box on the rattan chest at the end of her bed. Yep. Only a locksmith could get into that box without smashing it to bits. And she couldn't do that. Couldn't violate the past so obviously protected by a lonely widow. It didn't seem right.

I'll only open that box if I find the key, she promised herself.

There. That was settled. The box was now firmly in the hands of Providence.

Eight

The dog days of summer dragged by like a three-legged hound. As the seasons changed, the air cooled and the Shenandoah Valley breathed a sigh of relief. The mountains donned their most glorious colors. Russet-reds and brilliant yellows flirted with a cobalt blue sky. With the brisker temperatures of nightfall, the land was enveloped by fog, only to be burned off by the autumn sun come morning.

The inn was only moderately busy, so Natalie decided to close the dining room for a week to give the staff a well-deserved break after the busy tourist season. Beginning tomorrow.

"Old Silas Q. is an antebellum man, if there ever was one," Lu declared with a groan as she eased her tired body down in a kitchen chair after the last dinner guest had left the inn. "When he first came, I thought we were still fighting the Civil War."

Tika chuckled, remembering, and sipped on a cup of steaming hot lemon water as the others enjoyed her special cocoa. "The first night, Nattie, he ventured into the kitchen, saw me working furiously on dinner, and nodded smugly, as if a woman like me was in the right place. I kid you not."

Natalie shook her head. "Little did he know that a gourmet chef was fixing his corn bread and black-eyed peas."

"I make no apology for my race or gender. My talent speaks for itself."

Tika was still a bit miffed, Natalie could tell. "What made you decide to become a chef?" She reached for one of the oatmeal cookies on a plate in the middle of the table.

"Must be in the genes. My mother and grandmother were both unbelievable cooks. They worked miracles with seafood; I grew up in Maryland—on the Eastern Shore. And Grandpop, well, his specialty was Sunday breakfast. His gravies—" her huge dark eyes rolled heavenward—"put everyone else's to shame—including mine. I want Grandmom to put on his tombstone: 'Here lies the secret to the greatest gravies in the world.'"

Lu disagreed. "I think some of that must have rubbed off on his granddaughter. Your sausage gravy is the best I've ever tasted, Tika. And your biscuits—"

"Stop that, you two," Natalie scolded. "It's only midnight, and I'm already hungry for breakfast!"

Good-natured laughter flowed among the women, quietly though, so as not to disturb the guests. Oren, of course, had long since retired; gardeners were always up at first light.

"I'll make you some biscuits and gravy soon, Nattie," Tika promised.

Natalie sipped some more of her cocoa. "You're all so good to me. I still can't get over it."

"What's so unusual about that?" Lu chimed in. "In the first place, it's easy to be good to someone like you. Besides, I guess we're just born innkeepers. Right, Tika?"

"Absolutely. Service is our business. We love what we do, and we do it well."

"*Too* well." Natalie wrinkled her nose. "Now that I've done all the redecorating I'm going to do, I don't have any real duties to speak of."

Tika flipped her collection of black braids over her shoulder. "Do you miss computers?"

"Not really. At least not PluraNet." She tapped the tabletop with her short nails. "But that *does* give me an idea. Now that I've got Trinity up and running—technologically-speaking—what I need to do is design a Web page for this place. Advertise on the Internet."

Lu was all for it. Despite her years and her love of antiques, her ideas were anything *but* antiquated. "That's a wonderful notion.

And it will give you something to think about—all that programming and such."

"Sheesh, Lu, I can write HTML in my sleep."

"Of course you can!" Tika declared. "You're a smart lady." She leaned toward Lu and mumbled under her breath, "What's HTML?"

"Beats me." Lu shrugged, then turned to Nat. "What's HTML?"

"Hyper Text Markup Language."

"See?" Tika nudged Lu. "I told you she was smart. After all, she kept *us* on, didn't she?"

Natalie grinned. "Yes, and it's the best decision I ever made, bar none. Okay, it's settled then. I'll start working on our Web site tomorrow. If I'm persistent, I should have it up and running by the end of next week."

The kitchen clock struck one.

"Well, ladies," Tika sighed, downing the last of her drink, "tomorrow's a big day. I'd better be getting my beauty sleep."

"Oh?" Lu looked suspicious. "And just what big plans do you have up your sleeve for your time off?"

Tika assumed a mysterious smile—that African Mona Lisa look that could only mean one thing.

"You have a date!" Natalie said with an equal measure of incredulity and delight.

Lu was clearly flabbergasted. "I can't believe you didn't tell us before now! Do we know him?"

Tika crossed her arms and leveled them a long look. "Now *who* in this town would I go out with?"

Natalie acknowledged the dilemma with a nod. "There really aren't many eligible men down this way. Even at my church—" she shuddered in distaste—"they're all just trophy-hunters."

"Well, I'm not going on safari. But since you asked, the man is a friend of my sister. He's from Alexandria."

"Egypt or Old Town?" Natalie meant it as a joke.

"Egypt, actually."

Two mouths dropped open. It figured.

"He's an archeologist," Tika explained. "I've only met him once, but he seemed interesting enough, at least for one date. Then again, you may hear by next week that I've died of boredom. At least, I'll get to speak French for a little while."

And with that, she wished them a good night and headed for her quarters, a quaint stone cottage that had once been the springhouse.

"Imagine that!" Lu gasped. "An archeologist from Egypt! And who says exciting things don't happen in Pleasant Valley?"

"Yeah. Imagine that." Natalie was strangely silent as she clicked off the recessed lights over the kitchen cabinets.

Life had altered so completely. More so than she could have ever foreseen late last winter. In D.C., every day had been a rat race, although an exciting one, if she were honest. But here, only a few months later, all the really good stuff happened to other people—and the most exciting thing *she'd* done lately was design a brochure for the church bake sale! Maybe "settling down" hadn't been such a good idea, after all.

Yet, the town was beginning to feel a lot like family, and it *was* comforting to work with staff who acted more like a brother and sisters than paid employees.

Still . . . .

Lu shimmied her bare feet into her Birks. "You going to bed now, darlin'?"

"Yep. Maybe read a little Jeanine Beaumont first."

Lu smiled knowingly. "Good night then. And sweet dreams. . . ."

The next day Natalie logged on to the Internet via her laptop, downloaded the latest software, and surfed for some ideas. As reward for a morning well spent, she put the top down on her Jaguar and drove along the Parkway. On that drive an idea was born.

On her way back into town, she stopped by the Sherwin Williams store, then by Jonah C. Chord's office. Jonah was the local contractor she hoped to hire for some of the small remodeling jobs she'd deemed necessary to bring the inn completely up to par.

At her request, he climbed into his Blazer and followed her back to the inn.

On the way, she did some thinking about Jonah—a member of Trinity, unmarried, and too unassuming to mingle regularly in the "singles' market." His scratchy voice was subtly appealing, she thought, but decided it must be a source of embarrassment for him. He seldom said more than a few words—and then only in answer to a direct question. As a result, he seemed shy and a little lonely.

Renee had told her that both of Jonah's grandparents hailed from Cuba originally, escaping on a raft in the middle of the night. His mother had married a native Bahamian, and he was a stunning mix of the two islands. At six foot seven, he reminded Natalie of a mahogany statue. Caramel-colored skin was stretched tautly over his wide features. Close-cropped black hair covered his large head. His immense physical proportions made his shyness all the more charming. Jonah was a rugged man, at home in hiking boots, dungarees, and flannel shirts. But more than building and enjoying the beauty of nature, Jonah loved music.

Accomplished on a variety of instruments, including piano, he often accompanied the choir for special numbers. What endeared him to Natalie most, however, was his work with the mentally handicapped. Whenever the handbell choir from the local institution would play, she always found herself brushing away tears. Watching those huge, work-roughened hands directing so gracefully, the eager faces of the young musicians. . . . It was enough to melt the hardest heart.

If Jonah wasn't so utterly shy.

Or so utterly polite.

He should have been married a long time ago, Natalie thought, as he helped her carry in the wallpaper books and paint samples. Maybe he was just stubborn, like Tika, she hypothesized.

Tika.

Hmm.

"Just put that stuff there on the table." She shrugged off her shoulder bag, deposited her armload, and looked up. "How busy are you right now?"

"Not very."

"Do you have any men available?"

"A few."

"Then let me show you what I need. This pantry here off the porch—" she led the way through the screen door—"is awfully inconvenient for Tika, our chef. You've met her, haven't you?" He shook his head no. Natalie laid some groundwork. "She's a great gal and a terrific cook. Anyway, this spot would make a wonderful office for me. Private. Plenty of room for a computer desk and a chair."

"Shelves?"

"If you think they'll fit. Now, come back inside. See this bathroom off the kitchen here? No one ever uses it. It's really just a glorified broom closet. Can you tear out the fixtures and make it into a pantry?"

"Sure."

"When?" Now he had *her* speaking in monosyllables.

"Wednesday. Jeremy Davis is finishing up at Mike Mitchie's pub on Tuesday. Does good work. Could get you an estimate by tomorrow."

"Fine."

They shook on the deal.

A smile played on Natalie's lips as she watched him climb into his Blazer. *Look out, Natalie, you're getting to be as big a matchmaker as Lu.*

Still, it was mildly disheartening when she tallied the score. *Two* possible prospects for Tika: Jonah and the archeologist. Nat: zip. The only unmarried men in her life were old Silas Q.—and Andy . . . who didn't count.

On that depressing note, Natalie proceeded to make the biggest sandwich she could get her mouth around.

By mid-week, Jonah Chord was in and out of the house several times a day, moving with the lithe grace of a ballet dancer for such a giant of a man. Ever quiet, he and his small crew made a minimum of racket except when hammering or using the Skilsaw. With the reopening of the dining room and the influx of foliage-viewers spinning the staff in many directions, he was pretty much left to do his own thing.

By now, Natalie couldn't think of much besides the new Web page. Much to her dismay, she hadn't been able to come up with a single idea that suited her.

Yet.

She surfed the Net for hours, looking for the perfect backgrounds and finding new ideas. She wanted to say it all without the user having to download heavy graphics. There was nothing more frustrating than watching that little hourglass for minutes on end, seeing picture after picture eek its way onto the computer screen.

The format must be bright, snappy, elegant.

And *fast*.

At all costs the little stop sign icon must not be clicked on by those who came across the site.

Natalie sat back and took a breather. It was 2:45.

A.M.

After a dozen or more false starts, she'd finally found an interesting, parchment style background with the perfect, buttery tone, reflecting the warmth of the inn itself. Anxious to get the site up and running, Natalie was relieved.

Even *more* relieved to have Tika back in the kitchen and the dining room open for business again. Nat had caught more than a few interested looks passing between the cook and the contractor in the last few days. Good. Things seemed promising—at least on that front.

In spite of her fatigue, Natalie went to sleep with a smile on her face.

The alarm, making no concessions for late-night hours, sounded off with a piercing shriek at the same old time.

Natalie mashed the snooze button, but exactly nine minutes later, the clock had the audacity to buzz again.

Oh, all right. All right!

Irritated, Natalie pushed back the sheets, grabbed some fresh underwear, and headed off to shower.

The minute she emerged, Lu knocked on the door—the "breakfast-is-ready" signal—and Natalie hastily threw on khaki pants, an ivory turtleneck, and a fisherman's sweater.

Oren was already seated at the table, eyeing the grits and gravy and tapping his foot impatiently.

"Sorry," Natalie muttered, pouring a cup of coffee. "The snooze button was too tempting this morning."

Tika set down a plate of melt-in-your-mouth biscuits, then slid into her seat with a bowl of granola and skimmed milk for herself. "Know what you mean."

For a few minutes there were only the contented sounds of munching, the clink of silverware on the everyday china, and an occasional slurp from Oren.

Much to Natalie's surprise, it was he who broke the silence. "How's the computer advertisement coming?"

"Very nicely, thanks. Finally found a background worth using. Of course, it took me half the night."

"Thought you looked a little fuzzy around the edges this morning," Lu clucked with a shake of her head, her heavy silver earrings brushing against her neck. "No worse than Tika, though, after that week at her sister's—and her date with the archeologist."

"Let's don't dig up that subject again, Lu," Tika warned good-naturedly. "It's an experience I don't particularly care to relive."

"What?" Natalie laughed. "You mean having to pay for your own meal at *Roy Rogers* wasn't what you had in mind when he asked you out?"

Tika shook her head. "As if taking a chef to a fast-food restaurant wasn't bad enough," she moaned. "But then making me pay for my own burger."

"Not the feminist you thought you were, eh?" Oren put in, still grumpy at having his breakfast delayed.

"What a disaster." Tika shuddered. "He went on and on about his food allergies—as if I could help him. Good grief! Now I know how doctors and lawyers feel when someone is trying to finagle some free advice."

"Speaking of doctors and lawyers," Lu changed the subject. "Dr. and Mrs. Manley will be checking in today."

"They're still like a couple of newlyweds." Tika finished up her cereal.

Natalie agreed. "The cutest older couple *I've* met since I moved here."

Oren stood to his feet. "If folks aren't already hitched up when they come here, you women are schemin' ways to get 'em hitched up. I've got my rakin' to do." With that, he dredged one more bite of biscuit into the remaining white gravy on his plate and took off.

"Who else is scheduled for today?" Natalie asked Lu, who always seemed to have that register practically memorized. And later, as she checked in several new guests, she recalled the stories Lu and Tika had shared.

John Farrow. A very tired school principal, "swinging in out of the jungle for the weekend," he'd said.

Mr. and Mrs. Robert ("Rahhbeee," as his wife called him) Jessup. Newlyweds with the wide-eyed innocence of a pair of newborn lambs—and an encouragement to all who believe that some things are still sacred.

Callie Stein. Speech pathologist. A lovely girl with waist-length hair and glacier-blue eyes escaping the horrors of her work with stroke and accident victims—"for just a little while."

And more.

Always more.

From newlyweds to nearly deads, an endless procession of faces. Some masking pain, others radiating joy. All of them seeking a quiet haven—a place to heal, to be renewed, to love and be loved.

Many were reasonable. Some were demanding. But all came in search of a smile and a little friendly chat—and they never went away disappointed. Lu and Natalie made sure of it.

At the end of the month, two very cherished guests—Tommy and Renee Alcott—signed in to celebrate their anniversary. Natalie half expected Renee to take on the role of cruise director. But to her delight, the Alcotts—staying in the Gardenia Room—kept pretty much to themselves. They took long walks along the river, browsed the antique stores they had driven past all their lives, and chose a romantic little alcove off the dining room each evening.

Renee was positively glowing when they checked out before church on Sunday morning. It was her comment when she and her very happy husband left that sparked Natalie's first real creative streak in weeks. "Honey, do I ever have a great line for your new ad," she whispered behind her hand. "'Spicy, sweet, a honeymoon treat, Pleasant Valley Inn just can't be beat!'"

Natalie hooted, thinking of all the sophisticated ad copy she'd read in her day.

"Okay, okay," Renee defended herself. "I know it sounds like a cheer—old habits die hard, you know—but you get the idea." And she sailed off on Tommy's arm, looking ten years younger and almost that many pounds heavier after indulging in Tika's good cooking!

But Natalie's mind was already running at 64 megs of RAM. Why not advertise the inn as the perfect honeymoon spot? Jonah was still around—why not ask him about adding a gazebo out back in the garden, or maybe even a conservatory? It would be an ideal place for small weddings or for renewing vows. Reception following in the gardens or the dining room. Maybe even make it a package deal, with part of the honeymoon included.

She ran back to the kitchen to tell the others.

                                                     ∽

For the next two weeks, Silas Q., ensconced in his new rocker, surveyed all the goings-on with ill-concealed irritation. That the pale eyes were a little brighter each day was the only sign that he was secretly enjoying his front-row seat.

And on the day that Jonah completed the new addition to the kitchen, Silas actually took a tour of the area and gave it his blessing. A nod. A slight tip of his cap. And one corner of his mouth tilted upward.

Why not? Elva Jacks had never brought him tea or cocoa out on the porch when the weather turned chilly. Maybe this St. John woman wouldn't be so bad, after all.

Nine

The new pantry boasted pull-out shelves, baskets, and more bins than even a Cordon Bleu chef could have dreamed of. Tika was impressed with the gleaming white, well-lit addition. And Lu, not to be left out, was thrilled with her broom closet beneath the stairs, which was every bit as well organized as Tika's pantry.

After a detailed inspection—at Jonah's insistence—Natalie handed him a check. Without glancing at the amount, he folded it and slid it into his shirt pocket.

"Did you find a present for your niece's birthday?" Natalie asked, knowing he'd been worried about locating the perfect gift.

"Sure did."

"And what did you come up with?"

"An easy bake oven."

Tika, who had been scrubbing her butcher's block, looked up. "You took my advice, I see."

"Good advice, too." Jonah spread his lips in an easy grin. "She loved it."

"Well, you never know what that gift will lead to. It's how I got my start."

Natalie was puzzled. "When did you give Jonah this sage advice, Tika? Between his unwillingness to say more than two words at a time, and your keeping our guests well fed—"

"With you being Miss Ad Executive these days, just who did you think was going to help him design the shelves and drawers for the pantry?" Tika's dark eyes flashed.

"And the bins," Jonah added. "Don't forget the bins."

"*Especially* the bins." They shared a private joke, chuckling softly.

Natalie wasn't about to pry. She held out her hand. "Thanks for taking on the project, Jonah. And . . . I was hoping you might have time for another one soon."

He shook her hand. "We'll talk."

"Great. Guess I'll see you in church on Sunday."

"Yeah. The handbell choir is playing. See ya."

And he was gone.

Lu sidled up to Tika, hands on hips, eyes sparkling. "Now *there's* a nice young man!"

Tika was stirring the soup for the staff's lunch break. "Don't even *think* about it. Maybe he's everything I *should* want in a man, but he's one of Nattie's Jesus freaks."

"Oh, I wouldn't exactly call him a freak," Natalie said with a coy little smile. This wasn't the time to launch into a sermon. "*Hunk* is more like it, wouldn't you say?"

"Well . . . maybe," Tika agreed reluctantly. "At least, he's a far cry from that nerdy archeologist."

"Everything you could want in a man," Lu repeated with conviction.

Tika wiped her hands on a towel and flung it aside. "Enough about me. What about you, Nattie? What do you want in a man?"

"That's what I'd like to know, too." Lu began to put out the silverware, Natalie following with the napkins. "You read those Jeanine Beaumont novels all the time. I had no idea educated women like you ever read those things."

"I read them to make me quirky," she teased. "To give my personality a little edge."

"Nonsense," Lu scoffed. "Underneath all that big-city glamor beats the heart of a real woman. The right man just hasn't come along, that's all."

"And sometimes I hope he never does. Think of all the relationships that fail nowadays, Lu. I don't need a man for fulfillment or personal happiness, and I refuse to be one of those divorce statistics. Maybe it's smarter just to leave well enough alone."

"Now you sound like Tika." Lu looked around as Tika scooted through the doorway to fetch something from the pantry. She eyed Natalie with a solemn expression, then tugged her to a secluded corner of the kitchen. "You know, darlin', there's something really nice about being needed. It's always been that way with Oren and me."

"Oren's a jewel, Lu. You were lucky."

"Luck had nothing to do with it, and you know it. I'm surprised to hear a Presbyterian say such a thing." Lu herself, a devoted Southern Baptist, possessed a quiet, deep faith. "God made us for one another, I'm sure of it. And—" she peered at Natalie over her half-glasses—"I'm just as sure He has someone in mind for *you*."

Natalie wasn't buying that. "Marriage isn't for everyone, Lu. Besides, I'm only twenty-nine. A lot of career women don't get married these days until they're well up into their thirties."

Lu's blue eyes blinked wide. "Aha! So you're not giving up on the idea."

"Why is it so important to you anyway?"

"Oh, darlin', it's just that you have so much love to give. I can't imagine you going through life alone, without lovin' with a full heart. Why, even Silas Q. came down for punch and cookies at the Midsummer Night's Dream Party, remember? And if you can do that for a vinegary old man, just think what you could do for a *young* one!"

Lu was right. But Natalie wasn't about to confess just *how* right. She was lonely, true. But things could be worse. Like watching her mother cry herself to sleep night after night when "the geologist" left her for another woman. Like having her own heart broken again. . . .

"Lunch ready?" Oren called from the mudroom where he was washing up from his outside chores. "I'm starvin'!"

"Soup's on, and it's getting cold." Tika was back with a jar of pickled beets and cast Natalie and Lu a skeptical glance. "Butternut squash soup is the worst when it's cold."

"Just think about what I said," Lu mumbled, for Natalie's ears only.

"I will, Lu, although what does it matter? I'm not exactly winning a popularity contest among the singles in this town, am I?"

"You intimidate the men around here, darlin'."

"Well, that's their loss then," she said with a petulant shrug.

"There's always Andy," Tika piped up, overhearing the last remark.

Natalie gaped. "Oh come on, Tika. Andy and I have known each other since we were kids! He has no romantic interest in me whatsoever. Besides, Andy's not my type."

Tika narrowed her gaze, her disbelief plain to see. "A rich, smart lawyer who just happens to be your best friend—not your type? So just what kind of man *are* you looking for, Nattie? Some swashbuckling cavalier like the guys in those Jeanine Beaumont novels?"

"You leave Jeanine out of this! I don't know why I don't have any romantic interest in the man—I just don't. You, of all people Tika, should understand that. Especially after that date with the archeologist. There was nothing wrong with him, was there?"

"Not if you call feeling all creepy-crawly when he put his arm around me *nothing*." Tika shivered dramatically. "Or the fact that he was a cheapskate."

"You girls!" Lu clucked. "You're all just too picky nowadays. By the time I was your age, Natalie, I was married for almost ten years. And by the time I was *your* age Tika—" she folded her arms across her bosom—"I already had three children in school."

"*C'est la vie!*" Tika shrugged in her best Parisian manner and sat down to eat her own cooking.

By the beginning of November, the Web site was finished. It was all Natalie had hoped it would be. Gracious, elegant, timeless.

All that, and the recipient of a "Best of the Web" award as well. She chuckled to herself every time she saw the little icon proclaiming its status, and once again the thought of the technology that allowed her to reach out to people all over the world shot a thrill down her spine.

Business was as brisk as the weather, and so many reservations for next spring and summer were already being made on-line that once Jonah had finished the gazebo, Natalie had him begin construction on several cottages on the back two acres of woodland behind the house. Places for families, since children weren't allowed in the main house. She was planning on putting in a pool when spring came, well camouflaged of course, and a first-rate jungle gym. With Luray Caverns and the Shenandoah so close by, not to mention all the Civil War sites, she had predicted a boom by summer.

Lu was talking about hiring on another person to help her, and Tika said she'd definitely be needing full-time help in the kitchen since the dining room had been expanded as well. It didn't seem possible to Nat that she would soon have been an innkeeper for the better part of a year.

She turned her attention to the computer. The point cast screensaver blinked off as soon as she moved her mouse, and she clicked on the "send and receive" button of her E-mail program. The clock on the shelf said 1:31.

Just half an hour until my Jeanine Beaumont time, she thought, looking forward to "Love in the Afternoon," as Tika called it mockingly.

Natalie had recently picked up a copy of a new Beaumont novel at Walden's, and she planned to start reading it today. She would sit in her remodeled sunroom with a pot of Darjeeling tea and a plate of Tika's lemon scones. *Heavenly.*

Scrolling through, Nat saw that there was the regular assortment of jokes forwarded from friends, some replies to a question she had placed on a hoteliers newsgroup, and the normal number of inquiries regarding the inn. One caught her eye, a message with the address of "medievalman@jmu.edu."

Interesting.

She opened the file and began to read the entry entitled "An Inquiry."

To whom it may concern:

Having come upon your web site on the Internet, I am writing to confirm the room I reserved at your establishment for the month of December. If this is not agreeable, please contact me right away.

Sincerely,

Alexander S. Elbert, Ph.D.
Department of History
James Madison University

Natalie, remembering the enchanting English accent, quickly responded under the title, "An Answer," realizing at the same instant that she had failed to list the professor in the registry. She would take care of that just as soon as she'd finished the E-mail.

Dear Dr. Elbert,

Pleasant Valley Inn is pleased to be planning your accommodations for the month of December. Since this month is generally slow for us, you should find the atmosphere conducive to academic writing. If you wish, we would be happy to set up a computer for you. We are known for courteous, individualized service. Thank you for your interest in Pleasant Valley Inn. We look forward to serving you.

Sincerely,
Nat St. John, Proprietor

Automatically, she signed the abbreviated version of her name, then finished answering the mail she had neglected yesterday. Gail, her former administrative assistant at PluraNet, who was presently in the throes of planning a wedding, had sent a nice long, newsy note. And there was also an E-mail from a distant cousin—Nat's only living relative other than "the geologist"—who lived in Springfield, Illinois.

The registry was forgotten.

A light rap sounded on her office door, and Tika's braided head poked through. "Sorry to disturb you, Nattie, but I thought the time might have gotten away from you. It's two o'clock."

Natalie smiled. "Thanks. I was just finishing up. I'd better hurry and get that pot of tea made, or I won't have much time for Jeanine."

"I made it for you. Darjeeling. Is that okay?"

"You read my mind."

She followed Tika into the kitchen and took down a tray, a teacup and the sugar and milk. "Any lemon scones left from this morning?"

"Sorry," Tika called from inside her pantry. "Silas just ate the last one."

"Rats."

"If you wait just one minute, there's a batch of pumpkin walnut bread coming out of the oven."

Natalie hated walnuts. That bitter aftertaste, the way they squeaked between your teeth when your molars started to grind away. She shuddered. "No thanks. I'll just grab some of the biscotti from yesterday."

"In the jar on the counter!" Tika called, still on her haunches in front of one of the bins.

Nat grabbed several of the crunchy treats and threw them into a small bowl, then hurried to the chaise lounge in the sunroom. In no time, she was transported via the printed page from Pleasant Valley to a castle in Cornwall. Jeanine had set the mood perfectly with a fire glowing on the stone hearth, massive oak beams supporting a vaulted ceiling, and a soft rug, its rich colors muted with time, like the brushstrokes in a fine old painting. Catherine was sitting on a settee with the dashing rogue Nigel Pierce. Little did she realize that from across the room a brooding pair of eyes, belonging to American railroad millionaire, Jake Arlen, was already branding her as his own.

~~~

"I got an E-mail today from the history professor." Natalie broke that bit of news at the dinner table. "Please don't let me forget to write it down."

"You mean you didn't sign him in months ago?" Lu raised an eyebrow.

"No, I didn't. I can't believe I forgot, but I vaguely recall that I took that reservation during my first week at the inn—back when I was a real greenhorn." She waved a hand in dismissal. "Oh, well, no harm done, I suppose. December's a slow month."

"Unfortunately, that's not quite true any more—not since you brought us into the twenty-first century with your fancy Web page," Lu groaned. "I don't know where in the wide world we're going to put him."

Natalie rolled her eyes. "I guess I'll just have to give him *my* room."

It seemed that perhaps all college professors were like her father—taking what wasn't theirs.

Ten

<p>H e pushed through the carved double doors of the quaint inn, searching for some signs of life. "Hello? Is anybody here?"</p>

Not a sound.

"I say, is anyone around?"

Alexander Elbert tensed his jaw, his full bottom lip thinning in frustration. This was extremely awkward. Where was the innkeeper? That St. John chap. He'd hear a few choice words if the fellow ever did appear on the scene.

Alex had made his reservations a good eight months earlier, for goodness sake! Not only that, but he'd confirmed by E-mail just a fortnight ago, using the computer at the university.

He clicked open his pocketwatch. Seven A.M. Surely someone would be up and about at this hour. He could hear the rattle of pans from what must be the kitchen area. "Hello?"

"Just a minute! I'll be right there!" Clad in navy sweats, a most extraordinary-looking woman came running in from the back, her hair still up in a white bath towel. Escaping its confines, a dark, spiraling tendril brushed her cheek. "May I help you?"

"I should certainly hope so. I'm Alexander Elbert."

Alex's annoyance gave way to amusement as she shuffled quickly through the pages of the register. "Alexander Elbert, Ph.D. From JMU, right?"

He bowed stiffly, wondering why he was suddenly behaving like Mr. Chips. "Yes, madam." And sounding like Alfred to boot.

She was immediately contrite. "Forgive me. We didn't realize you'd be coming quite so early or we'd have—"

He waved away her attempted explanation. "Just show me to my room, please. I have a lot of work to get done today." *Why am I acting like an idiot?* he thought. *A pretty woman walks into the room, and I suddenly feel like I've been hit by a cyclone!*

He watched as she unlocked a cabinet, grabbed a key, and motioned him down a corridor. "I put you at the back of the house. It's more secluded there. Quieter, too, and more conducive to concentrating. Unfortunately, I'm afraid we haven't had time to clean it after . . . the previous occupant."

He followed, noting the trim lines of her figure, enjoying the slightly husky quality of her early-morning voice.

"There's a lovely sunporch where you may wait until your room is ready," she was saying. "I'll be putting up the Christmas decorations outside today, so if you need anything, you'll know where to find me. There's a bell just inside the door." She put the key in the lock, turned it, and reached around for the bellpull. "See? It rings in the kitchen, and one of us will be in to take care of whatever you need. Lu, our housekeeper, will be around shortly."

"I'd be very grateful."

"Have you had breakfast yet?"

"An hour ago."

"Do you need help with your luggage?"

"This is everything I brought with me." He held in one hand an ancient leather suitcase. Tan. Hard-sided. In the other was a portable typewriter in a black carrying case. "And it is getting rather heavy, so if you don't mind, I'd like to settle in."

Alex could have kicked himself six ways from Sunday when he noticed the woman's downcast expression. She was not only going to conclude that he was a stuffed shirt, but an obnoxious one at that.

"Oh, please—come on in and make yourself at home." She moved ahead of him into the room, opening up a luggage rack, clearing a space on the dresser for his typewriter.

"If you're planning on eating lunch with us, we'll need to know," she said, somewhat apologetically. "The dining room is usually only open for dinner."

At least, he could set her mind at ease on that score. "All I'll require is a pot of strong tea delivered to my room every afternoon at two o'clock. No milk and sugar, no lemon or cookies, just a nice hot pot of tea and a china cup."

She nodded. "We'll do our best to accommodate you. The bathroom's through that door there, and there's a walk-in closet. Remember, if you need anything, I'll only be—"

"—outside. Yes, I remember. Good day then."

She turned to go, and he felt a moment of panic. "Oh, miss . . . I didn't catch your name."

She turned again to meet his gaze, and the towel slipped back from her head like the hood of some medieval knight's fair lady. A riot of auburn curls, dark and wet, tumbled down around her face, her eyes an emerald green.

"I'm Natalie St. John."

Startled, he caught his breath. So this was Nat St. John. A *woman*!

"Uh . . . Ms. St. John, may I say I'm surprised . . . that is, more than pleased . . . with the rooms. They're quite adequate . . . and the large windows will afford the perfect lighting for my work. I'm sure I'll find here everything I . . . uh . . . need." Why was he stammering around like a schoolboy?

The proprietor of Pleasant Valley Inn nodded pleasantly, turned once more, and closed the door softly behind her.

"Blast you, man!" he muttered to himself, as he began to unpack. Placing his toiletries bag on the back of the commode, he leaned forward to study his reflection in the mirror. Tweed jacket, oxford cloth shirt, school tie. "What a frump she must think you," he said, laughing. "Well, old boy, you've an entire month to show her you're not the pompous prig you appear to be."

"Lu!" Natalie careened into the kitchen, the towel now draped around her shoulders. "You've got to make up my room. The professor is here!"

Lu swirled her hair up into its bun, secured it with a couple of chopsticks, then shoved her feet, encased in heavy, rag wool socks, into her Birkenstocks. "Oh dear. An early bird. He and Oren should have a lot in common." She heaved herself to a standing position and quickly finished her cup of coffee. "It's a good thing you got your clothes out of there yesterday."

"I know. Talk about awkward."

"Awkward is sleeping up in the attic like you'll be doing for the next month," Lu frowned. "I keep telling you you're welcome to stay with Oren and me."

"I know, and I appreciate the offer, Lu, but one of us should be in the house during the night in case someone needs something."

"Suit yourself." Lu was getting her baskets together—one, filled with cleaners, little soaps, shampoos and mints; the other, with bed linens and towels.

"Lu, he doesn't seem to be the talkative type," Natalie warned.

"Okay, okay. I promise not to talk his ear off, if that's what you're worried about. But I *was* looking forward to hearing his accent!" With that, she was on her way.

"So tell me about the new guest," Tika asked when Natalie, dressed and dry, came in for some breakfast. "He's a professor, right?"

"Medieval history. From James Madison."

"Now *that's* a scary thought. The word *medieval* conjures up only two things: torture chambers and ladies in pointy hats. What's he look like? Is he an older man?"

"Hardly," offered Lu, who had just finished cleaning his rooms. She slid into her place with a bowl of hot cereal.

"That's exactly what I'd expected . . . with a name like *Alexander Elbert.*" Natalie buttered a biscuit. "But he's young—around thirty-five or so, I'd guess."

"Is he 'cute'?" Oren mumbled over a bite of pancake, baiting them.

She chuckled. "Oh, I suppose. Sandy blond hair. Ruddy complexion. Medium height. But he's every inch the professor—right down to his Hushpuppies."

Tika burst into laughter. "Hushpuppies? *Hushpuppies?* You've got to be kidding. How old did you say this guy was?"

"Well, as peculiar as he seems, he certainly won't be any trouble," Natalie said. "Tea at two is the only thing he asks out of the ordinary. 'Just tea.'" She imitated his very patrician-sounding voice. "'No milk and sugar, no lemon, no cookies. Just a pot of strong tea and a china cup.'"

Lu's eyes widened. "Did he really say that? He was already hard at work in the sunroom by the time I got there, so there was no chance to chat."

"He sounds just like the old-time Hollywood film stars. Very cultured—an accent somewhere between British and American. Heavier on the British, I think. It's actually quite nice."

Tika waved her hand impatiently and got up from the table. "You would think so, Nattie. Your mother must have been a hopeless romantic. I mean, she named you *Natalie,* for heaven's sake. Not exactly a Seven-Eleven kind of name."

Natalie ignored the comment. "As I was saying, I don't think we'll even know he's around most of the time. By the way, Oren, thanks for hauling that desk to the sunroom. The professor had a portable typewriter with him—no computer in sight. He's obviously still living in the Dark Ages."

Oren's eyes twinkled appreciatively. "Sounds like an old-fashioned kind of lad to me. Up early. Ready to get going with the sun. I like that in a fellow. Behind that accent there might just be a real good man."

"We'll see," Tika put in skeptically as she began to rummage in the pantry for the ingredients for the day's breadbaking. "Hey, Nattie, how about some cranberry bread?"

"Perfect. After I put up the outside decorations, I'm planning on curling up with a good book in the parlor. Tea and cranberry bread will be just the thing."

"Did you finish that Jeanine Beaumont book you were so excited about?" Lu asked, returning from the dining room with the remnants of Old Silas's breakfast—eggbeaters, fake bacon, and wholegrain toast. Always the same.

"It was one of her best." Natalie twisted her mouth in a wry grimace. "The only problem with being faithful to an author is that once you've read all her books, you have to wait until the next one comes out."

"Maybe the anticipation is half the fun." Lu took Oren's empty plate and refilled his coffee cup. "By the way, I read something interesting in the paper this morning. Kind of funny in a way, at least for a Baptist."

Natalie was curious. "What was it?"

"There's this office building down in Miami where the streaks left by the window washers look like the Virgin Mary."

"Not your everyday sidewalk scene, I'll admit." Still, some people seemed to find the spectacular in the mundane. Could be an admirable quality. She'd have to ponder that one.

"They're calling it a Christmas miracle. Folks are making a pilgrimage down there, bringin' all sorts of gifts and everything. Some are even hoping to be healed."

Tika spooned some yeast into a bowl of hot water. "Hmph! Just another example of looking for hope in all the wrong places, if you ask me."

"I know where my *hope* lies. But I suppose I have more experience in looking for *love* in all the wrong places," Natalie confessed with a rueful grin.

Lu sighed and sat down to rub her fallen arches. "Back to men again, huh?"

"Yeah . . . the wretched creatures. But I have about as much hope of finding true love as I do of being healed by a window washer's Virgin Mary."

She left the kitchen, the solace of her attic room and her mother's Bible calling softly around the edges of her loneliness.

⟋⟍

"I don't know, Tika." Lu pulled out her trusty broom. "Seems to me there must be somebody out there for Natalie. Some knight in shining armor who'll love and cherish her."

"She's a solitary sort when you get right down to it, Lu. Maybe she likes it that way."

Lu continued to sweep, sliding the crumbs from breakfast into a dustpan. "Nobody really likes to be lonely." She emptied the pan and cocked an eye in Tika's direction. "Now, on the other hand, maybe that professor is here for something more than writing some stuffy old paper. Maybe he was sent by God."

"Oh, right, Lu. Some moldy guy with a sissy accent? No, what Nattie needs is someone really strong, someone to come along and sweep her off her feet—like one of the heroes in those novels she's always reading."

"Can't argue with you there. Too bad Jeanine Beaumont can't find her a husband!"

⟋⟍

Somehow, even with all the new holiday guests, Natalie managed to get the porch decorated. Lighted garland spiraled round the pillars and looped from the railing. Great burgundy-colored bows accented the wreaths that hung at each window.

On the doors were two larger wreaths Renee had helped assemble the day before.

"Give me a glue gun," she'd boasted, "and I could put Ford Motors out of business!"

Renee had gotten to work, and the effect was breathtaking. Airy French-wired gold ribbon intertwined with the burgundy velvet bows, pine cones, holly, and a lovely angel robed in gold. Afterwards, she'd grinned and quipped, "Your own guardian angel."

Oren was a big help, too, whistling "It's Beginning to Look a Lot Like Christmas," filling the air with his own brand of holiday cheer.

Down the street, the boys at the Volunteer Fire Department were hanging the obligatory brightly colored lights and exchanged waves every so often. When Tika delivered a steaming copper pot of cocoa, the firefighters happily convened on the porch to wrap their hands around the earthenware mugs.

For the town of Pleasant Valley, the Christmas season had officially begun. Natalie's favorite time of the year. Yet, this year it felt different. Maybe because this was her first without her mother. Maybe. . . .

Professor Elbert had sent word that he wished to dine early, at 6:00. He arrived at precisely 5:59. Natalie, in a simple wine-colored crepe dress, seated him by one of the fireplaces and presented him a menu. He opened it quickly, and before she could itemize the specials or ask if he wanted to start with an appetizer, he ordered his meal.

"The chops, please. Not overdone. Baked potato and broccoli. Bleu cheese dressing on the salad. A glass of ice water. The torte for dessert, with a cup of coffee. The real thing—not decaf."

"Uh . . . certainly." She had absolutely no idea how he'd read the menu that fast or had known that the vegetable of the day was broccoli. Keen eyes and a keen sense of smell, she suspected. And the self-assurance to trust his instincts.

"Are you expecting many other guests tonight?" His glance took in the entire room, coming to rest on the painting over the mantel.

"Not until seven. I'll be right back with your salad."

"Oh, before you go, can you tell me who did that painting there?"

"A local artist, Drew Bordan."

"Primitive. I like it."

Natalie smiled. "I suppose its lack of perspective would appeal to someone who specializes in the Middle Ages."

He didn't respond, just continued to study the picture.

Natalie retreated into the kitchen to fetch his salad, rolling her eyes as she walked through the door. "Well, I think I just put my foot in my mouth with the professor."

"What did you do this time?" Tika asked as she artfully arranged the field greens on a depression glass plate.

Natalie admitted her faux pas, adding, "The problem is, I don't know if he understood which one I think lacks perspective—the painting . . . or *him*!"

"Uh-oh." Tika gave her a sympathetic smile. "But I doubt if he noticed. That type is usually too preoccupied with his own narrow field of study. Here you go." She handed over the plate of greens, garnished with yellow cherry tomatoes and toasted pecans.

Natalie whisked the dish out to the dining room. "Your salad, Professor Elbert." His nose was already in a book, so she set the plate in front of him and quietly removed herself from the room, letting the wait staff take over from there.

She was aware that Alexander Elbert's eyes followed her retreat . . . every single step of it. She could feel his gaze on her back. It was disturbing—both stimulating and frightening. She could only pray that December would melt into an early spring.

Eleven

*A*lex let himself out the front door of the inn. He breathed in the crisp morning air, then exhaled, his breath a visible cloud of steam, perfumed by Colgate. After a couple of deep kneebends, he sprang to his feet. Nothing like a brisk morning walk to get the circulation going and the mental wheels turning.

Over in the side yard, Oren Luckadoo was already out raking, gathering up the last of the stragglers from the sugar maples.

Alex sprinted over to greet him. "Tenacious little fellows, eh?"

The gardener straightened and crossed his arms over his rake. "Well, a good mornin' to ya. Another early bird here at the inn is always welcome."

"Are the others late risers?" Alex hunched his shoulders against a sudden chill breeze and shoved his hands into his pockets.

"Not really. Up by six-thirty, all of 'em. I have to hand it to our new owner. Don't expect more out of us than she's willin' to put out herself, though she does hold up breakfast now and again, skimmin' the Net, or whatever they call it, until all hours the night before."

"A good boss, I take it?"

"You're darn tootin'! Pretty, too."

"I'd have to agree there." Actually, Alex hadn't been able to think about much of anything else for the past three days. That sweet face, those green eyes, the glorious hair. "I must admit to a certain fondness for lovely redheads."

Oren's blue eyes caught the morning light, and his gaze was suddenly piercing. "Natalie St. John's a fine woman. You'd do well to remember that."

Was that some kind of veiled threat? What did the man take him for?

"A young fellow who's up this early is either gardenin' or huntin'—and I don't mean the four-legged variety."

Alex laughed aloud, the sound reverberating through the quiet streets. The noise of it surprised him pleasantly, and after bidding Oren a good day, he broke into an easy run.

Four weeks, he mused. Not much time. Not much, indeed.

"I wish Tika and Lu would get off my back about this love and marriage thing," Natalie fumed aloud as she made her attic cot. The truth was, though, she was beginning to feel more restless by the day. She figured it had a lot to do with her mother's death—and the fact that Christmas was such a family time. Maybe it was just sleeping on that cot!

Down to the parlor she went to sulk. Turned on *The Morning Movie.* Watched the screen as Jimmy Stewart materialized with his lanky frame and his sweet-boy face, pretending to be standing beside a great white rabbit. Myrtle Mae was making an egg and onion sandwich for her prospective suitor, played by the original Maytag repairman. Dr. Chumley dreamed of lounging beneath a tree in Cincinnati while a lovely young woman patted his hand, saying, "Poor thing. You poor, poor thing."

Natalie recognized the movie at once—a rerun of *Harvey,* another of her all-time favorites. The inside decorating she'd planned to do could wait until after lunch.

She sat without blinking, her gaze riveted on the screen.

Finally, the soliloquy in the alley outside "Charlie's Place"—a rare portrayal of the human condition by an actor she had always admired. Jimmy Stewart as Elwood P. Dowd, the harmless eccentric, and his invisible friend.

"Harvey and I sit in the bar and have a drink or two . . . play the jukebox," Stewart drawled. "And soon the faces of all the other people, they turn toward mine and they smile. And they say, 'We don't know your name, Mister, but you're a very nice fellow.' Harvey and I warm ourselves in all these golden moments."

Natalie smiled and tucked the throw pillow up under her chin as he continued.

"We've entered as strangers, but soon we have friends and—and they come over and they sit with us and they talk to us and they tell about the big, terrible things they've done and the big, wonderful things they'll do. Their hopes. Their regrets. Their loves. Their hates. All very large—because nobody ever brings anything small into a bar."

Jimmy pauses for dramatic effect.

"And then I introduce them to Harvey. And he's bigger and grander than anything they offer me. And—and when they leave, they leave impressed."

So who was crazy—Elwood P. Dowd or the rest of the world? Natalie chuckled softly as the picture faded to a toothpaste commercial.

"A fine movie." The professor's distinctive voice came from the doorway. "And *that,* in my opinion, is one of the most memorable scenes in all of filmdom."

Unaccountably, the day brightened. "So you're a Jimmy Stewart fan, too."

Professor Elbert sauntered over to the television set, hands plunged into the pockets of his jacket, a lock of tousled blond hair spilling over his forehead. He glanced back at her over his shoulder. "Isn't everyone?"

Maybe it was the way he was dressed today but . . . why hadn't she noticed before? Alexander Elbert was the best-looking man she'd ever seen! In this light, she could see that his eyes were brown. A luminous light brown, with flecks the color of sunlit honey. . . .

"Did you know that this was one of his favorite roles?"

"Wh-what?" She blinked, clearing her head. What had he said? "Oh . . . uh . . . yes. I have the video that tells about the making of the film."

"So do I. So you're a lover of old movies."

She sighed. "A junkie, I'm afraid."

"Too bad that's a luxury I can ill afford just now." Alex unzipped his parka, revealing a broad expanse of chest under a turtleneck. "But I came to write, and write I shall."

She rose to put another log on the fire, brushing against him accidentally. To cover her confusion, she said the first thing that came to mind. "Well, cheerio, as they say back home in England."

Despite the cheerful fire, the atmosphere chilled a couple of degrees, and he was the stiff professor again. "Good day."

"Cheerio?" St. John, you're an absolute imbecile! Natalie chided herself as he stalked away. *The man must have thought you were making fun of him.*

A little while later she heard the furious tap-tapping of his type-writer and wondered just what subject stole him from society. Was it really the distant past—or something just over the horizon?

∽

"Hi, Nat. It's Andy."

Natalie's lip curled in dismay at the voice on the other end of the line, but she forced a cheerfulness she didn't feel at the moment. "Andy! How have you been?"

"Fine. I was just wondering if you were busy this Saturday."

"Well, as a matter of fact, I am." Boy, she hated to do this, but she really was busy. "The inn is completely booked this weekend, and with the Christmas activities I've got planned, there's just no way I can take the time off."

"Oh."

"I'm sorry, Andy. I hope you understand. It's just going to be bananas around here during the month of December." She didn't offer a later alternative.

There was a long pause. Poor guy.

"Okay. Guess I'll see you later then. It's just that there's someone I want you to meet."

"Oh, yeah? I hope it's not some guy creating motherboards in his garage who needs financing."

Andy's chortle had a different quality about it. She wondered why. "No, definitely not that, Nat. In fact, it's not a guy at all."

"I thought I knew all your relatives. . . ." She pondered a moment. "So. You must have a new girlfriend." That would be the day, Natalie thought, smiling to herself. Good ol' Andy. He'd be true—even without the slightest encouragement from her—till the end of time.

"Make that fiancée, Nat . . . as in—I'm gonna get married."

If he had announced his decision to run for president, she couldn't have been more flabbergasted. Andy was her best friend. She'd always known what he was thinking—usually even before he thought it! Granted, she'd been pretty busy lately. . . . "When did this happen?"

"Last night. But I met her at the closing on your inn, Nat. It's Elva Jacks's lawyer—Lori Chester."

The room was spinning around her. "I can't . . . believe it, And."

"It all happened sort of fast. I ran into her a few weeks ago . . . and well, things just clicked. Sheesh, Nat, I'm thirty years old, Lori's thirty-two . . . at our age, when you know it's right, there's no sense in waitin' around."

"Have you set a date?" Natalie's hand on the receiver was trembling. She'd never expected this—not in a million years. She'd always been able to count on Andy being there for her. And now. . . .

"Next week. She wanted a Christmas wedding. Can you come?"

"To D.C.?" The room tilted again, then righted itself. Was this really happening?

"Where else? Lori's a widow—she hates it when I use that term—and she just wants something small. We're havin' it here at the house. Ma's makin' a big dinner afterwards—lots of pasta and meatballs, you know. If I could ask you to be my best man, I would, Nat."

There was a small silence while Natalie blinked back tears. Andy . . . getting married?

"Lori's a wonderful lady, Nat. The whole thing took me by surprise. But it's so right."

His tone was warm and calm—the tone of a man in love and confident he was making the right decision.

Natalie finally found her voice. "Andy, I'm happy for you. I really am."

"So you'll come?"

She broke into a wide smile. Why not? Just because he was getting married didn't mean he wasn't the same old Andy. "You'd better believe it, pal! Wouldn't miss it for the world."

Andy gave her the particulars, then added, "You know me . . . we're not goin' in for anything real formal, so don't get too dressed up. We're havin' a little jazz quartet at the reception, and you know Ma's cookin'. It's going to be a lotta fun. And, Nat—"

She waited, hoping she could manage to sit through the wedding when the time came.

"—bring a date if you want." He rang off with a "Too much to do and not enough time to do it. But we'll stay in touch. I'll call . . . soon."

Natalie sat, stunned, receiver in hand. She'd just lost her best friend. Memories of a brokenhearted seven-year-old came rushing back. Her parents' shouting matches. The growing distance between them. Then, finally, the day her fun-loving father had left for the last time with a kiss and a promise to call. . . .

No sooner had she cradled the receiver than the phone rang again. Maybe Andy had forgotten to tell her something—

But it was an operator's voice, cool and impersonal. "I have an overseas call from the UK for Miss Natalie St. John."

Without a reply, she hung up.

Maybe it was time to make amends with "the geologist." But not today.

⁓

"You ladies need something more to think about," Oren declared with a scowl. It was Friday morning. He hated Fridays because it meant the weekend was here, and on weekends, he was banished to the house. Mrs. Jacks had never wanted him bustling about the yard while the inn was busy, and Natalie continued in the tradition. "That poor man in there seems like a normal enough fellow to me. Why don't you just get on with your cookie-making and leave him be?"

"Now, Oren," Lu snapped, "if we didn't dream a little now and again, we'd be a mighty dull bunch."

"True," Natalie sided with Lu. "Keeps our jobs interesting."

"Speak for yourselves!" Tika retorted, adding some baking powder and salt to the mixture in the bowl. "I happen to love my job."

Natalie liked the sound of that. "Keep talking, Tika. I'd be foolish not to realize that your cooking is ninety percent of the reason for this inn's success."

Lu feigned annoyance. "Is that so? Tell me how long you'd stay in business if the sheets were never changed, missy! Just tell me that!"

Oren let out a grunt of disgust. "You gals can gab all you want. I've got chores to do."

"Good idea!" Lu snapped again at his retreating back, then muttered to the others, "You'd think he'd appreciate a little change of pace, but that man's addicted to fresh air, I do believe."

"Better that than a lot of other things I can think of," Tika drawled. "But back to this professor of ours—he really is a creature of habit for somebody so young." She turned on the mixer, and the paddle began to rotate in the stainless steel bowl. "I saw him walk by the greenhouse yesterday morning when I was snipping some thyme. I'll have to admit, Nattie, he is cute."

"Even in his Hushpuppies?"

"Actually, I believe he was wearing jeans and Timberlands at the time."

"Oh, you don't fool me, Tamika Monroe," Lu cut in. "You like him because he's never sent back anything but an empty plate yet. The way to Tika's heart is through a man's stomach," she parodied.

Tika grinned. "Every morning I keep adding a little more just to see if I can get him to say a gastronomic 'uncle,' and every morning the plate comes back clean."

"Rises at 5:40 every morning, in for breakfast at 8, then takes a walk down by the river, wearing those old boots." Lu laughed. "And when I go in to tidy his room and clean the bathroom, the towels are always hanging just so—just like I left them the morning before. They're damp, all right, but neat as a pin."

"A real neatnik, huh?" Natalie pressed down on the cookie cutter, forming a bell in the dough. Jingle bells . . . or wedding bells?

"I'd say so. He has one of those Walkman things by his typewriter, and the wires are always wrapped neatly around the headset. His CD's are all lined up perfectly, too."

"What kind of CD's? Harps and lutes?" Tika snorted.

"Do you think I'd go snooping around like that?" Lu looked shocked.

"Oh, come on, Lu. Don't play high and mighty with us. We know you read the titles. And don't think you can get away with not letting us in on it." Tika was spooning spheres of peanut butter oatmeal dough onto a baking sheet at the rate of two a second, Natalie figured.

"Don't look at *me*," Natalie responded to Lu's pathetic expression of appeal. "I want to know, too. What kind of music does he listen to?"

Lu shrugged, conceding defeat. "*Best of Bread,* Tony Bennett, Perry Como. He's even got a Carpenters' CD and some classical stuff—Chopin, Debussy . . . and the soundtrack from 'Camelot.' Seems our proper young man is actually a romantic at heart."

Unaccountably, Natalie felt a weird little flutter in the area of her rib cage.

"And there's a lovely picture of him on the nightstand—taken in London, I'd wager—with a *woman*," Lu went on. "She was looking up at him like she could eat him with a spoon."

Natalie felt the flutter again—this time with a sinking sensation. "Figures. Probably one of his students, if I had to guess."

"She's probably a Britisher," Tika surmised dryly. "What would a man like that want with an American girl?"

Plenty, Natalie thought.

"Now, Tika," Lu scolded, "let's not jump to conclusions. She could be his first cousin once removed, for all we know. And he mightn't be an Englishman, either."

"Let's say—" Tika's eyes danced—"that he's really an American, a fugitive on the lam for murdering one of his luscious graduate students in the heat of a passionate argument!"

"Or—" Natalie chuckled—"maybe he's not a professor at all, but an FBI agent, come to stake out Old Silas, who's running a counterfeit operation out of his room in the middle of the night!"

Oren stepped into the room just in time for that last exchange. "You're at it again I see," he remarked with a look of disdain. "I'm tellin' ya, you women obviously don't have enough to do."

"Fret all you want, my dear," Lu called as she rummaged in the drawer for a spoon, "but tomorrow's Saturday, and *you'll* be the one with nothing to do!"

The phone rang and Natalie hopped to. "Pleasant Valley Inn." Her brow creased. "No, I will not accept a collect call from the U. K.!"

She slammed down the phone in disgust.

"What on earth?" Tika wondered aloud. "Who could be calling from the United Kingdom?"

"Wrong number," Natalie stated flatly. "Definitely the wrong number."

Twelve

❧

The weekend guests began pulling in around 4:30, a steady stream that didn't let up until 7:00. To escape the worst of the traffic, most of them had taken the afternoon off and had already begun to unwind on the peaceful drive down. They were in for a real treat—a special weekend package Natalie had advertised in the *Washington Post* and on the Web as "A Holiday Revelry."

In the afternoon, when she had served the professor's tea, he'd been a bit more talkative than usual. "The decorations outside look lovely, Ms. St. John."

"Thank you, Professor. I finished up the inside today. Everything, that is, except for the Christmas tree. I'm saving that for the week before."

He seemed to be studying her with a peculiar intensity. "I have a request. With all the extra people, I was hoping my meals could be brought here to the room."

Natalie was surprised to find a little disappointment mixed in with her relief. "Beginning with dinner tonight?"

He ducked his head half-apologetically. "That's what I had in mind, if it wouldn't be too much trouble."

She could hardly refuse him—not with him looking at her with that small-boy expression in his eyes. "Well, I think I should mention that tonight we're offering something different for a Friday night—an informal fireside buffet. Would you prefer to come fill your plate, or should I?"

"Why don't you do it. I'm feeling a little whimsical tonight. Surprise me." If he were joking, his expression didn't betray it. But he did seem to be fidgeting with his silver pen more than usual.

"All right then. I'll be by a few minutes before six. I hope you have a productive afternoon," she added, noting the sheaf of papers stacked neatly beside his typewriter.

Apparently following the line of her vision, he shrugged. "Sure hope the noise isn't a bother."

"Not at all. I'm all the way—" she cut herself off lest she reveal that he was occupying her quarters—"upstairs. But then we only hear the typewriter when things are quiet in the afternoon. Never at night."

"Oh, that's when I prepare notes for my next day's writing—in longhand."

"Very thoughtful of you. Thank you for your consideration."

Natalie left, at a loss as to what to say next. The man was an enigma. He didn't act like any professor she'd ever known. But it wouldn't do to let him know how baffling his behavior was, how unsettling his presence.

She didn't hear the door click shut right away. And when she reached the end of the hall, she turned to find him standing at his door, his clear brown eyes watching her.

~⌒⌒

Mr. and Mrs. George Pilcher were effusive in their praise of the fireside buffet. "Natalie, dear, your chef outdid herself this time." Violet Pilcher was a typical Southern gentlewoman. Soft-spoken, kind, always ready with a gracious compliment. Stylish white hair that had never once been tinted blue by Agnes down at the Beauty Spot. "Did you help her plan the menu?"

"Oh, Tika's far more capable in the kitchen than I. In fact, Martha Stewart could take a few tips from her. Did you enjoy the leg of lamb? I remembered that it's your favorite."

"Scrumptious. Wasn't it, dear?" She turned to her husband.

"You've got that right, Vi. I enjoyed every bite." In the afterglow of Tika's feast, George seemed relaxed and ready to move into the parlor nearer the fire.

Natalie enjoyed playing host. It was part of what made her tick. "Don't forget the cookies over on the sideboard or the cocoa and mulled cider in the silver urns on either end."

"Your new musician—the piano-player—" Vi gestured toward Jonah, who had agreed to play for the gathering—"is divine!" she gushed, putting her arm through George's and steering him toward one of the plush new couches, upholstered in a deep burgundy and navy with plump cushioned backs, that flanked the fire.

All of the regulars had congratulated Natalie on the improved seating arrangement, which had proven to be one of her most popular changes. By making the parlor area more comfortable, folks gathered at all hours, playing one of the many board games, watching the television recessed in an antique armoire, or just chatting in front of the fire.

What Violet had said was true. The music was perfection. Jonah sat comfortably at the shining black baby grand piano, clad in tan corduroys and an ivory turtleneck. He had played softly all during the dinner hour, rambling melodies that seemed to flow out of his fingertips. Delightful improvisations from his soul. But now that the dinner guests were gathering in the homey room, he struck a series of chord progressions to introduce some of the oldies— "Blue Moon" and "You and the Night and the Music."

While Jonah was entertaining the crowd, Natalie looked around frantically for Erin Higgenbotham. She and Tyler made dinner at Pleasant Valley Inn a monthly date night, and Natalie knew they'd finished eating awhile ago. Tonight Erin had promised to lead a sing-along. Her voice, smooth and slidey, was perfect for old songs and warm carols. But where was she?

Natalie was about to panic when someone tapped her on the shoulder. "Sorry," Erin whispered. "I had to use the ladies room. Should I just start quietly, and then encourage others to join in?"

"Sounds good to me, but you know more about this kind of thing than I do. I think almost everyone is here. Except for Silas and the professor."

"Well, you didn't expect either of them, did you?"

Natalie gave a wry grin. "About as likely as Santa Claus putting in an early appearance."

⁓

Tyler smiled from his spot near the fire as his wife strolled over to lean against the piano. Erin didn't sing much in public anymore. A former Las Vegas lounge singer, she said it brought back too many painful memories. But tonight was different—a chance to redeem it some by helping Natalie out. To tell the truth, they were both glad to do something for the woman who had single-handedly taken Trinity Presbyterian from a two-typewriter, one-copy machine operation to a networked, online computer playground.

Miss Delia Bloodworth, the church secretary and an institution in the town, had fought the board of elders every step of the way when the plans were announced. But once Natalie had the equipment up and running, and had taken a week to walk the eighty-two-year-old through the word processing and spreadsheet packages, Miss Delia Bloodworth became the chief proponent of technology as Pleasant Valley, Virginia, knew it.

"One is never too old to learn," Natalie had reminded her gently the first day. "And besides, I'm here to see that you do. Just relax and know that there's nothing you can do to these machines that I can't fix."

The normally sassy octogenarian couldn't hide the fear in her eyes. "You really mean that? I could pound away on the keys and make a mess of things, and you could still fix it?"

"Absolutely. And besides, I'll be right here beside you, Miss Delia."

The old woman had breathed in through her nose, pushed back her shoulders, and flexed her fingers. "All right, then. Let's go for it."

And here she was on this festive Friday evening, outfitted like the rest of the group in a ski sweater and corduroys, sitting next to Tyler and telling him how to dump all the files permanently out of the trash bin. "There's nothing to it. You click on the 'Recycle Bin' icon...."

Miss Delia Bloodworth's gaze found Natalie's across the room, and they laughed softly, feeling like co-conspirators in a cyber adventure, Tyler figured.

❧

"'There's a somebody I'm longing to see'," Erin began, Jonah following easily on the piano, her rich, throaty voice drawing the group into a mellow mood. A hush descended as they listened, spellbound. A *preacher's* wife?

Deftly she moved from one old favorite to another—"Night and Day," "Stardust"—then, as Jonah picked up the tempo, the crowd got the idea and joined in heartily on such tunes as "Don't Sit Under the Apple Tree" and "Pretty Baby." With a subtle shift, they slid into the old familiar carols, "Hark the Herald Angels Sing," "O Come All Ye Faithful," and when Erin, with a nod to Jonah, broke into the standard "O Holy Night," there wasn't a dry eye in the place.

Natalie, catching Tika's frantic wave from the doorway of the kitchen, was looking for an excuse to escape the room. "The cookie plate," Tika mouthed with exaggeration. "Time for a refill."

Back in the welcome haven, she sank into the first available chair.

"Sounds like it's going well in there," the chef remarked as she heaped more goodies onto a Delft platter. "That woman can sing ... and," she added nonchalantly, "I didn't know Jonah could play the piano like that."

Natalie nodded over the lump in her throat. The song Erin was singing reminded her of her mother.

Tika brought out a pan of gingerbread that was cooling in the pantry. "Wait just a second while I sprinkle confectioner's sugar on this and cut it up."

"Umm. Gingerbread. Until I moved here, most of my baking was out of a box."

"Christmas isn't Christmas without gingerbread. My grandmom always made a gingerbread house with all the trimmings—icing for the snow on the roof and lots of gumdrops." As she talked, she was working quickly and efficiently, placing several lacy doilies on top of the golden brown surface of the bread and sifting the sugar lightly over the top. When Tika lifted the doilies, Natalie noticed the airy pattern that had been created—like a fall of snowflakes.

"You're the best, Tika." She meant that—in more ways than one.

Back in the parlor, Natalie arranged the platter on the sideboard and turned to take her seat in the far corner.

She was surprised to find that it was occupied—by none other than Alexander Elbert, Ph.D., lured from his work by the music, no doubt.

He sat back, eyes closed, following along as Erin led them in a nostalgic rendition of "I'll Be Home for Christmas." One hand rested on the arm of the overstuffed chair; the other held a mug of mulled cider. He seemed lost in another world, another time.

He sat there for the next hour, singing so softly as not to be heard, never opening his eyes. Though he remained aloof, Natalie was glad he'd joined them. No one should be alone at Christmas. Not even a professor.

With his eyes still closed, she had an opportunity to study his features. For the first time, she noticed a bit of silver woven into the golden strands of hair at his temples. His youthful face was unlined, but there was a confidence and maturity to the set of his square jawline that was profoundly reassuring. And the bottom lip, slightly fuller than the top . . . she pushed aside the direction that thought was leading. Right now he needed a shave—a faint shadow of stubble that was disturbingly appealing.

Again her gaze lingered on his hands—not at all what she'd expected of a professor. Not soft and pampered—unused, except for bookwork. After all, what did professors do that could possibly rough up their hands?

But Alexander Elbert's hands were strong and had obviously seen hard work. The fingers were marred by small cuts and scrapes, and a jagged scar stood out on his left wrist. Maybe he'd had a run-in with a chalkboard or a pull-down map.

Natalie concluded as she sat there that, although Dr. Elbert was an academician, refined and scholarly, he was definitely very masculine. So far, he'd given no reason for her to assume that he was anything like the geologist. And despite her inbred suspicion about all men in the profession, she was intrigued.

She found herself wondering what his voice sounded like as he sang. Was it the carols that had brought him in from his work? Was he remembering Christmases past?

The similarity between Alex sitting there quietly in his chair, and Jonah, playing "Silent Night" made her heart jump, spin, then soften like a pat of melting butter. Quiet strength. It's what she had always wanted in a man. A stability she could count on. . . .

The moment she saw him, she'd sensed that rare quality . . . though until now, she hadn't been willing to admit it, was still half afraid to believe he wasn't like all the others. . . .

Another urgent summons from the kitchen jolted her from her thoughts, and she helped Oren set out an urn of decaf coffee and a plate of hot doughnuts, fresh from the fryer. And when she walked back into the parlor to announce that a new feast had been prepared in the dining room, the professor had disappeared.

Natalie recalled the picture on his nightstand. The woman laughing up into his eyes. Who was she, and where was she now?

Oh, well. So much for any romantic notions brought on by the season. Even if the professor was nothing like her father, he was obviously very much taken.

~~~

Just as the last guests were leaving around midnight, the phone rang at the desk in the foyer. She reached for it automatically.

"Pleasant Valley Inn."

The accent was unmistakable. "Overseas operator here. I have a collect call for Miss Natalie St. John. Will you accept the charges?"

Thirteen

◦────◦

In the sober light of day, Natalie was appalled. What had she been thinking?

Last night, lulled by the mellow mood of the crowd gathered in her parlor, the lush music, the nostalgia of the season, she'd allowed her imagination to run away with her. And by the time the professor had appeared, she'd been ripe for the picking—emotionally and mentally speaking.

He'd never known, of course. Had not been aware that she'd sat staring at him, entranced by the chiseled lines of his face, his profile backlit by a parlor lamp, causing his blond hair to glow like some Renaissance angel. And then he'd disappeared. . . .

It figured.

When the phone had rung, she'd been rudely awakened from her little daydream. That third phone call from the British Isles—or the attempted call, for she wasn't about to accept it—was all it had taken to put everything back into perspective. To remind her that men—especially charming professors—were deceptive, manipulative, and utterly untrustworthy. How could she have forgotten?

Well, it wouldn't happen again. She'd steer clear of *this* professor as often as possible. Besides, she wouldn't have to put up with him for very long. He'd be gone by the first of the year. And if she were lucky, maybe he'd have plans to spend Christmas elsewhere, too.

But she couldn't avoid teatime, it seemed. Tika was at the meat market, selecting filets for the main entrée at dinner, and Lu had some errands to run. The wait staff wouldn't be arriving until four-thirty. So. . . .

❧

Alex had been expecting her, had clocked her arrival from the time she left the kitchen till the moment she reached the threshold of the door of his suite. He knew virtually every move the woman made.

Her light rap sounded at his door. He opened it. Planted in front of him, holding tightly to the handles of her serving tray, was Natalie St. John. She couldn't possibly have known how lovely she looked. Wisps of auburn hair had escaped her loose ponytail and curled about her bare face, flushed with healthy color. Even in blue jeans and a flannel shirt, she was utterly enchanting.

Alex assumed a look of surprise. "Ms. St. John! Two o'clock already?" He eagerly held out his hands for the tray, feeling her fingers slide beneath his. "I could use the break." Casting about for some way to delay her awhile longer, he blurted out the very thing that was on his mind. "You look like you might have just come in from the cold. Your cheeks are rosier than a two-year-old's."

For some reason she wouldn't look him in the eye. "I was walking along the river."

"An enjoyable exercise at any rate. I wouldn't miss my time out in the fresh air each morning. Does wonders for one's concentration."

She took a step backward, as if she couldn't wait to get on about her business, and he rushed on before she dashed away. "In fact, I can't think of a better spot to accomplish what I came here to do."

He noticed her glance at the nightstand. "And that is?"

"To meet my next deadline. They seem to roll around rather regularly. At this stage I rarely allow myself a distraction, but I must confess that last night's musicale was quite delightful."

Her smile stopped a little short of her eyes. "That's nice to hear. We do our best here at Pleasant Valley Inn to keep our guests' comfort and satisfaction uppermost."

Blast! She sounded like a television commercial. What had happened to the spontaneous young woman who'd greeted him that first morning, her hair all done up in a towel?

"Enjoy your tea," she said. And before he could think of a sensible reply, she turned around and closed the door firmly behind her.

~

"I'm telling you . . . that man's not all he seems," Lu insisted, looking around to make sure Oren was out of the room.

"Oh, please," Tika drawled, putting away the groceries she had purchased earlier. "I hate it when people say that. It's so . . . so . . . "

"Vague?" Natalie supplied.

"Exactly. For once, I'd like a real, genuine, hit-me-where-I-live example."

Lu didn't appear to be the least bit offended, Natalie thought, wishing she could come up with an answer—any answer. Instead, she sat down at the table, poured herself a cup of tea, and listened.

"How's this?" Lu began, unaware of Natalie's dark mood. "We all go about our day thinking we're standing . . . on the earth, you know. But in actuality, we're on the *side*—sticking *straight out* of the planet—not at all like it seems."

Lu and Tika looked at each other in disbelief, thinking that they had just heard what might possibly be the weirdest statement ever made.

"Well? It's true, isn't it? Don't you go around thinking you're on top of things, when really you're on the side of things? Do you ever once stop to thank God for gravity? If not for gravity, we'd have all fallen off into space a long time ago!"

For a moment there was a loud silence. Then Tika rose and braced her hands against the metal surface of the table. "Lucinda

Luckadoo, sometimes I think I've got you all figured out, and then you go and say something to blow the image."

"As it so happens, I think she's right . . . about the professor," Natalie said with a shrug. "Have you two noticed his hands?"

She had their attention immediately. "What do you mean?"

"They're not smooth, professorial hands at all. Nicks and cuts. Ragged fingernails. What do you think he does when he's not lecturing or writing?"

"Oren's hands are like that," Lu declared. "Maybe the professor gardens on the side."

"Sounds as if *someone's* showing more than a casual interest in the professor-man," Tika said with fond accusation.

Natalie wasn't about to bite. "I couldn't care less what he does with his spare time."

"It's true, then!" Lu clapped her hands in triumph. "I *told* you, Tika. She wouldn't be so defensive if she weren't a little interested."

They were talking about her as if she weren't even in the room. "You're both crazy," Natalie said. "Certifiable. I've barely spoken to the man. Besides, you know those academic types—" She thought of her father and changed the course of the conversation. "He could be an existentialist or even an atheist, and you know how I feel about that."

"There are plenty of mixed marriages these days," argued Tika. "Religiously as well as racially."

"True. But my beliefs are too important for me to risk compromise."

"Oh, Saint Natalie, are we?" Tika challenged.

"Leave her alone, Tika," Lu interrupted. "It's one of those things we believe. It's just not an option."

"Well, excu-use me, but I think it's closed-minded and discriminatory."

Natalie couldn't help wondering if this had something to do with Jonah.

Lu defended the position. "It may sound that way. But when the kids come along, it makes everything easier. And like it or not, to be 'unequally yoked,' as the Good Book says, is disobedience, pure and simple. Would you want that on Natalie's conscience?"

"I guess not. My grandpop always used to tell me that we have to respect one another's consciences."

"I'm sorry we've been kidding around, Nattie," Lu said. "You're not in junior high anymore, and whether or not you have a crush on someone is strictly your business."

"Believe me . . . if I ever had a crush on anyone, the professor would be the last man on earth." She left the kitchen without a backward look.

~

Lu sighed. "I don't know, Tika. She just seems to fall deeper and deeper into her fantasy world—those books, the old movies. I'm afraid no one in the real world's ever going to be good enough for her. You couldn't find a nicer young man than Andy, here in Pleasant Valley or anywhere else. And she hasn't even given that good-looking professor a chance."

"I'm not sure what to make of Nattie's attitude toward our newest guest," Tika said, rolling out some dough for a mincemeat pie. "I'm not convinced it's just the religion thing—if that turns out to be a problem. As much grief as I give her about it, I do respect her faith. But sometimes a woman needs more than church to warm her heart . . . or her bed."

"Tamika Monroe! Nattie's not that kind." Lu sighed. "But I can't help thinking she's missing out, too. Of course, that's easy for me to say—being married since I was eighteen." A mischievous look crossed her face. "I think I'll call JMU."

"Why?"

"Do a little detective work. Find out a little more about this professor. You know how some secretaries are. Maybe she'll spill the beans about the woman in the picture."

Unfortunately, Mrs. Ledbetter, the professor's secretary, was tight-lipped and just as adamant as Lu was persistent. Lu had to admit she'd finally met her match.

After church the next day, a snowstorm hit the Shenandoah Valley, making it impossible for Natalie to make the drive to D.C.

Andy would just have to get married without her.

But she'd have to call and let him know. "Hi, And, it's me—Nat."

"I heard about the storm down there. You're not going to try to make it, are you?"

She was amused to hear him sounding worried. "With my little car?"

"Yeah, yeah, I know. It may be a Jag, but it's not exactly a snow-mobile."

"How are you holding up?"

"A little nervous." To prove it, he laughed nervously. "But then, that's natural, isn't it?"

"How about Lori?"

"Don't know. She won't let me see her today. Says it's bad luck or something."

"A traditional type, eh?"

"Yeah. A nice girl, Nat. Like you."

Natalie's heart warmed. "And?" Her voice was tentative.

"Things won't change between us, Nat. I promise." He knew. "You'll always be my best friend."

She let out a long sigh. "I guess I couldn't expect you to make me the only woman in your life."

"A man needs a wife, Nat. It's just as simple as that."

Natalie suddenly wanted to hang up—to remove herself from any further pain. But she had to know. "You're sure Lori is right for you?"

There was not a second's hesitation. "Absolutely. Committed believer . . . smart . . . kinda pretty. And nice. Lori is really nice."

Natalie arched a brow. "And she's a lawyer, you say? Except for you, I don't know any nice lawyers."

Andy laughed. His regular old laugh. Natalie's tension melted away. "Still don't trust our kind, eh? Besides all that though, Lori loves me." He paused, and Natalie could hear Mama Gatto rattling on in Italian. "Listen, I gotta go. Sorry you can't be there, Nat. Other than Lori, you and Ma, there isn't anyone else coming who really means anything to me. I'll miss you."

"Take lots of pictures."

"Will do. We'll have you up for dinner real soon. After all, if you hadn't bought that inn, we'd never have met in the first place."

She let the tiny flutter of bitterness pass. "Be happy, And."

"Thanks, Nat. I'll be thinkin' about you."

"Yeah, right." She chuckled. "I'll just bet you will."

They rang off. Natalie slogged into the kitchen, looking for company. But no one was there. She heard the soft tap-tapping of Alex's typewriter and felt some small measure of comfort.

Lori loves me. Andy's simple words haunted the empty corridors of her heart.

Fourteen

⤴︎

Shivering into her old fleece robe, Natalie shoved her feet into her slippers and dragged her tired body down to the kitchen. Lu was up, breaking eggs into a bowl. Dressed in a tie-dyed caftan and wearing her signature sandals and wool socks, she reminded Natalie of an aging Mama Cass.

"What a weekend!" Lu remarked cheerfully.

"Tika already gone?" Natalie asked, then yawned. A long, wide yawn that came from the very back of her throat. The weekend had been more exhausting than usual.

"Yep. Gone up to Baltimore for the day to visit her grandparents. I hate her days off."

"That makes two of us. Thanks for doing breakfast. I'll get Old Silas's eggbeaters going."

They worked in quiet harmony—Lu, making the professor's Smithfield ham and eggs, while Natalie fried up Silas's turkey bacon and egg substitute. Heating on the stove were two pots, one containing Tika's spiced apples and the other bubbling with cheese grits.

"Biscuits in the oven?" Natalie inquired, as she slid two slices of crusty oat-bran bread into the toaster.

"Yep."

"You're a saint."

"Not really. Tika made 'em before she left."

"Then *she's* the saint."

Lu sighed. "Wish that were true."

"I know." Natalie opened the door of the fridge and removed the butter dish and milk carton, then swung the heavy door closed with her hip. "Tika doesn't seem to be *anti*-Christian. She just seems to have no real place for the Lord in her life."

"I've been prayin' for that girl for years. I keep hoping her grandparents can get through to her. They're wonderful people. Came down to visit once. A tiny little couple, but giants of the faith. Raised three children and six of their grandchildren, so Tika tells me."

"Wow. You don't hear of that kind of thing much anymore." From my own personal experience, exactly *nothing*, Natalie thought bitterly.

"That's what I call dedication to family."

The word *family* had failed to conjure up warm feelings for quite awhile. But Natalie quickly shoved it all aside and forced a cheerful comment. "Maybe Jonah is heaven-sent. Tika sure seems to take notice whenever he's around. She's been to church every Sunday for the past month."

Lu dished up the professor's plate. "I've known Tika a long time and I've never seen her turn to Jell-O at the sight of anyone before."

"Gelatin, you mean. Tika would hate being referred to by a brand name." Natalie chuckled. "Have most of the weekend guests checked out?"

"Everyone except our two bachelors."

As if in confirmation, hearty male laughter rang out from the dining room.

"They must be two peas in a pod," Lu remarked with a shake of her head. "Imagine that."

Natalie wasn't about to voice her opinion on the matter. "I have a couple things for you to do today, Lu."

"Fine with me." The stout housekeeper wiped her hands with a tea towel.

"The first is to finish serving breakfast." She handed Lu the two plates. "The second is to take the day off."

"But, Natalie, it's Monday. And Mrs. Quigley isn't coming today, remember?"

"It's just for one day. The dining room is closed for dinner—except for Old Silas Q. And since this is Christmas week, we have only two guests. I'll be fine. Besides, I gave Oren a list of things we need from Staunton. It's a beautiful day for a drive, Lu. And—" she pulled an envelope from her pocket—"here's a little early present."

Lu's face lit up like a neon sign. "Hold on, while I deliver these plates."

And she was back in a flash, ripping open the envelope and pulling out a slip of heavy paper. "A gift certificate to the Belle Grae Inn. I love that restaurant! How did you know?"

Natalie grinned. "Oh, a little gardener told me. I want you and Oren to have a nice lunch—on me."

"Nat, you didn't have to—"

"Sure I did. You two are pretty special to me, you know."

Lu, her lovely hazel eyes misting over, gave Natalie a hug. "You're an angel, Nattie, darlin'. I can't tell you how much nicer it is working for you than for that Mrs. Jacks."

"Just enjoy yourselves."

"Oh, we will, we will. We can see our daughter Annie and finish our shopping for the grandkids. . . ." Natalie could see Lu mentally ticking off her list. "We'll get going just as soon as the men are finished with their breakfast."

"Go on. Scoot! I'll clean up."

Lu threw her a kiss, snatched off her apron, and breezed through the swinging door.

Truth was, Natalie really wanted the inn to herself. A very special delivery would be arriving sometime this afternoon.

~~~~~

It didn't take Natalie long to finish the morning chores—a result of years of doing the housework her mother was always too tired to do. One more strike against her father. He'd been the one responsible for her childhood spent in after-school programs and then home alone—doing laundry and making sure supper was on the table by the time her mom got home from the shop, dead on her feet. Well, no time to brood. There was work to be done.

Lunch was easy enough. The professor, of course, was cloistered in his rooms, typing away. And now Silas, after a hearty bowl of chowder and some of Tika's good corn bread, was back in his old rocking chair, Merriwether snuggled in his arms, sleeping in a shaft of sunlight that spilled over the front porch.

Natalie sauntered over and sat down on one of the other rockers, a weekly ritual designed to irritate the old man enough to get his blood pumping firmly through his old body. "Was your lunch to your liking?"

"It'll do."

"It's Tika's day off, you know."

"I thought that corn bread tasted like sawdust."

Natalie couldn't resist a smile. "She made it before she left."

The old man scowled. "Shoot, girl, why do you insist on provokin' me?"

"Because you won't let me be nice to you." She paused, watching the people passing by on their way to holiday parties or shopping excursions on Main. "Do you look forward to Christmas, Mr. Wethington?"

"Just another day, if ya ask me. Usually spend it with my brother in Washington. The old buzzard is grouchier than I am."

Now *that* was debatable.

❧

The truck from Kelsey Farms—an ancient Ford that was more rust and rattle than anything else—delivered the Christmas tree just before dusk.

Silas, who was still enthroned in his wicker rocker, looked on as Fred Kelsey unloaded the seventeen-foot Frasier fir. "How you think you're goin' to do that all by yourself—an old geezer like you?" he yelled out, much to Natalie's dismay. Maybe she should call on the professor for help. . . .

"Just watch me!"

And Fred proceeded to hoist the evergreen onto a dolly and maneuver it into the foyer, where it nestled in verdant splendor in the curve of the staircase. "There you are, Miss Natalie." He stood back to eye the tree and make sure it was properly positioned in its stand. "The finest of the lot."

"I appreciate doing business with you, Mr. Kelsey." She paid him—an extra twenty for his trouble—and sent him away to enjoy this, her very first Christmas tree ever, in privacy.

She'd spent a small fortune on the tree and trimmings, but it was worth every cent. It was to be a Victorian style tree—ornaments that would make a rainbow green with envy. Many in various shapes—grapes, birds, houses, even a pickle!

Janet St. John had never celebrated Christmas, so Natalie had been deprived of the memory. Just why her mother had chosen to ignore the season was never quite clear since she attended church, at least irregularly. Perhaps she regretted the commercialism. Or maybe it was just because the day also happened to be her ex-husband's birthday. Well, now Natalie would never know.

Dragging her CD player down from the attic, she put in an Andy Williams' holiday disc and turned up the volume until the chandelier vibrated. Removing the lids from the boxes of ornaments, she lifted them out one by one, admiring the delicate prisms, like so many jewels. Strands of multi-colored lights trailed down the hallway. If she were lucky, maybe she could keep them untangled until she coiled them around the tree.

White lights would have been in better taste, she thought, carefully placing each bulb on one of the lower branches, *but I've been wanting colored ones ever since I can remember.* Never having been one to give undue consideration to public opinion— if her own was right and just—she hadn't hesitated at the Shenandoah Lawn and Garden Center when choosing the lights for her tree. She did draw the line at the flashing ones, though. They reminded her too much of the gaudy shop windows in some parts of D.C., or the little hole-in-the-wall Chinese restaurants she'd loved. She still hadn't tried the Chinese carry-out down the street, and promised herself that tonight would be the night. Put on an old movie perhaps. Or catch *It's a Wonderful Life* on TV. This week the classic would be airing daily.

Emerging from the back side of the fir, she was shocked to find the professor standing there.

"Oh, sorry!" she hollered over the din of the music, smoothing her disheveled hair. "I didn't mean to disturb you."

She couldn't read the expression in his deep-set eyes. How could she have been so thoughtless?

She stumbled over the clutter to turn down the volume.

"Sorry about that." She seemed genuinely contrite, with the music now down to a more conversational level. "I guess I got carried away."

He tore his gaze from her face, glowing in her little-girl excitement, and tipped his head to take in the full height of the tree. "Very impressive. I like a Frasier fir." He paused for a moment. "Ornery clan, though, the Frasiers."

She seemed to ignore the aside. "I really prefer a blue spruce myself, but I hate to see them cut. They deserve to be left in their natural setting, with snow on their boughs."

He shoved his hands in his pockets. "Colored lights, eh?"

She smiled . . . and blushed. He hadn't realized women did that anymore. "They may not be in vogue, but they're so much more cheerful than the white ones, don't you think?"

"Umm. They remind me of home. Mum always used colored lights on our tree." He scanned the topmost branches. "Need a hand?"

Natalie frowned. "Well, I wouldn't want to take you away from your work. . . ."

He waved away her concern. The book could wait. He wasn't ready to leave such extraordinary company—not just yet. "I could use a bit of a break. I've plugged away ever since arriving here, and except for my morning jogs, I haven't taken much time for relaxation. Mustn't risk burnout, you know."

"I know . . . all too well. And thank you for offering to help. I was wondering how I'd ever make it all the way up there—even with Oren's stepladder."

He took the strand of lights from her hand. "Allow me. I'm an old pro at this sort of thing. We can start at the top of the tree and work our way down." Mingled with the pungent smell of evergreen was a heady, yet light perfume that drifted from that cloud of hair as she moved nearer to steady the ladder.

Most definitely he would take the rest of the day off.

~⁓

He was a take-charge sort of man, Natalie could see that. But his manner wasn't at all imposing or pushy. Only helpful. It was obvious he had decorated a lot of Christmas trees in his day—tall ones, if she was any judge.

Soon a rhythm was established, the music was turned up just a bit more, and the conversation began to flow. They worked together so beautifully, Natalie felt almost giddy and wondered what Bobby Lewis, her first crush, would think if he knew he was firmly replaced in the butterfly department. Or maybe it was just the wonder of the season. . . .

"You mentioned home." She handed Alex the last strand of lights. "Just where is that?" she couldn't resist asking.

"England, actually, though I suppose I'm a product of two continents. Mum was a war bride—World War II. Dad was an American GI stationed in London. They met during the Blitz. After the war, he brought her to America. I was born here. Then, later, after he died—when I was only six—she took us back to England."

Natalie knew a sudden kinship. "It's tough growing up without a father around, isn't it?"

"Yes it is. But Mum is one of those people who always puts the best face on things. A cheerful sort, great fun. She always made Christmas a fine celebration, and since I was so young. . . ." She caught his quizzical glance. "I take it you've lost your father, as well."

"You might say that. But it would be more accurate to say he lost *us*. He left us when I was seven, and that's the last I've seen of him."

"I *am* sorry."

Natalie shrugged. "You adjust. You have to. Unfortunately, my mother, although I loved her very much, *wasn't* a very cheerful sort." She flinched with the pain of remembering. "Do you have brothers and sisters?"

He nodded, intent on fastening an ornament on a branch of the tree. "One of each. My brother lives in Denver—works for an environmentalist group. He's into meditation and yoga—that kind of thing. And my sister lives in Missouri with her preacher husband and five children. They met when she was at Washington Bible College studying sacred music. She and my brother are poles apart philosophically. She's a fine Christian, homeschools her children, grows her own vegetables—the whole program. Bakes the best bread in the world if I may luxuriate in hyperbole."

"And you? Where do you fit in, if you don't mind my asking?" Natalie felt her heart rise in her throat like a lump of dough. She dreaded the answer.

"My sister and I share the same basic beliefs. Although she's more orthodox in practice than I, she hasn't lost the joy of her salvation. I'm not opposed to the organized church, but I'm content with my relationship with the Lord—very intimate, very real." There was a long pause as he stretched to hang an ornament on a far branch. "How about you?" He tossed off the question almost too casually, though inwardly she gave a sigh of relief.

"I'm a Christian first, a Presbyterian second—a member of Trinity just down the street. It's a good fellowship. True to the Bible and responsible to the community."

"Sounds like the proper combination to me."

She moved an ornament he had just placed, to space it more aesthetically, and she noted his quick, slightly lopsided grin. "We sponsor a soup kitchen for the poor and a ministry to the elderly. And there are plans for a daycare by next fall."

"That's where the church can really do some good these days."

"I agree. If women need to leave their children in daycare . . . well, at least the church can love these kids while their moms are away. Speaking of moms, will your mother be coming to the States for the holidays?"

"Unfortunately, no. Grandmum is still living—she's quite ancient, actually—and this may be her last Christmas." He turned to regard Natalie solemnly. "Which leads me to something I've been meaning to ask ever since I arrived. I know the inn is normally closed on Christmas Eve and Christmas Day, but I was wondering if I might stay over."

"Oh." She caught her breath, completely off guard. "I'd assumed you had other plans."

"Not at all. My brother doesn't celebrate Christmas, and while I usually go to my sister's house, this year I have a rush job I really must finish. . . . It would be just the *room* I'd need, you understand. I wouldn't expect meals or maid service."

Her mind whirled. What in the world would she do with a guest underfoot over the holidays—when she'd planned on a mini-vacation for herself? But she covered her confusion. "Of course. You're more than welcome to stay. And feel free to make use of the kitchen if you'd like."

"And will you be joining your mother?"

Natalie felt her face flush. "My mother died last year. So it'll be nice to know you're . . . someone's . . . in the house."

He brightened, looking considerably younger than a history professor had any right to look. "Well, that's wonderful then." In his effort to reach the topmost branches of the tree, a lock of thick blond hair had slipped down over one eye, and he shoved back the wayward hair with his fingers. "We can celebrate together."

"Why not?" she found herself saying with a little lift of her heart.

"I must say I'm quite relieved. I was dreading the thought of spending Christmas by myself."

By this time, the tree was heavy with fanciful decorations, and Natalie was feeling more comfortable with the professor by the moment. "Would you like to take a break? For tea?"

His laugh was infectious. "I'm beginning to suspect that you've British blood somewhere in your line. Tea would hit the spot."

"Would you trust me to brew it? Tika, our chef, has the day off, and the housekeeper has gone to Staunton with her husband. But you've met our groundsman."

"Does a wonderful job about the place, doesn't he?" the professor remarked on the way into the kitchen. "We've had some interesting conversations in the mornings."

"Do you garden?" Maybe she'd find out about those hands.

"Not a bit. Love to look at flowers, could care less how they got there. So you say your cook is gone for the day?"

"Yes, I'm sorry to say. That is, the restaurant is closed to the public on Mondays, so I'm afraid you and Silas will have to put up with my cooking."

"Nonsense! There's a little Chinese place down the street, isn't there? Why don't we order some carry-out and dine together in the parlor? I noticed a video of *White Christmas.*"

"What about Silas? He only eats heart-smart food."

"Yes, well, it so happens I poach a chicken breast like nobody's business. If you can steam some rice and a vegetable, we'll have him set up in no time."

"You're on, Professor. Chinese it is."

She put out her hand, and he took it in his. She could feel the strength of his grip, his warmth.

"Please . . . call me Alex. I may look the part of a stuffy old academician, but I can assure you I'm anything but."

She nodded with a smile, regretting the moment he withdrew his hand. "In that case . . . I'm Natalie."

"I know. 'Born on Christmas Day.'"

"July 5." She laughed at his look of consternation. "Sorry to disappoint you. The geol—my *father* was born on Christmas Day. I was a summer baby."

"Of course. With that red hair of yours, I'd say you'd been kissed by the sun and surrounded by all that's warm and full of life."

"You can tell that about me, can you? Perhaps you're jumping to conclusions."

His smile was almost secretive, as if he knew something about her she didn't. "Oh, no. Remember, I'm a scholar. I only deal in facts—an especially easy task when they're staring you right in the face." He cleared his throat. "Now, how about that tea?"

She smoothed her hair and hurried to put on the kettle, her scalp tingling as though her hair really were aflame. She filled the awkward silence. "What does Alexander mean?"

He leaned against the counter, his arms crossed. "'Great protector.' A bit grand for a simple scholar like myself, I must confess."

"There's not a simple person alive, is there?" She got down the teapot and cups from the cabinet, then turned to face him. "We all just wear different faces for different people."

"That's what makes life interesting. Surprises around every corner."

"I'm not so sure. I've never much liked surprises."

His brown eyes sparkled merrily. "It depends on the surprise, doesn't it . . . Natalie?"

Fifteen

"I'm gone for one day, and this place turns into a zoo!" Tika folded her arms across her flat chest. "Strangers cooking in my kitchen! Old Silas joining you for a movie and spilling popcorn in the parlor! What next?"

Natalie smiled to herself, thinking how she'd awakened sometime in the night to find herself tucked up on a couch, the parlor lights dimmed and the fire banked. Someone had been thoughtful enough to cover her with an afghan and prop her head on one of the tapestry pillows, too. Surely not Silas, who'd taken off to his room right after the late news. . . .

"And there you sit, grinning like a Cheshire cat," Tika pointed out. "Just what went on while the three of us were conveniently out of the picture anyway?"

"Well, for one thing, we trimmed the tree," she replied, hedging.

"That's plain to see—especially with those lights! But you know that's not what I meant, Boss." Tika was obviously not about to let up on the third degree. "Give with the details—about you and the professor, I mean."

Natalie shrugged. "There's absolutely nothing to tell. Except that he's very nice and accommodating and—and a perfect gentleman."

Tika rolled her eyes. "It's that British reserve. Or maybe he does have a girlfriend stashed somewhere. Did you ever ask him about that picture in his room?"

"Are you kidding? Of course not. It's none of my business. He's a guest here, and I treat all my guests the way I'd want to be treated. Period. End of paragraph."

"Liar." Tika grinned, pouring milk in the cup of tea Natalie had made for herself. "I may not have known you long, Natalie St. John, but I know a woman whose heart is hungry when I see one."

Natalie gasped and blinked . . . and to her utter amazement, felt tears welling up, then began to track a slow path down her cheeks.

In a rare moment of sensitivity, Tika rushed over to give her a hug. "Oh, Nattie, I'm so sorry. You *are* lonely, aren't you? Even with a houseful of people. This isn't altogether about Professor Elbert, is it?"

She allowed Tika to comfort her. But briefly. Then, without another word, she retreated to her attic room.

The rest of the week—despite all the last-minute Christmas shopping and wrapping—seemed to drag by like molasses on a winter morning. The professor only emerged from his room for his morning hike, seldom for a meal. And an obvious preoccupation precluded any real conversation when Natalie served his afternoon tea.

Lu noticed a change in her employer's behavior as well, and she told Oren as much. "I think it's got something to do with the professor. He seems to be avoiding her."

Oren waved a stiff wire-bristled brush in the air. "Maybe he's just busy with his project, Lu," he suggested reasonably, although it was obvious that his wife didn't really want his opinion. "He's probably trying to beat some kind of deadline."

They were sitting on crates in the potting shed, vigorously scrubbing moss off the four large terra-cotta pots that adorned the front steps from spring through fall. The temperature had turned warmer than Sy Brown, the weatherman on WPLV, had been calling for that morning, and they were both working up a real lather.

At Lu's disdainful look, he went on. "I know when spring comes I can't think of anything else but getting everything in on schedule. It's the way we men are."

"The way you men are!" she scoffed, sweetening her tart words with a light caress on his hair. "I don't know why that professor in there can't see this perfectly charming young woman right under his nose. He must be blind!"

"Or busy." Oren said it again.

"There must be some way to get those two together. . . ."

"Oh no ya don't, Lu! I'm putting my foot down right now. No matchmakin'!"

"But, Oren—"

"She's our *boss*, Lu! Don't forget that."

"But she's a woman first. Maybe I could—"

"Don't even think about it!" Oren was as emphatic as he ever got, but he might as well have saved his breath, for Lu was already on her way to the house.

Two days before Christmas, Alex came running down the corridor. Natalie, sightless behind an armful of bed linens, cried out as they narrowly avoided a collision.

"Oh, terribly s-sorry," he stammered, reaching out a hand to steady her.

"It's really all right, Professor. I should have been watching where I was going."

"I know I've been out of touch lately, but you see, my manuscript took a rather unexpected turn, and I had to rewrite almost the entire second half. I've been under it, really."

Natalie hated herself for feeling so relieved. "I'm sorry it's been such a stressful time for you."

"No need to be sorry. All's well that ends well." He held up a sheaf of papers, bound with rubber bands. "And now I'm off to meet with my editor. Is there a copy shop about?"

"I use the one on Commonwealth. Just continue down Main, take a right, and go all the way to the end. It's just a small shop, but they're very helpful in there—and reasonable."

"Wonderful! Thanks." He gave a little salute. "Now I'd best be off. We're meeting down in Warrenton at noon. Luncheon at Napoleon's."

She knew the place. Very classy. Very . . . intimate and romantic. "Then you'd better hurry. Warrenton's a good drive from here."

He grinned at her—that lopsided grin—shoved back his blond hair with strong fingers, and hurried down the steps to his car. From inside, Natalie watched him place his manuscript carefully in the trunk of the old Triumph. Much to her surprise, he put down the rag top, made sure his scarf was wound securely around his neck, his hat on tight, and sped down the gravel lane and on to Main Street.

The sight of his dashing figure was shadowed by a sudden speculation: What if the editor waiting to rendezvous in Warrenton was not a male—but a female?

⌒

"Darling!" Celine motioned to Alex from her seat in the lounge, then rose to greet him, hands extended.

Too much jewelry cluttered the slender fingers but, curiously enough, her nails were neither polished nor shaped. Funny he'd never noticed before.

Very thin and chic, she was wearing a shocking pink suit with a skirt shorter than Toulouse-Lautrec.

"Celine! Wonderful to see you."

"I can't believe you insisted I fly all the way from New York, then take a rental car to this little one-horse town, darling, but as you can see, here I am." Her laughter was brittle, and a little too loud for the conservative crowd of business people meeting here for lunch.

"Do you mind if we eat before we go over the changes? I'm famished."

"You always are after writing a book, darling. Always." She put her arm through his and followed the maitre d' to a dining room on the second floor of the renovated old home.

When the waitress came to take their order, Celine asked for a dinner salad and a glass of tonic water. "You'll never gain any weight eating like a bird," Alex chided her, then ordered a hefty burger for himself—with bacon and cheddar.

Putting the menu aside, he leaned forward, hands steepled. "Now, let me tell you about the most significant change in the manuscript." Celine's eyes brightened and she got out a Daytimer and jeweled pen. "There's a new heroine."

She was clearly astonished. "Are you out of your mind, Alexander? Introducing a new heroine at this stage?"

"Her name is Natalie . . . an auburn-haired beauty with plenty of savvy. . . ."

Celine drummed her fingertips on the table. "Is there anything else you think your editor should know?"

"As a matter of fact, there is." He couldn't suppress a wide grin. "I think I'm in love."

Sixteen

~

"*I* don't believe it!"

"It can't be possible!"

They sat side by side on the edge of the professor's bed, struck motionless by shock.

"You don't think he'd still be at the copy shop, do you?" Lu stared at the paper Natalie was holding.

She shook her head. "By now he must be in Warrenton. You're sure you found it lying by the desk?"

"Propped against that front leg—in plain view. Let me see it again."

Natalie handed her the stray sheet of paper, and Lu read the header out loud: "*A Day For Love,* by Jeanine Beaumont. Page 22. I *told* you there was more to him than we thought, Nat. But I didn't expect—"

Natalie began to laugh and Lu joined in, their shoulders shaking. It was absurd. More preposterous than anything they might have imagined during all their late-night guessing games. And soon they were producing such gales that Tika ran in from the kitchen.

When she saw the page, she hooted. "So our medieval man is also a romance writer! This is rich! Oh, Nattie, you really do know how to pick 'em!"

"Me? I didn't pick him. He picked *us,* remember? Oh, Tika, this is too bizarre. This man who has been living here all month—and sleeping in *my* bed no less—is none other than my adored Jeanine Beaumont!"

134

"And who said English people were stuffy," Tika remarked, still holding the paper. "Alexander Elbert, Ph.D., AKA Jeanine Beaumont. Specializing in medieval torture devices and Victorian romance. This is definitely a man with two faces, Nattie."

Natalie arched a brow. "Two faces? I'd put him in the double *life* category!"

Lu rose from the bed, dabbing at her eyes with a hankie. "Well, let's just put this page back where I found it and go get one of his/her books. Might as well find out what all the fuss is about."

"Count me in." That was Tika. "Nattie could be pretty prejudiced, you know. We ought to judge for ourselves."

"All right, you two, enough with the jokes."

Lu sashayed into the bathroom to hang the fresh towels. "Who's joking? We've got a celebrity in our midst. It's time we found out why."

The inn was empty, except for Silas, who was playing a game of Solitaire in his room. Natalie and her two partners in crime sat before the fire in the parlor, each reading a book from her Jeanine Beaumont collection. Oren was at the table tying flies, already anticipating the fly fishing season.

The front door flew open, the stiff December breeze causing the fire to flicker in protest. In through the door, accompanied by a flurry of snowflakes, came the professor.

"Hello there!" he hailed them cheerfully. "Quiet evening by the fire? Lovely."

Natalie laid her book in her lap. "And how did your meeting go?"

"Fine. Fine. Just need to tweak the manuscript once more."

"Who publishes you?" Lu asked, her eyes wide and innocent.

"Oh, nobody you'd know. It's a small house. I write for a very specific audience."

And how, Natalie thought with a wry smile. *Starry-eyed females.* Although she did not count herself among that group. No self-respecting woman ever did!

He began to unwind his muffler and she watched, fascinated. If he could write such gripping, heartfelt romances, he must be a real catch.

When they all continued to stare at him, he looked up, meeting each of their gazes in turn. "Is something wrong? Have I a spot on my tie?"

"Don't mind them!" Oren called. "They've been sitting there reading those silly Jeanine Beaumont novels all evening. Beats me how women will gobble up that kind of pablum."

"Oren!" Lu was aghast.

But the professor only nodded. "I suppose you're right, sir. But I once had a professor of literature tell me that the greatest of all human experience—whether male or female—is love. It's true, you know. And books like Miss Beaumont's simply reflect that truth." He strode over to the fire to warm his hands. "As for why more women read them—well, I rather suspect it's because they're smarter than men. Seem to know more about the meaning of life and love than we do."

"Maybe," Oren admitted grudgingly, tying off a caddis fly.

Natalie and Lu flinched. But it was Tika who spoke up. "This is the first romance novel I've ever read. But Nattie here is such a big Jeanine Beaumont fan, I thought I'd see what steals her away from us every afternoon."

"That's right!" Lu echoed effusively, while Natalie, embarrassment warming her face, tried to fake a nonchalance she didn't feel. "Do you know she has every Jeanine Beaumont book ever written? How many are there, Natalie?"

She shrugged. "Oh, I don't know. Twenty-five or thirty, I think."

The professor leaned against the doorjamb. "And you have the hardbacks, I see. Purely out of curiosity, Natalie, what is there about her books that you so enjoy?"

Oh, wow! How do I get myself out of this? With her two unsympathetic cohorts looking on, Natalie decided she'd better answer honestly, or he might suspect they were on to him. "It's her dialogue, I think—so natural and believable. But more than that, I like the way the heroes and heroines always battle an outside conflict. So many romances focus on a love/hate relationship that it's refreshing to read books where the main characters actually get along with each other."

He frowned in concentration. "Hmm. I think I see what you mean. I've always been under the impression that if a relationship gets off to a rocky start, chances are it's never going to change."

"That Jeanine Beaumont must really be something," Tika put in, her chocolate eyes dancing. She aimed a question in Natalie's direction. "What have *you* heard about her in real life, Nattie?"

Tika Monroe, I'll get you later! she promised, darting her friend a meaningful glare. "Well . . . nothing concrete." It wasn't exactly a lie. "I don't suppose anyone knows much about Jeanine Beaumont."

The professor nodded. "All part of the mystique, I imagine. A calculated marketing technique, if I don't miss my guess. Well, goodnight, everyone. Lots of work left to do. Enjoy your reading."

"Oh, we will!" Lu actually cackled. "You can believe we'll be hanging on every single word!"

When they heard the door to his room close, they let out muffled shrieks at which point Oren looked up, shaking his head in disgust.

"I couldn't believe he asked what you thought of his books!" Tika said.

"Oh, I can." Lu nodded. "What author wouldn't love to hear rave reviews from a fan?"

"Notice he asked me what I enjoyed about them, not what I didn't enjoy," Natalie pointed out, remembering what her mother had said about academics and their egos.

"Can't fault him there, Nattie," Tika said. "He's a man, after all. With a man's need for praise."

"And a woman's way with words." Lu waved her book. "He's definitely got a woman's way with words."

Oren scowled. "What in the world are you women talkin' about now?"

Lu got up to draw the blinds for the night. "As usual, Oren my dear, you haven't a clue."

When the clock chimed midnight, Lu put down her book and rose from her armchair. "Well, it's officially Christmas Eve," she declared and left the room.

Tika laid aside her book and sprang toward the kitchen.

Oren went into action as well, clearing the coffee table of its requisite ash tray, coasters, and magazines, then leaned over to stoke the fire.

Natalie was puzzled. "What's going on?"

"It's a tradition here," he explained. "Since we're all leaving in the morning, we exchange gifts at the stroke of midnight on Christmas Eve, have a cup of cocoa and a piece of Tika's special hazelnut torte."

"Why didn't anyone let me in on it?"

Oren's shrug told Natalie she should have known better than to ask the poor man.

There was the sound of clinking and clattering coming from the kitchen . . . water drumming into the bottom of the kettle . . . an opening of drawers . . . and Lu's and Tika's lowered voices as they chattered away like two magpies. Natalie hurried up to her attic room, thankful she'd finished her shopping only a few days before on a trip to D.C.

When they all reappeared, Tika led the parade, bearing the torte on a silver platter garnished with holly. Behind her was Lu, carrying a tray with the chocolate pot and four Lenox mugs. Bringing up the rear was Oren, only his eyes visible—twin stars adorning the top of a pyramid of brightly wrapped gift boxes.

"Let's open them by the tree," Tika suggested as she and Lu deposited the luscious spread on the coffee table. They filed into the entry hall.

The meager Christmases of Natalie's past were forgotten the instant the paper started flying. No one waited for the others in a dreary "one-at-a-time" process. It was a free-for-all of "oohs and ahs and thank-you-ever-so-much," and Natalie choked back tears when she opened a pair of soft leather gloves from Tika; a new ledger, embossed in gold, from Lu; and Oren's IOU for an English garden outside her bedroom window in the spring.

Lu proudly displayed an antique doll quilt Tika had found for her collection. And Tika was soon poring over three new cook-books. Oren declared a hat was just what he needed for those frigid winter mornings, but would Natalie mind if he exchanged the plaid hat for the red one he'd seen in the window at Phillip's Menswear.

One present remained to be opened. For Natalie, from the others. The box was large and flat . . . and very heavy. They looked on in anticipation as she pulled off the bow and began to strip away the star-strewn paper.

"Now what could this possibly be?" she asked, slowly peeling back a piece of tape.

"Just open it!" Tika urged, knotting her slim fingers.

Following instructions, Natalie ripped off the paper and yanked open the lid.

There, nested in gold tissue paper, was a sign—a beautiful wooden sign—handpainted on both sides with the words: *Pleasant Valley Inn. Natalie St. John, Innkeeper.*

"So you'll let me stay, after all?" she whispered.

"You bet!" Oren said, and hugged her impulsively, the Christmas spirit getting the better of him.

Lu followed suit. "You belong here, Natalie. Here with us."

"Yep." Tika embraced her as well. "I had my doubts at first," she joked, "but it's true. This inn belongs to you, Nattie. From the crawl space to the rafters, you've given the old place heart."

Natalie wiped her eyes. "Thank you—all of you. You couldn't possibly know what this means to me."

Tika hopped to her feet. "Uh-oh, before it gets too deep in here, let's go eat."

"Amen!" cried Lu, always ready for dessert.

"God bless us everyone," Oren quipped.

Natalie kissed him on his weathered cheek, not trusting her voice at the moment. It had been the perfect Christmas. . . .

But it was about to get even better. For after the torte was only a fond remembrance, and the mugs were left with beards of foam, the doorbell rang.

"Who on earth would be visiting at this hour?" Lu wondered aloud as Oren ambled over to the front door.

"Well, well, if it isn't Jonah!" he called to the others. "Come on in and set yourself down with us by the fire. Tika, can we find some extra cocoa for Jonah here?"

"Did you do it? Did you tell them?" Jonah moved over to stand beside Tika.

"Tell us . . . what?" Natalie was instantly suspicious.

The slender young woman, suddenly shy, opened her mouth, but closed it again. Turning her dark eyes on Jonah, she croaked, "You tell them."

It was probably the longest speech any of them had ever heard from Jonah. "I asked Tika to marry me . . . and she did me the honor of saying yes."

There was a chorus of excited chatter. "What?!" "When?" "Why didn't you tell us before?"

By now Tika had recovered her voice. "Jonah proposed last Monday, up in Baltimore. He went up with me for a wedding. . . ."

"You didn't say anything about any wedding. Whose was it?" Lu voiced Natalie's question.

"My own," came the quiet reply.

Natalie, Oren, and Lu exchanged confused glances. "You two are already married?"

"What Tamika is trying to tell you is that she became a bride that day—a bride of the Lord Jesus Christ."

"You mean—?" Lu began.

Tika nodded, eyes brimming with tears. "I was sitting in the living room with Grandmom and Grandpop not long ago, and it suddenly all made sense. All those years of teaching, all the prayers. I can't explain what happened exactly, but God got hold of me. I trusted Jesus as my Savior and put everything—body and soul—in His hands." Tika walked over to Lu and hugged her as tightly as she could, the contrast between the tall, thin, dark woman and the short, plump, fair one a wondrous thing to behold. Sisters now in the Lord. "Thank you, my friend. Thanks for never giving up on me."

Lu fell to her knees and sobbed, while Oren, subdued by the news, joined her there on the floor, patting her awkwardly.

"I'm so happy for you," Natalie told Tika. "You deserve all the happiness in the world."

Jonah put his arm around his fiancée, and their eyes met. He caressed her taut cheek with his large, calloused hand. "In this world," he said, "and the next."

⁓

Natalie's prayers that night were prayers of thanksgiving. The greatest gifts of all this Christmas had not been wrapped in silver foil and tied with a bow. In this season of miracles, it was the gift of eternal life, with Tika's name on it. And for Natalie, from her new family, the gift of love and acceptance.

It was all so unexpected really. Nothing like the plot of a Jeanine Beaumont novel. With all the romance books and old movies, Natalie had thought the answer to her loneliness would come in the form of a man—a husband to love and cherish her. But now she knew better. And the realization freed her heart for love of another kind.

Seventeen

*N*atalie—her friends all on holiday vacation—sat alone in the kitchen with a pot of tea and a plate of sugar cookies. There was a snowman, two trees, and another that resembled a deformed Santa. Tika, the consummate perfectionist, had wanted to throw it out, but Natalie wouldn't hear of it.

"Look, I don't expect you to be the African-American Martha Stewart, Tika," she'd said. "I don't care how he looks as long as he tastes good."

A light snow was falling outside, and the radio was calling for a storm later in the day. With the kitchen lights off, the room was cast in blue shadows. But there was a peace that she'd been missing lately.

She bit off Santa's hat and turned the page in her Bible. With no one stirring—she hadn't heard a thing from the professor and Silas had left for his brother's house—she'd finally have time for morning devotions.

In the frenzy of Christmas preparations—entertaining, cooking, decorating—it was easy to forget what the season was all about. Reading the simple story of an average couple from Nazareth, she rested in their joy when the extraordinary Babe was born, the joy that was now her own.

God had sent His Son that first Christmas so long ago, that she—and Tika and Lu and Oren—might know the Father.

Yes.

She had believed on His name as a child, had felt His forgiveness, His healing touch. She knew His love. Even without the rest of her new family, He was enough. It had just taken a break in the noise of her life to realize that He had been with her all along, holding her hand, seeing her through.

The Father who was always there. . . .

She basked in God's love, and time escaped her.

"So sad to be all alone in the world."

Natalie remembered the line from the screenplay and looked through the window to the snowy skies above. "I never really was alone at all, was I, Lord?" she asked aloud.

No, Natalie, never alone.

Lonely perhaps. But never alone.

~~~

An hour later the corridor outside the kitchen echoed with the sound of booted feet. She looked up to see a tousled head peering tentatively through the swinging door. "Forgive me for intruding, Natalie, but I wondered if you might be up for a walk before the storm hits."

"So you heard?"

He ducked his head in mock embarrassment. "Weather channel freak. What do you say?"

She hesitated only a moment. The professor would be leaving soon, and she did owe him an innkeeper's hospitality, at the very least. "Just let me get this bird in the oven. We've had power outages before in these storms, and I'd better not risk it. They're counting on this for the main entrée at the Christmas Eve dinner at the church tonight."

Alex waited while Natalie turned on the oven and proceeded to take the stuffed goose out of the refrigerator. She popped open the door and slid in the roaster. "I'll get my gear. There's another cup of tea left in that pot there if you'd like some. Cups are in the cupboard over the sink to the left."

"Thanks."

When she returned, outfitted in old Wellingtons, a parka, knit cap and gloves, the teapot was drained and cookies had disappeared as well. "Sorry." He grinned, wiping his mouth with a napkin he had apparently found on his own. "No breakfast."

She felt a twinge of guilt. "I could have made you something."

"Absolutely not. I expect no special privileges over the next couple of days, remember?"

They eased out the back door, through the courtyard garden, and down to the river. "Are there any restaurants open tonight or tomorrow? I thought you might like to go out to dinner."

"This is a small town, Alex. Even the Minute Market closes on Christmas. As for tonight, would you care to join us at church for the Christmas Eve dinner? There's a candlelight service afterward."

"I accept—gratefully. But what about tomorrow? Shouldn't we stop by a store and put in some supplies for Christmas dinner?"

She had to laugh at his earnest appeal. "Never fear, Professor Elbert, tomorrow's meal is already planned, and it's a surprise, so don't bother trying to weasel the menu out of me."

He held up his hands in mock surrender. "All right, all right. I recognize the tone my Mum uses with me when I'm meddling where I have no business. I just wanted to do my part, that's all."

She slanted him a speculative glance. He had to be the most considerate man she'd ever met. That is, if he were what he appeared to be. . . .

The bare limbs of the trees clacked softly in the wind, and the clouds sent down a few dancing flakes to accompany the rhythm. A fleet of ducks swam by, paddling in time to nature's subtle percussion.

Both Natalie and Alex breathed in deeply, then smiled at the synchrony of their movement.

"It always affects me like this," he confessed. "Nature, I mean. I love all her faces as the seasons change—her perfume, her music. . . ."

"Now you sound like a poet."

"My mother's influence, I suppose. She introduced me to Browning and Donne almost before I left the cradle. It was Dad—"

he looked out over the river, rippling under the sluggish sky—
"who taught me the more basic skills. I think he was hoping that
one of his sons would become an engineer or a doctor—do something really useful in life, you know."

Her own expression matched his pensive mood. "You're a man
of many surprises, Alexander Elbert."

"Deep down I suspect I've wanted to shatter the illusion that
college professors are mealy little milquetoasts who care about
nothing but books and papers and such."

Natalie's bitter laugh echoed off the water. "Ha! If you knew
some of the professors I've known, you wouldn't be talking like
that. Some of them had very strong interests outside the classroom—among the females in their classes, to be exact."

There was a long silence, and she wondered what he might be
thinking. "Unfortunately, that's sometimes true. Some of my colleagues have trouble with a wandering eye."

"Wandering eye! More like a drooling tongue. Do you know
how many times I had to tell a professor to bug off during my college days?"

He turned to regard her, and his gaze swept her from head to
toe. "I can imagine. You must have many male admirers."

This was dangerous ground. Best to move on. "Tell me about
life in England. I must admit I'd love to see a real castle."

"Oh, they're nothing special. Just cold, drafty old things that
were obsolete well before the end of the centuries for which they
were built to last."

"I'd still like to see one someday. My mother and I traveled
quite a bit, but mostly around the North American continent. She
was afraid of flying."

"I love planes," he said enthusiastically.

"Don't tell me you're a pilot, too?!"

"Not at all. The closest I come to flying on my own is in my
little Triumph."

Laughter easing the tension, they walked on, the silence
between them growing as comfortable as an old pair of loafers. But
when the snow began to fall more heavily, they decided to make the

trek back home for a quiet afternoon of reading by the fire and numerous pots of strong tea.

⌒

Renee was flitting about the church gymnasium, looking like an illustration out of a children's storybook. When Natalie spied her in her gold lamé blouse and full white taffeta skirt, set off by lots of bangles and beads, she could think of nothing other than "The Christmas Fairy." Alex's take on the vision was more appropriate: "Trinity's own Spirit of Christmas, eh?"

Natalie's vivacious friend spotted them right away, and in a matter of minutes, the room was abuzz, with heads turning in their direction. She'd have some explaining to do come Sunday. But for now she was savoring the sensation of being escorted by the handsomest man in the room. Alex looked very British in a tweed jacket, tattersall shirt, wool slacks, and leather brogues.

"Where's the bow tie?" Natalie had asked earlier when they'd met in the entry hall of the inn. "I thought professors, especially history professors always wore bow ties."

He'd run his fingers along the length of the olive green silk tie and quipped, "Precisely why you won't find one anywhere in my closet."

Natalie wondered if he was as proud to be with her. She'd dressed carefully, choosing a Black Watch plaid dress with a simple velvet bodice. Black velvet shoes and tights. Small emeralds in her ears. Holiday simplicity. Had Alex even noticed?

If he was like other professors, it wouldn't matter what she wore, she thought as he helped her off with her coat. *Come on, Nat. Don't let the geologist spoil Christmas Eve as well!*

⌒

After the candlelight service, Renee pulled her aside and into the kitchen. "Tell me *everything!*" she demanded, turning on the faucet to soak a pan of dishes. "Where did you find such a dream-boat in Pleasant Valley?"

Natalie fished for the dishwashing liquid under the sink. "He's just a guest, staying on over the holidays. His family's in England, and his work prevents his going so far."

"So he'll be all alone for Christmas?"

Natalie didn't dare look Renee in the eye. "I guess it will be the two of us. The staff is off for the holidays."

Renee dropped her mouth and braced her hands on her ample hips. "You mean you weren't planning to celebrate with family?"

Natalie shook her head. "There is no family . . . at least, none close by. And the inn reopens two days after Christmas."

Renee was appalled. "Then you and the professor must come to our place for dinner tomorrow afternoon. Believe me, it's a full house with all of us around the table, but there's always plenty of food, and we have a great time together. If this snow keeps up, we'll have Granddad get out the old green sleigh and hitch up the horses."

As soon as she could get a word in edgewise, Natalie broke the news. "As lovely as it sounds, Renee, I've got an incredible meal already underway. Roast beef, Yorkshire pudding—the works."

Renee darted a curious glance at Natalie. "You really like him, don't you? You wouldn't be going to so much trouble if you didn't."

Natalie lifted a brow and tried to keep her composure. "He's a fascinating individual. A professor of medieval history and an author. . . ."

"Wow! And he looks like something out of the movies. You'd better hang onto him, Nat."

"He's a guest, Renee. Besides, he's leaving to go back home the first of the year."

"Better work fast."

The very idea of exerting effort to nab a man—particularly this man—reminded her of her father and threw a damper over the entire evening. Still, she couldn't resist a peek at Alex, who was playing indoor soccer at the far end of the gym with a gang of teenagers.

"Looks like he's in the right line of work," Renee observed. "He certainly gets along with young people."

Alex's cheeks were flushed and his hair was tumbling over his forehead as he traded places with the goalie. At that point, he began communicating loudly with his team members, his distinctive accent causing a stir among the onlookers.

"Another side of him I've never seen," Natalie said later as they were giving the counters a final wipe-down. "Really, Renee, there's nothing that man can't do. Except cook." She laughed, remembering. "He poached the sorriest looking chicken breast for old Silas I've ever seen. It was positively beige!"

"No doubt you'll find a few more flaws as your relationship progresses, honey. Nobody's perfect."

"What relationship? Don't go jumping to conclusions. I—" Her comment was cut short as Alex loped over, breathing heavily.

"Whew! Those kids sure gave this old man a run for his money! I'm not in shape like I used to be."

"You looked great out there to me," Renee purred, extending her hand. "I'm Renee Alcott, a friend of Natalie's."

"Pleasure to meet you. Alex Elbert here."

She handed him a glass of water. "Oh, I know. Natalie's told me all about you."

Alex turned to Natalie, who was wishing she could vanish into thin air. "I can't imagine the sorts of things she was forced to report," he said, smiling down at her. "I haven't been much fun since coming here, I'm afraid."

"You must have been pretty busy. Natalie tells me you're an author."

"She did, did she?" He looked surprised. "I don't recall mentioning that."

Natalie dropped her head sheepishly, and he laughed. "So you saw page 22, did you?"

She nodded, eager to beat it out of there. "We'd better be going, right, Alex? The snow is getting thicker by the minute."

"That's not all that's getting thicker," Renee replied with a knowing look. "Would either of you care to tell me what this is all about?"

"Frankly, no." Natalie meant it.

They started to shrug on their coats.

"Remember my invitation," said Renee as they turned to leave.

"Thanks, Renee, and Merry Christmas."

"Merry Christmas to you . . . both."

They passed a group of carolers on the way back to the inn, and Alex tucked her hand in the crook of his arm. She allowed it to rest there, secretly enjoying the warmth of his body.

"This is nice, eh? A far cry from the way I had originally planned to spend Christmas."

They rounded the corner and saw the inn, its new sign proudly displayed where Alex had hammered it into place earlier in the afternoon. "I didn't know you were such an athlete," Natalie said.

"The soccer? Oh, I'm not. I just look good compared to American teenagers. Believe me, when I was in public school in England, I was one of the last to be picked for a team."

Feeling his firm biceps beneath her hand, she found that hard to believe.

"It's why I enjoy walking so much. I'm not much good at other sports." They approached the front porch in companionable silence. "But I have to say that tonight was quite special. Thank you for inviting me, Natalie."

By this time they had reached the steps and were making their way to the front door. "And thank you for coming, Alex."

They paused at the doorstep, trying to avoid looking at each other. Natalie held her breath, every nerve in her body alive. Alex, standing so near. . . .

The moment stretched into eternity, it seemed before he finally cleared his throat. "Yes . . . well . . . it's getting late, I suppose."

She nodded and stripped off her gloves, her breath pluming in the frosty air. "I suppose so." Her entire being sang with tension, silently begging his lips to come closer.

He gazed into her eyes. "Until morning, then?"

Natalie mentally shook herself. "Uh . . . yes. Morning. Breakfast . . . at nine."

He reached for her hand, led her inside, and lifted her fingertips to his lips. "Thank you again, Natalie—for everything."

She couldn't speak. Could only feel . . . the firm, yet gentle contact of his flesh.

Then he was gone. She stood rooted to the spot, listening for his bedroom door to close, feeling as though her fingers, so recently caught in his grasp, were on fire.

Delilah the cat walked around the corner just then and gave her a baleful look. But Natalie paid her no mind. Her thoughts were filled with the memory of Alex's face, his voice, his touch. . . .

"Merry Christmas," she whispered to the stars as she closed the front door and leaned against it.

Yes. It promised to be a very merry Christmas indeed.

Eighteen

~

"Y ou were right, Natalie," Alex conceded with a wry grin. "The power must have gone off sometime around 2 A.M."

They were huddled in the parlor, mufflers wrapped around their necks, Natalie chafing her mittened hands together.

In the early-morning light, Alex looked ruggedly handsome—a stubble of beard shadowing his face. He had wisely chosen to layer his clothing—a tan turtleneck under a thick wool sweater.

"The storm must have knocked out the electricity." She moved the drape aside to take a look at the side lawn, frozen into a wintry still life. "But there's plenty of firewood out back. Oren cut some just before he left. And there are some old newspapers in the box on the hearth."

He chuckled, a warm, rumbling sound deep in his throat. "I could contribute quite a few paperwads, where I've discarded some false starts on my latest writing project."

She laughed, feeling herself beginning to relax as he shrugged on his parka and headed for the back door. He reappeared a moment later with an armload of wood. It was as if she were watching some old movie, the plot having not yet unfolded. In spite of a familiar feeling of apprehension, she was intrigued to find out what would happen next.

Alex arranged the logs on the hearth, rummaged in the chest for the paper and kindling, then laid the fire—expertly—before touching a match to the paper.

Natalie was impressed. "Where did you learn how to do that?"

"Lay a fire?" Rocking back on his heels, he glanced over his shoulder, his cheeks ruddy from the vaulting flames. "Oh, that little accomplishment harks back to my childhood." He rose and dusted off his hands. "One of those fundamentals I gleaned from my dad. He also inspired in me a love of carpentry—building things, actually. In my spare time, I'm working on a log cabin."

She envisioned a model—perhaps a miniature replica of some historic building. "Will you display it in your classroom?"

He slanted her a look of amusement. "Oh, I doubt that it would fit. This is a full-scale house, though a small one. A one-bedroom. A retreat of sorts. A place where I can get my writing done, 'far from the madding crowd,' so to speak."

The man never ceased to amaze her! No ordinary professor, this. "And how far along are you on the construction?"

He paced in front of the fire, his enthusiasm and the warmth from the hearth reaching out to enfold Natalie. "Almost finished. Felling the trees and planing them into shape was the greatest challenge. Then I had to hire some local carpenters to help me raise the walls and put on the roof. But it was great fun all in all. Energizing, really. Helped clear my mind of illuminated manuscripts and battle details."

So that's how he'd gotten those nicks and cuts on his hands. "Just where is this cabin located?"

He took a seat on the couch opposite her and leaned forward, spreading his hands toward the blaze. "Not far from Lynchburg. About three years ago, I bought a parcel of land overlooking the James River, north of Big Island. Lovely spot."

Natalie made a quick mental calculation. Lynchburg was at least a hundred miles away. When the cabin was completed, there would be no reason for the professor to book a reservation at Pleasant Valley Inn. She couldn't explain the sudden overwhelming sense of loss.

"Well, I'd best go see what I can scare up for breakfast," she said, leaving the cozy parlor to forage for food in Tika's immaculate kitchen.

"Guess it's my turn to make like a pioneer." When she returned, Natalie brought with her a heavy cast iron pot and a plate of blueberry muffins. "Tea and toast. That is, if we can figure out some way to toast these muffins."

In the glow of firelight, her hair had taken on a sheen that almost took his breath away. Alex decided to occupy his mind elsewhere. "Well, the American pioneer era is not exactly my speciality, but between us, we should be able to come up with something."

He'd noticed the iron arm with a hook on the end attached to the side of the fireplace, attesting to the true age of the house. Taking the kettle of water from her, he hung it and swung the black pot over the flames. "Tea for two . . . coming up. Then if we can rig up some coathangers—a la campfire style—we might even manage that toast."

Her answering smile was dazzling. "I'll go see about the coathangers, get the teapot and cups, and bring back a little butter. Let it never be said that Pleasant Valley Inn shirked its responsibility to a guest—particularly an English guest who needs his tea—even in a snowstorm."

She darted through the door, trailing that delicate fragrance that sent his senses reeling. He *liked* the woman. She was obviously competent—running this place as profitably as she did. Resourceful and witty, too. And completely feminine. In this day, that in itself was something of a miracle.

Time flew as they enjoyed their simple meal, enhanced by the flow of conversation.

Natalie, propped up on the couch across from him, sipped her tea and stroked Delilah, who had wandered into the parlor and was now curled in her mistress's lap. "Just what prompted you to begin writing romance novels anyway?"

"It all started as a dare, believe it or not, during my undergraduate days—Worcester College, Oxford." He responded to her lifted brow. "While a group of us were sitting at our favorite table at the Eagle and Child discussing literature—my major as an undergrad—one of my mates confessed to reading one of his little sister's Barbara Cartland novels. Said he'd enjoyed it, actually—much as one might enjoy hearing a folk tune as opposed to a symphony."

"Variety is the spice of life," Natalie interrupted. "But do go on."

"I was quite the pompous bloke in those days, and I laughed at him. Well, he got all huffy and said, 'If you think it's so easy, go ahead and write one yourself. Then we'll talk.'"

"So you accepted the challenge?"

"That very night. It wasn't exactly easy, but I took to the genre right away, I must say. And though some may think me an oddity, the craft has brought me a fortune—and much satisfaction—so I shouldn't write it off altogether."

"Which book was your first? I've read them all, you know."

He watched her for a moment, the light playing on the lines of her face. If ever there was a model for a heroine.... "That was *Love's Sweetest Song.*" He felt the heat rise to his face and wasn't sure whether to blame the fire, the subject ... or Natalie herself. "I try to give them all names fairly dripping with honey."

Her soft laughter reminded him of tinkling windchimes. "I loved that one, but it definitely isn't one of my favorites."

He shrugged. "First novels are filled with mistakes the author would correct if given the chance. Nevertheless, in my ignorance, I sent off the manuscript to a publisher, was rejected, advised to rewrite, and after a dozen tries, finally landed a contract with a London house. Not exactly an overnight success story."

"But you must have been thrilled when it was accepted."

"To be honest, I was, but very few people were in on my secret. In fact, you and your staff are among the handful who know Jeanine Beaumont's true identity."

She smiled an endearing smile. "Your secret is safe with me ... Jeanine."

"It had better be, or I'm through!"

Delilah roused and blinked disdainfully at the burst of laughter, then settled back down to her long winter's nap.

~

With no hope of a break in the weather before morning, according to the reports on Alex's transistor radio, there was nothing to do but make the best of it. Christmas dinner turned out to be soup, heated in the black kettle over the fire, a can of tuna fish and crackers, and tea. As fine a feast as Tika had ever produced with all her modern conveniences, Natalie thought. On the other hand, maybe not. But neither she nor Alex complained.

Still sitting in the parlor, they whiled away the afternoon with talk. Lots of it. The current controversies over abortion and assisted suicide. Medieval class structure vs. modern. The uses—and misuses—of the Internet. "Jeopardy" vs. "The Wheel of Fortune." Sometime, just before dusk, Alex abandoned his couch to join Natalie on hers. Delilah meowed in protest, then leapt to the floor to doze by the fire. And sometime later, Alex's arm found its way around Natalie's shoulders.

She leaned back and let her lashes drift shut, hearing the music of Christmas from the transistor, turned low so as not to subdue their conversation. Hearing the music of her heart as it beat a steady rhythm.

"I've never experienced a Christmas like this one," she murmured, keeping her eyes closed lest she open them to find the parlor deserted, the images only a dream.

"Nor have I," he rumbled beside her. "But there's one tradition we haven't yet observed."

Her eyes flew open and she turned her head to stare at him. "What's that?"

Alex reached behind his back and pulled out a sprig of mistletoe he'd filched from some arrangement no doubt. "May I?" he whispered.

"Yes . . . please."

With one hand he held the mistletoe above their heads; with the other he gently cupped Natalie's chin and tilted her face toward his. Breathlessly, their lips met in that timeless expression between a man and woman—a kiss that meant more than Natalie cared to admit. How long it lasted, she could only guess, so swept away was she by tides of pure joy.

Hushed and still, the world waited as the snow continued to fall.

When Alex lifted his head, Natalie's eyes were shining. "You're not really a prince, are you, in the guise of a professor?"

"No, Natalie. Only a hopeless romantic in the guise of an ordinary man."

They kissed once more. And before they said goodnight, Natalie St. John was completely and irrevocably in love.

The next morning Alex was already back to work on the revisions of his novel. Natalie breathed a sigh of relief when the lights flickered back on, and was genuinely heartened when an employee of the gas company showed up to ignite the pilot light of the furnace. By noon, the inn was as warm as a busy tea cozy.

Natalie slid the roast beef into the oven and made a pot of coffee to sip on while she waited out the afternoon. The roast began to broadcast a delicious smell an hour later, and by the time it was almost done, Alex shuffled in. Natalie had just thrown the Yorkshire Pudding into a very hot oven to puff to a delicious, golden brown. She hoped.

"I knew the aroma would bring you in sooner or later. You're turning into a regular workaholic," she teased, noticing his tired eyes.

"Roast beef?"

She nodded. "I'm making yesterday's dinner today. Here," she said, handing him a cool cloth, "this should soothe your eyes."

"Thanks." He accepted the moist rag and held it to his eyes for a moment. "Got anyone in mind to help you eat this feast?"

"I was counting on you to do that job."

He glanced appreciatively at the professional kitchen, made less sterile by the beamed ceiling, bunches of dried herbs perfuming the air. "This is a wonderful room. No matter the country, the kitchen is the heart of the home. And how nice to share my meals. Since I'm batching it, I usually take my meals by the television set after a hard day in the classroom. Fast food, more often than not."

"There was nothing fast about *this* food." She laughed. "It took us two days."

"May I tell you again how wonderful you've made Christmas for me?" At his approach, all chit-chat ceased, and there was no longer denying last night's kisses. She straightened as his hands encircled her waist, and he turned her around to face him. "You're a very special woman, Natalie St. John. I don't know why someone hasn't grabbed you long before now."

"No one's ever been quick enough—" she gave him a coy smile— "'til you."

He tugged her into his embrace, all the love of the home in which he'd been brought up rising to the surface to fill his arms. True affection and caring—not just mistletoe and magic. Steady warmth and light—both needed for growth.

"I'm so happy," she mumbled against his chest, the nubby wool of his sweater scratching her cheek. "So very happy."

"Mmmm."

The timer going off at that moment pulled them apart, and she and Alex began to set out the meal. But things were different between them—a new closeness, fresh and alive, which precluded words.

Throughout the meal, eaten at the little table in the kitchen, their gazes locked, exploring, seeking. She might have been eating hamburger instead of tenderloin, though he declared the roast beef "excellent." She loved the way he held his knife and fork in the

Continental manner, never setting them down, cutting the bites and moving them to his mouth in a single deft motion.

"This is superb, Natalie."

"Thank you. I hope it was worth waiting for."

"Very definitely." His eyes, looking deep into hers, never wavered. "The best things in life always are."

Natalie opened her mouth to speak, but before she could utter a word, the phone came to life with a shrill voice of its own. "Excuse me," she said, springing up to take the call. She'd had a sneaking suspicion that Jonah and Tika might elope during the holidays. Maybe this was someone with the news.

"Pleasant Valley Inn."

Hearing the voice on the other end of the line, her heart sank. "What do *you* want?"

She noticed Alex wheel around at her strained tone, and turned her back on him to speak more softly into the receiver. "Look, I told you never to call me again!"

Pause.

"You walked out a long time ago without having the guts to say goodbye."

Pause.

"If you didn't have the nerve to face me then, then why should I see you now?"

Slam!

Natalie felt her eyes prickle with tears and dashed out of the room before Alex could see. Upstairs in her attic retreat, she threw herself on the bed and cried her heart out.

"He couldn't even call me on Christmas Day," she sobbed into her pillow. "It had to be the day after." She cried until the well of tears ran dry.

Too late. The geologist was always too late.

~⌒~

Meanwhile in the kitchen, a bewildered Alex put away the food and loaded the plates into the dishwasher. From time to time, he shook his head, wondering about the strange turn of events.

And the next day, before anyone was awake—not even Oren, who was back from his Christmas vacation—Professor Alexander P. Elbert gathered his belongings and left, as silently as he had come.

Nineteen

⁓

"A clean break is a much easier wound to heal," Lu said one morning in March, relieved that Natalie was finally willing to talk about it. The staff had all agreed that it was best not to bring up the subject until she was ready.

Natalie's face was expressionless, but they all knew how she felt. "He just seemed so nice—so different from all the others."

"I really liked him." Tika squeezed Natalie's hand from her seat next to hers at the kitchen table. "I didn't think he was the type to cut and run."

Natalie grimaced. "I guess my little act after the geologist called was too much for him. Men have little sympathy for theatrics."

"You had every right, darlin'," Lu insisted. "Tika and me can neither one of us understand what it must be like to have such a father. All the same, Nat, maybe you'd feel better if you'd take his call next time. He could have done a lot of changin' in the last twenty-three years."

"I don't want to know about it if he has. I really don't."

With a huge sigh, Natalie left the kitchen, heading back to the sunporch, where she'd put in a new supply of books and reading material—not a Jeanine Beaumont novel in the bunch, Lu happened to know.

⁓

After that scene in the kitchen, Tika was determined to speak to Lu. And she did, during a morning break, just after she'd gone over the evening's dinner menu.

"You know Jonah and I have been taking some counseling sessions at the church," she began when Lu had settled down for a cup of coffee. "We've been studying about forgiveness."

"Know all about that," Lu was quick to put in. "It's one of the basic teachings of Christianity—God forgiving us for our sins; then we, in turn, forgiving 'our brother,' as the Good Book says."

"But what about *fathers?* Does the Bible say anything about forgiving fathers?"

"Well . . . ." She gave it some thought. "Jesus said we're to forgive anyone who offends us, and I'd think that would include fathers. In fact, now that I think about it, He even mentioned how many times we're to forgive. Somethin' like 'seventy times seven,' or some such way-out number."

Tika did a rapid calculation in her head. "Maybe He means we're just to keep on forgiving." There was a long pause as they sipped their coffee. "I've been wondering if Nattie is ever going to be happy with a man—*any* man—until she gets things straightened out with her dad."

Lu cocked an eyebrow. "Maybe you're right."

"Why don't you have a talk with her, Lu? I'm so new at all this that I'm not sure she'd welcome any advice from me. I still have so much to learn."

"Ha! You've grown more in three months than any new Christian I've ever known." There was an approving gleam in Lu's eye.

"Well, there's Sunday school and counseling . . . and Jonah's tutoring me on the side." She stared out the kitchen window at the crocuses on the lawn and felt a surge of love and gratitude. "Oh, Lu, God was so patient with me all those years. I guess I'll never understand why—I was just plain *stubborn*, or maybe stupid is the word for it. But then He sent Jonah . . . and . . . well, I guess it took someone like him to open my eyes. I never thought I could love a man the way I love that guy. And now I just want Nattie to find the same happiness."

"I'll talk to her tonight," Lu promised, "after things settle down. We were going to rent a video anyway since you'll be out with Jonah and Oren will be with his fisherman buddies." She polished off a piece of banana bread, hot from the oven. "You still going into D.C. tomorrow to shop for your dress?"

"Uh-huh. Time is flying, and May 1 will be here before we know it!"

Lu had never seen Tika so happy. She was positively blooming. "I can hardly believe it."

"Oh, *I* can!" Tika exclaimed. "I've been making and freezing hors d'oeuvres for so long I could do it in my sleep."

"No one said you had to prepare all the food for your own reception."

"But Jonah loves my cooking."

"Who doesn't?"

"That's my point."

"By the way—" Lu rose to take her dishes to the sink—"have you been out to the greenhouse lately?"

"Uh-huh. Oren's doing us proud in the flower department. I'm not quite sure why he's going all out like this, but I'm not complaining."

Tika noticed the faraway look in Lu's eyes. "When we eloped all those years ago, Oren never got over the fact that I had no bouquet. He plum forgot to get me one. Surroundin' you with beautiful flowers on your special day is one way of makin' it up to *me*."

"He's a good man—your Oren." Tika felt an unfamiliar moisture misting her eyes. "Now if we could just find a good man for Nattie."

~~~

An infant in a long white christening gown. Two smiling parents.

A toddler in a red bathing suit, wearing her father's hat and her mother's high heels.

A leggy teen, looking lost and lonely, sitting in the porch swing . . . on the side of the pool . . . in a lawn chair with a book in her lap. . . .

Natalie leafed through an old photo album, reading her life on its pages. One of the saddest things about being the only child of a single parent, she decided, was that it meant you were almost always by yourself in pictures. Someone—usually Mom—had to man the camera, right?

Lu rapped softly on the door, then peeped inside. "Nat? Are you ready to start the movie?"

"In a minute . . . ." She placed the album on the nightstand.

"Oh, pictures!" Lu cried, spotting the book. "I love family pictures. May I?" At Natalie's nod, she sank down on the bed beside her and paged through without comment. Then, "You want to hate him, don't you?"

Natalie's eyes welled with tears. "It would make it so much easier."

"Then why won't you talk to him, darlin'? He calls at least once a month. Give him a chance."

"I don't think I could stand another rejection, Lu. I don't know what I'd do if he left me again."

"Oh, darlin', he won't leave you again. He's been trying so hard to get through to you."

"I'm not so sure about that. Mom always said he was a man who enjoyed the conquest, but he didn't stick around long afterward."

Lu sighed, and Natalie could tell there was something on her mind. "There's more to this than just your father, Nat."

She waited.

"It's about getting on with *your* life." Lu seemed hesitant. "I—that is Tika and me—we've been thinkin' that until you at least see your father again, you'll not be able to get on with . . . other things. You know . . . another man. You don't trust them."

Natalie shot to her feet. "Well, why should I?" she snorted, pacing. "If Alex couldn't understand—"

"This isn't about Alex, Nat," Lu went on softly. "It's about a lot of unfinished business. It's about forgiveness . . . and it's about trust."

Natalie turned to look at her friend, feeling the raw anguish in her heart. Sighing, she sank back down on the bed and opened up the album again. "See? This is my father. Good-looking, isn't he? All the women were after him—" she broke off with a choking sound in her throat.

"So your Dad had a way with the ladies."

"That's one way to put it. My mother was Wife Number Two. There was one more . . . the one he left my mother for."

"And he never tried to contact you in all those years?"

"Not until after his third wife divorced him. As far as I know, he's never married again. But that tells me plenty—that I've always been his lowest priority . . . that he never wanted me as long as he had a woman in his life. Lu, there's just no way I could trust him after that. . . ."

She sat, staring into space. "There's one more thing. When he walked out on my mother and went straight into the arms of another woman—it was a woman with a little girl two years younger than I." She turned to look at Lu, no longer trying to hide her naked pain. "Why, Lu? Why did that little girl get to have him as a father . . . and I didn't?"

Lu put out her arms and drew Natalie's head down on her shoulder. "I don't know, darlin'," she crooned, rocking her like a baby. "I don't know. I can't answer that. Sometimes all we can do is pray."

Natalie pulled away, indignant. "So I can end up forgiving him? No way. Lu, he's never ever admitted he did anything wrong. He's never asked for my forgiveness."

"Maybe that's what he's been trying to do all these years, Nattie, darlin'."

She was her cool, collected self again. "Listen, Lu, I know you mean well, and I appreciate your concern. But a lot of years have gone by, and it's too late. It's just too late. Besides, I'd never defame my mother's memory by running to him."

Lu sat there, not saying a word, and Natalie thought the matter was ended. But she was wrong. "Nattie . . . you're his flesh and blood. Your mother's gone . . . but your father is alive. And as long as he's alive, there's always hope. We can't live our lives for the dead." And with that, she left the room.

The movie forgotten, Natalie got ready for bed, Lu's last words echoing in her mind. *We can't live our lives for the dead.* . . .

Maybe it was worth a try. She refused to think beyond that tentative commitment.

Besides, she thought, flipping off the lamp beside her bed, *he'll probably never call again.*

Twenty

It was when Natalie was putting away her winter sweaters that she spotted it again. The box. The brightly painted affair that had provoked Elva Jacks's mysterious yearly ritual. Calling a locksmith was a serious temptation, since no key had shown up. At least none that fit the small lock on the front.

There were plenty of keys, of course, on rings found in various drawers of the house. One ring of embossed leather with the initials E. G. J.; one with a Precious Moments figure; another from Niagara Falls. Natalie was reminded of her own key ring collection at the age of ten.

Ten-year-olds often do funny things when they're reaching for their own identity, Natalie thought, and she herself was no exception. She'd collected at least twenty key rings, all hooked together to form a clacking wad of plastic, metal, leather and wood. All of these issuing from one ring that held a single house key. Twenty key rings for one little house key.

Now, looking back, Natalie wondered if she'd feared losing that key. Maybe home wasn't an ivy-covered cottage, smelling of chocolate chip cookies when she came home from school each day—but she didn't want to lose the way in.

The box had been with her for months now, a familiar object perched among her sweaters. It was a quirk and she understood quirks. Her father had many of them, according to her mother, and it was something Natalie had done her best to emulate as a teen. She'd tried to be like him—both eccentric and English—until one day it suddenly dawned on her that he hadn't called for two years and wasn't likely to any time soon. She'd put away all the black, European clothes she'd had her mother buy for her, and for some time had stopped drinking hot tea and calling crackers, biscuits and biscuits, scones.

Today Natalie sat at the kitchen table, sorting the mail. Bills to pay. Receipts to file. Letters to read and answer.

At that moment Lu walked in with a pile of clean tea towels to be folded. "Still haven't gotten into that thing?"

"Nope."

"What are you waitin' for?"

"I really don't know. Strange, but I still feel I'd be invading Mrs. Jacks's privacy if I broke into her box. Maybe I need to learn a little more about the woman." She paused. "I know only that she was a widow, always wore black, and had very few contacts, except for her lawyers. But what about her habits. Anything unusual?"

Lu pondered. "There was one thing that made her halfway human. She liked to slip out on the back stoop now and again and smoke a cigarette—when she thought no one was looking."

Natalie laughed. "We all have our vices."

"You got that right. Some smoke, others drink, and others gorge themselves with food." She chuckled, eyeing her own ample figure. "They all put you in your grave before you were meant to be there. I keep tellin' Oren if he doesn't lay off the Hershey bars, he's goin' to meet his Maker ahead of schedule.

"Mrs. Jacks wasn't a heavy smoker though. Wasn't a big eater, either, and never touched a drop of alcohol that I know of."

"From remarks you and Tika have made, I take it she wasn't the most agreeable sort."

"Well, she wanted things done the way she wanted them— whether it was the best way or not. But she wasn't nasty or unkind—just distant. I always felt a little sorry for her, Nattie. I think she was lonely." For the first time, Lu seemed to notice the stack of envelopes and stamps on the table. "There was one other thing . . . but I'm not sure it's important. She always wanted to be the one to get the mail—never let any of the rest of us do it for her. . . .

"The more I think about it, Nattie, the more I think you should take a look in that box. It might answer all your questions."

Natalie shrugged. "I don't know. When it comes right down to it, Lu, it's not *my* box just because I own the inn. Maybe I should call her lawyers. After all, her estate had to have been left to someone who may want the contents."

"Especially if it's money," Lu said sarcastically.

With that in mind, the decision was easy. "I'll call right now."

She rose from her seat, walked into her office and dialed the number on the business card she pulled out of her Rolodex. Five minutes later she was back in the kitchen.

"I have an appointment in the morning—nine o'clock—with someone from the firm of Dekker, Freese, and Groff. In Reston."

"So you see, Ms. St. John," the lawyer drawled in a very lawyerly way, a slight hint of a Virginia accent softening her words, "after a quick phone call, we've learned that her one surviving niece doesn't want the box."

She slid the box across the polished surface of the conference room table. Natalie couldn't help noticing how incongruous the battered box appeared on the expensive cherry wood surface. Couldn't help noticing, either, the attorney's meticulously manicured nails, matching her lipstick and enhancing the look of chic sophistication.

Lori Chester-Gatto. Andy's new bride. So professional . . . so courteous . . . so *distant.* The lawyer had kept things on a strictly professional note ever since her polite greeting in the lobby. No chit-chat, no "Andy's told me all about you." Nothing but business.

Natalie couldn't function this way. Andy was her best friend, for pity's sake. Lori knew that. So instead of making it some kind of competition, she'd welcome Andy's wife into the club.

Maybe they'd even start a little club of their own.

"You have lovely nails, Ms. Chester," Natalie remarked with an open smile, and the big-city lawyer let her mask slip from her bright blue eyes and suddenly became one of the girls.

"Are you sure this pink is not too bright? It's a different shade from the one Delores usually uses."

"Trust me. It's the perfect touch—feminine, yet professional."

The air was suddenly a lot more breathable, and the conversation drifted back to business, but with an easy camaraderie. "You know," Lori Chester said, pulling out a little mason jar of candy and setting it between them, "Mrs. Shaber was quite adamant about not wanting anything to do with her aunt's possessions."

"Didn't she inherit the money from the sale of the inn?"

"Yes. But all personal effects were left at the inn, as I'm sure you know."

Natalie nodded. "Lu Luckadoo told me they were instructed to take all the clothes to Goodwill. But we still don't know what's in this box. There may be something valuable—money or jewelry. . . ."

"If you want, I'll call a locksmith in and we can clear up the mystery right here and now."

"It would be a relief. I've had this box hanging around for so long, I'd like to get things resolved. Andy always thought I was crazy not to open it sooner."

There, she'd said the "A" word. What would Lori Chester have to say now?

The woman's unaffected laughter was Natalie's answer. "Anything Andy doesn't quite understand is 'crazy,' in his opinion."

Their eyes met in mutual understanding.

"He loved you for years, you know," Lori acknowledged frankly.

"I know."

"I'm glad you couldn't love him back—"

"Oh, it's not that Andy wasn't a great catch—" Natalie was feeling distinctly uncomfortable.

"I understand. For some people, love must come in like a flood, not a gentle rain."

Lori Chester-Gatto was wise as well as smart. Natalie couldn't help admiring her. "Which was it for you?"

There was that laugh again. "A deluge! Those liquid brown eyes of his. His wit. His quick mind. I was a goner in no time."

"I'm glad you found each other, Lori." Natalie meant it.

"Me, too. I thank God every day for Andy. It was time. For both of us."

While the locksmith was on his way, Lori ordered sandwiches from the deli just off the lobby. When the delivery was made, they spread their fare on her desk and took the time to get better acquainted.

"Did you ever meet Elva Jacks?" Natalie asked.

"Yes, I did. I visited the inn many times. Great place to unwind. What caused you to leave D.C. and take up innkeeping?"

"I had the money—from my computer business—and I hated the corporate scene."

"Too much stress?"

"Too little real living."

Lori thought about it and nodded. "People people everywhere and not a single one who gives a fig about you."

"Exactly. Not to mention the traffic and noise."

Lori bit into her tuna sandwich. "I hate city life." Her declaration surprised Natalie. "I grew up in western Virginia. My daddy was a tobacco farmer. But after law school, this place made me the best offer."

"You seem too nice to be a lawyer," Natalie said candidly.

"And you seem too normal to be in computers," Lori shot back with a grin.

"So much for stereotypes," Natalie remarked and unwrapped her pickle. "You and Andy should come back to the inn sometime. We've made some changes."

Lori sighed. "Poor Elva, she was never big on change. If only her sister could have forgiven her, she might have died a far happier woman."

Natalie leaned forward in her chair. "What do you mean?"

"She and her sister had a royal falling-out. Apparently Elva's husband was engaged to her sister Lova at one time."

"Lova?"

Lori chuckled. "Yes, their mother picked some weird names, didn't she?"

"Yechh. What happened with the husband?"

"The only thing I can figure, from piecing things together here and there, is that Elva and Richard eloped sometime before his wedding to Lova. Lova never forgave them—not that I blame her—so they moved from New York State, where they grew up, down to some place in central New Jersey. She had quite a bit of property there. After he died, she bought the old house in Pleasant Valley, did some remodeling, and opened the inn. You know the rest."

"So her niece doesn't want to have anything to do with her? Seems kind of strange to harbor her mother's anger after all these years."

"Especially when you consider the fact that if Lova had married Richard, Mrs. Shaber wouldn't even *be* here!"

Natalie laughed. "True."

The conversation continued in an easy vein. "I wish we'd met years ago," Natalie said.

"Yes, we've been missing out, haven't we? It isn't easy making friends in the city—not like back home."

An idea sprang to life at that moment. "Listen, we're having a special weekend at the inn next month to celebrate the cherry blossoms. Why don't you and Andy come down? As my guests."

Lori's eyes lit up and she pounced on the idea. "We'd love to! And I'm sure I speak for Andy."

"The new courtyard cottages will be done by then, and you two guys can launch one of them."

"We'll be there. Believe me, I could use the break. And Andy will be delighted to see you. I can't wait to tell him I met you today."

A light tapping sounded from the other side of the door.

"Come in!" Lori called and the door opened, a sour face appearing around the frame.

"You the lady who called for a locksmith?"

"I'm the one." Lori rose from her chair and handed him the box. "We need this opened right away."

He rolled his eyes as if to say, *And you couldn't have brought this down to the shop?* He took the box from her outstretched hand and, with a deft twist of a tool, had it opened a couple minutes later. Natalie wrote out a check, and he left, muttering under his breath. Reminded her of Oren.

She set the box on the desk and stared at it.

Lori leaned over the desk with an expectant glow in her eyes. "So . . . are you going to open it any time this year?"

Holding her breath, Natalie lifted the lid. . . .

Twenty-One

*L*etters! Ivory vellum envelopes stacked neatly in two even rows. The handwriting on the front fading gradually from firm to spidery.

"What do you think these could be?" Lori asked, reaching in for a handful. Natalie did the same.

"They're all addressed to Lova," Natalie stated the obvious. "And look, they were never opened."

Angrily scrawled across the face of each envelope were the words *Return to Sender.* Black letters in felt tip. El Marko letters that grew progressively larger and bolder as the postmarks recorded the passing years.

"Boy, oh boy—" Natalie whistled—"she really *didn't* want to hear from old Elva, did she?"

"I think you could effectively say that. Well, Natalie, go ahead and take the box. I doubt if there are any valuables in here. Just looks like old letters. Will you read them?"

"I'm . . . not sure."

"Elva Jacks is dead," Lori reminded her gently. "She won't be caring whether or not you read her mail."

"That's true, of course. Still . . . "

"You'll have to make up your own mind. But the truth of the matter is that legally you can do with them whatever you want."

"I guess I'll have to think about it." Natalie got to her feet and put out her hand. Lori grasped it firmly. "See you next month then?"

"Absolutely. I'm looking forward to it."

173

This unlikely friendship had popped up in the most unexpected of places. Natalie was well aware that she had been granted a gift. She really liked Lori. After Alex left, she'd decided not to date for at least five years. But she could really use a friend right about now. Even if that friend happened to be Andy's new wife.

"I'll give you a call," Natalie promised, "and send along a brochure."

"And I'll mark the date on my calendar right now."

They said goodbye and a few minutes later Natalie was on the Metro, headed toward the museum area of the Mall. The anonymity one could achieve on the grassy expanse that stretched between the Capitol and the Washington Monument was not to be found anywhere else—definitely not in a small town like Pleasant Valley. She'd seen people doing just about everything on these lawns, but on this unseasonably warm day, most of them were lolling about on blankets to sleep, or read. Some of the more active threw Frisbees or footballs. No one would think twice about a woman reading some letters.

Natalie emerged from the dark Metro station into the blinding sunlight near the Smithsonian Museum of American History. With the wind blowing briskly, she sought the protective sculpture garden of the Hirshhorn Museum. The hedges and the large pieces of art would provide a perfect setting in which to muse. And after grabbing a cup of coffee from the museum's Circle Café, Natalie sat down to read. As much out of curiosity as the fact that Tika and Lu would never let her live to see the end of their scorn if she didn't.

She opened the lid and took out the first note dated August 3, 1932.

Dear Lova,

I don't expect you to write back, but I just can't bear the thought that we aren't speaking to one another. Please forgive us, me. I knew you and Rich were having problems, and I guess I thought that justified what we did. I kept telling myself I was saving you both from future heartbreak. Ridiculous, I know.

*Lova, you were my favorite sister. What's done is done,
but perhaps there are still pieces left to gather of what was
once a beautiful relationship.*

I love you,

Elva

There was more. News of the move to Clinton, New Jersey, a
pregnancy, a miscarriage. A new job for Richard Jacks, a trip to
Las Vegas and hitting the jackpot. The diagnosis of cancer for
Richard, a timeline of his digression, his death. All the news Lova
never learned. All of the envelopes taped up tightly like the thin,
hard line of an angry mouth. And through the years, the theme
remained the same. Elva continued to beg her sister to forgive her,
despite the fact that the letters were always returned.

But Lova never forgave.

And now the bitter seed had been passed on to another generation. Like mother, like daughter. A perennial resentment that left
destruction in its wake.

How could Lova have hung on to her hatred all those years?
Natalie wondered. After all, she and her sister had loved each other
once. According to Elva's letters and the memories she'd recalled,
they had been closer than most.

Natalie skimmed through the file and picked out a letter near
the end:

*I know I failed you, Lova. I betrayed you, and you have
every right to hate me forever. I don't know why I did what
I did. It was a sin of the moment—a time of weakness
when my own selfish desires were more important than
doing what was right. When it was all said and done, I
realized I had thrown away one of the few things that ever
meant anything to me—your love and respect. If it's any
consolation, Richard and I never really got along after
those first deliriously happy weeks. It was probably a
blessing that he died early on, although I hate to say such
a thing. But it's true. Maybe it would have worked between*

*the two of you. Now we'll never know. But I regret that I
robbed you of your chance to find out.*

*Please, Lova, please read this letter. At least, give me
a chance to explain. . . .*

The letter was written only three years before Elva Jacks's
death—1994—sixty-two years after the day she made the decision
to put her own wants ahead of her sister's. Apparently, she hadn't
noticed that the thick black scrawl of *Return to Sender* had begun
to change twenty years before. The handwriting was messy—no
longer the studied hand from the days when penmanship was an
art and cursive wasn't a subjective maneuver.

Natalie read every letter until she noticed that the early spring
breeze had resumed its wintry chill, and the sunlight was slanting
across the garden, sending long shadows crawling out from the
bases of the sculptures.

Still, she wasn't quite ready to head back to Pleasant Valley.
There was too much to think about, pray over. Lova . . . Elva . . .
Lu's admonition . . . the geologist. . . .

A banner, hanging over the entrance to the National Gallery of
Art, caught her eye. *Medieval Man and His Expressions.*

She decided to check it out, deliberately putting aside any
thought of Alexander P. Elbert, Ph.D., who would delight in such
an exhibit. Besides, she'd always wanted to know more about castles.

She hurried across the Mall and up the steps to the museum.
Passing the painting of the "Last Supper" by Salvador Dali, she
wondered, as she always did, how the man could have captured the
essence of such a spiritual happening. The face of Jesus was so
right—at least to her mind's eye—so tenderly compassionate
toward his disciples, even knowing that shortly one of them would
leave that gathering to betray Him.

She paused beneath the great dome, thinking how it must
resemble the architecture of heaven—like a canopy arching over
the mansions being prepared by the Lord Himself. Heaven. Mom's
home now. Her own someday. Would Elva Jacks be there . . . or

Lova, the woman who had never learned how to forgive? Could those who harbored hate and unforgiveness see the kingdom of heaven?

Suddenly realizing that the museum would be closing soon, Natalie hurried toward the gallery. Following the signs, she found the exhibit, struck by the muted tones achieved by the artists. Tri-paneled triptychs displayed gilded figures, so two-dimensional in their rendering. Stained glass, brightly backlit, splashed the highly polished floor with prisms of rich color. Gargoyles leered from atop pedestals. She shivered.

But what took her entirely by surprise was the sign announcing a lecture going on at this very moment, in a room to the side of the exhibit hall. *"Medieval Man and the Arts,* a lecture by Dr. Alexander P. Elbert."

Her heart lurched, pounded. She felt flushed, then chilled. The very sight of his name after all these weeks was enough to bring on cardiac arrest!

Feeling drawn, in spite of herself, Natalie ventured inside. This was much too coincidental to walk away from, for what the world called chance or fate, she'd learned to call Providence.

He was standing on the podium, one hand in the pocket of his tweed jacket, the other braced on the lectern, the familiar British brogue calling up all the emotions she had tried so desperately to deny.

She slipped into an empty seat at the back, listening intently, hearing nothing. All she could think of was the touch of his hand on her face, the feel of his lips on hers. . . .

Once, she thought he'd seen her, his gaze coming to rest on the back row, a glint of recognition sparking the brown eyes. But when he moved on to encompass his appreciative audience, she couldn't be sure. She'd leave before the lecture ended. He mustn't think she'd chased him down. Mustn't suspect there was a shred of feeling for him. . . .

Still, mesmerized by the sound of his voice, she waited, frozen in place as surely as the sculptures in the gardens on the Mall.

~~~

When the lecture ended and Alex left the podium to stride to the back, she was panicky. Apparently there was to be no escape.

"Natalie!" Her name rolled off his tongue in that musical cadence that left her knees weak.

"Professor Elbert." She gave him her most professional smile and clutched her totebag to her side to still the trembling of her fingers.

"Whatever are you doing here?"

"It all happened quite by accident, I can assure you. I had business in the city . . . but that's a long story. Very nice to run into you again." *Keep it up, Nat, old girl. If you can pull this off, you can do anything.*

He surveyed the crowd forming around him, and he frowned. "Don't go away," he whispered. "I've got to hang about and chat for a bit, but afterward would you join me for dinner? If you have no other plans, that is," he amended hastily.

She hesitated, then allowed a reluctant smile. After all, she hadn't been *forced* to come here. And she did owe him a chance to explain his abrupt departure at Christmas. "I have no other plans."

But this had better be good. He'd better have a really good reason for walking out on her that night in December.

~~~

"And so," Alex finished up his explanation, "when I heard you tell your old boyfriend never to call again, and when I saw how devastated you were after hearing from him, I figured I must have misread your actions."

He raked his hand through his hair in a familiar gesture, expression open and frank. "Natalie, I don't know what it is about you, but I seem to have no choice but to tell you exactly how I feel." He gave a little self-deprecating laugh. "Although I'll be dashed if I'd ever let one of my heroes behave in such a way."

"Oh, I understand perfectly. Real people never act like the characters in romance novels. I'm just glad to know what happened. Still, I wish you'd asked me about it at the time."

"Why? Would it have made a difference?"

She lowered her voice, and he leaned forward. "That was my *father* who called."

"Your *father*?" He did have the grace to blush—all the way to his hairline. He peered at her through the shock of blond hair that had tumbled over his forehead. "I can only pray . . . that is to say, I hope my leaving so hastily didn't spoil. . . ."

Suddenly they were both talking at once.

"I couldn't believe it. I wanted to E-mail—"

"My stupid pride . . . I should have called—"

Laughing, Alex tugged her to her feet. "Let's get out of here. We've a lot of catching up to do."

He left a generous tip, then pulled her through the door of the restaurant. Hand in hand, they strolled Pennsylvania Avenue, the lights of the Capitol piercing the blackness of the night. Too soon for declarations of love, they shared bits and pieces of the past few weeks—Tika's and Jonah's wedding plans, Old Silas's change of heart—ending with the reason for Natalie's trip to the city. The box. The tale of two sisters.

"Tragic, isn't it?" she said. "Elva, begging for forgiveness all those years, and Lova, never granting it. Never even acknowledging her sister's letters. And now they're both gone—and it's too late."

"Sad how some families seem destined for sorrow and separation." He gazed down at her as they walked along the broad avenue.

"What Elva did was wrong—terribly wrong—" she insisted.

"But one might wonder why the other sister's heart never softened. One, living in bitterness; the other, cutting herself off from the only family she had left. What a waste."

There was nothing left to say. She felt the stinging irony of that story. Was Alex saying that she was anything like Elva Jacks?

He wouldn't dare. And if so, then he didn't know her father like she did!

They walked on in silence, feeling the balmy breeze against their cheeks. By the time they reached the Washington Monument, she'd cooled down. Hand in hand, they stood by the reflecting pool. The sickle moon shone in wavy wisps of light on the water and the petals of the cherry trees danced in the light breeze.

"What a beautiful sight," he said, standing so near that she could feel his warm breath on her hair.

"I do love Washington at night," she said, hardly daring to breathe.

"It's *you* I was speaking of, Natalie St. John. I'm so glad you came."

She turned to look up into his handsome face, laughing softly. "And I'm glad *you* came . . . to my inn, Jeanine Beaumont."

His answering smile faded as he lowered his lips to hers. In that moment all the lonely hours of their lives were blown away with the cherry blossoms in the wind. It was more than a kiss. It was a meeting of minds . . . and hearts . . . and souls. She closed her eyes and gave herself up to the delicious sensation. "Alex," she murmured into his jacket. "Alex, I was afraid I'd never see you again."

It was a moment to remember, a moment she would cherish for a lifetime—or for as long as this relationship lasted. . . .

Feeling hesitant again, she pulled away and walked over to the pool, seeing a few delicate cherry blossoms floating on the mirror-like surface. So tender. So fragile. Like her heart. Was she ready to trust him with it?

She'd never know if she didn't give him a chance.

With a prayer for guidance, she turned and held out her hand.

⟋⟋⟍⟍

Unwilling to end the evening so early, Alex suggested a drive to Great Falls. The full moon illumined the rocky falls of the

Potomac River, and the night was cool. They walked to the cliffs
and sat at the edge of the river, holding hands, subdued by the
breathtaking spectacle before them.

Alex broke the silence. "Will you always hang up on your
father?"

"What is there to say?"

He tightened his arm around her. "I just wouldn't want things
to turn out for you and your dad like they did for Elva Jacks and
her sister."

She leaned her head into his shoulder, the small action telling
him he hadn't overstepped his bounds. "Do you ever dream you're
falling?" she asked, her face turned to his, the moon washing her
features in its soft light.

"Doesn't everyone?"

"Those dreams always wake me up with a start, and places like
this—" she eyed the distant drop to the river below—"frighten
me."

"I'm holding you," he reminded her, his voice husky with emotion. "I'd never let you fall."

She smiled and closed her eyes, her head still resting on his
shoulder. "I remember going to Niagara Falls with my parents
when I was about six. Standing there . . . I got an insane urge to
jump. The powerful water rushing nearby, the little boats that take
people up to the Horseshoe Falls looking so small, so far from the
shoreline . . . I was afraid they'd be suddenly sucked under the
falls . . . and no one would ever see them again."

Alex waited for her to finish, knowing that what she was about
to say was very, very important.

"I remember holding my daddy's hand and telling him I didn't
want to fall. And I remember what he told me." Alex had to lean
over to hear her whispered words. "He said, 'If you do, Natalie,
honey, I'll be there to catch you.' And a year later, he was gone
. . . and I've never seen him again."

There was a heartbreaking pause while Natalie caught her
breath, then choked out, "A voice on the other end of the line just

isn't the same. I'm so scared of falling, Alex . . . knowing that no one is there to catch me anymore."

She was sobbing now, softly, and he waited it out. "But there's another kind of falling, Natalie. The kind one never does alone." He lowered his head and touched his lips to hers, lightly, briefly. "Are you falling now, love?"

"Yes . . . and I'm scared to death."

Twenty-Two

FROM: Alexander P. Elbert, Ph.D., medievalman@JMU.edu
DATE: Monday, April 4, 12:03 A.M.
TO: Natalie St. John, pleasantinn@vanet.com
SUBJECT: Easter

Hello, Natalie!

Your Web site looked so enticing for the coming season that
I was inspired to inquire about an opening over Easter weekend.
Once again I cannot make the trip to Missouri to visit my sister,
and since there's no one I'd rather spend the holiday with than
you....

I enjoyed this past Saturday. It was a lovely day for a drive,
and the fact that you gave my cabin an innkeeper's thumbs-up
gave me great pleasure. It must be true. We are soul mates. I don't
say that easily, have actually scorned the term . . . until recently.

But just in case someone else has found you as enchanting
as I, I'd best get my bid in early. First of all, would you be free to
attend the Book Fair with me next weekend? I'll be traveling
incognito, of course.

And, because I was able to get tickets early, I'll ask now if you
would be interested in a concert at the Kennedy Center—in May.
The fifteenth, to be exact. Do hope you haven't already made plans.

Will call to confirm the room for the Easter weekend.

A. E.

FROM: Natalie St. John, pleasantinn@vanet.com
DATE: Monday, April 4, 1:45 P.M.
TO: Alexander P. Elbert, Ph.D., medievalman@JMU.edu
SUBJECT: Re: Easter

There's always room in my Inn for you, Professor. You Brits! So stiff and starched. I do look forward to the day when you learn the fine art of casual communication.

As for the concert at the Kennedy Center—after checking my calendar, I find I'm all clear for that date. But only if we dress up and have dinner at "1789" in Alexandria first. My treat. Although—consummate gentleman that you are—I'm sure you've already figured a way to pick up the tab over my protests. And I suppose I'll have to admit—90s woman that I am—I'm enjoying every minute of it. The flowers, for instance. Incredible! I put them on the sunporch, and they're outblooming Oren's garden outside. Don't tell him I said so!

The Book Fair this weekend should be a blast. I went last year with a friend, but it will be even better in the company of a famous author—undercover though you may be. Incidentally, thanks for being so up front with us about your dual identity. At least, after we stumbled onto your little secret, *Jeanine!* With your inventiveness, you could have come up with a doozy of an explanation. But you didn't. How refreshing. I've had it with guys who don't shoot straight.

Come early, and Tika will fix you a nice, big breakfast, or we could stop at Cracker Barrel along the way.

Natalie

⁓

FROM: Alexander P. Elbert, Ph.D., medievalman@JMU.edu
DATE: Friday, April 8, 7:59 a.m.
TO: Natalie St. John, pleasantinn@vanet.com
SUBJECT: Tomorrow

Looking forward to our jaunt together. Don't put Tika to any trouble on my account. I love Cracker Barrel breakfasts and can already taste the horrifyingly fat-filled wonder of "The Sunrise

Sampler." Who knows, that "Ode to a Country Ham" I've been working on over the past few years might just come together.

I'll be putting the top down on the Triumph, so bring a jacket. And lunch is already planned. A surprise. Even Jeanine would be impressed.

A. E.

~~~

FROM: Natalie St. John, pleasantinn@vanet.com
DATE: Sunday, April 10, 1:45 P.M.
   TO: Alexander P. Elbert, Ph.D., medievalman@JMU.Edu
SUBJECT: Book Fair

What fun! Everything about our day was spectacular. Springtime in the Valley. All the tulips and daffodils taking over. The picnic at the scenic overlook—yes, even Jeanine would have enjoyed that spread! The Fair itself. . . .

Seeing all those people who'd come, I was reminded of shoppers at a bargain basement sale. Elbows everywhere. People pushing and shoving, looking for their favorite books. And you, pacing the history section like a hungry lion, waiting to pounce when you spotted the title you were hunting.

Thanks again! It was a day to put away and take out to enjoy again and again . . . like a rare book. One of my favorite Jeanine Beaumont titles, as a matter of fact!

Natalie

~~~

FROM: Alexander P. Elbert, Ph.D., medievalman@JMU.edu
DATE: Monday, April 11, 5:19 P.M.
   TO: Natalie St. John, pleasantinn@vanet.com
SUBJECT: RE: Book Fair

Speaking of Jeanine, glad you found some hardcover titles you were missing in your collection. But I must confess to being somewhat taken aback to find you sitting cross-legged in the romance section, stacks of books around you—and they weren't all Jeanine Beaumonts!

Don't tell me I'm not the only author in your life!

A. E.

❧

FROM: Natalie St. John, pleasantinn@vanet.com
DATE: Monday, April 11, 9:09 P.M.
   TO: Alexander P. Elbert, Ph.D., medievalman@JMU.edu
   RE: Your Last Comment

Sorry 'bout that! A couple of *other* female authors come close. Trudi Chevalier and Helen Bogart. They've been on the *New York Times* bestseller list and have won tons of awards. But then so have you!

Nat

❧

FROM: Alexander P. Elbert, Ph.D., medievalman@JMU.edu
DATE: Monday, April 11, 9:15 P.M.
   TO: Natalie St. John, pleasantinn@vanet.com
SUBJECT: The Last Word

There's at least one major difference between me and Trudi Chevalier and Helen Bogart. (Well, *two,* now that I think of it!) They can accept their awards in person!

A.

❧

FROM: Alexander P. Elbert, Ph.D., medievalman@JMU.edu
DATE: Wednesday, April 13, 2:20 P.M.
   TO: Natalie St. John, pleasantinn@vanet.com
SUBJECT: Surprise! Surprise!

Big news! Or at least one can hope. I've been invited to spend the summer in England. Guest lectureship at Oxford. The sister of an old school chum set it up.

There's only one hitch. It seems I've met this fascinating creature Stateside and wouldn't even consider accepting the invitation unless she'd agree to come with me. At least for one of the three months. You will, won't you?

You could stay with Mum—there's more than enough room, and she enjoys playing the hostess almost as much as you. We could take side excursions on the weekends, see a play in London ... and if that's not tempting enough, there's an excellent Chinese restaurant in Marylbone that rivals the carry-out in Pleasant Valley!

How about it?

A.

❧

FROM: Natalie St. John, pleasantinn@vanet.com
DATE: April 13, 2:25 P.M.
TO: Alexander P. Elbert, medievalman@JMU.edu
SUBJECT: RE: Surprise! Surprise!

What a wonderful opportunity. I'm delighted for you, of course ... although I'd thought you were planning to spend time at your new cabin.

But there's absolutely no way I could get away from the inn. Summer is our busiest time. Tourist season, remember?

And, Alex, who is this "sister of an old school chum"? Should I be jealous?

Natalie

❧

FROM: Alexander P. Elbert, Ph.D., medievalman@JMU.edu
DATE: April 13, 2:30 P.M.
TO: Natalie St. John, pleasantinn@vanet.com
SUBJECT: RE: RE: Surprise! Surprise!

No contest. If I recall correctly, Cornelia—at twelve years of age, when I last saw her—was as leggy as a young colt, with big teeth and curly black hair scraped back into pigtails. One of the most unattractive children I've ever seen. I can hardly imagine that her looks have translated much better into adulthood.

As for the cabin, there will be other summers. . . .

And I *would* enjoy the challenge of Oxford, revisiting old haunts, meeting up with my mates, spending time with Mum and my Grandmother . . . not to mention a certain young woman without whose inspiration I would be worthless to the university, I fear.

Turn the inn over to Lu and Tika, and come away with me.

A.

～

FROM: Natalie St. John, pleasantinn@vanet.com
DATE: Wednesday, April 13, 9:15 P.M.
TO: Alexander P. Elbert, Ph.D., medievalman@JUM.edu
SUBJECT: Pesky Professors

Sorry I'm just now getting back to you, but we're gearing up for the big Easter weekend, or had you forgotten? You're still booked, beginning tomorrow night, unless you've changed your mind.

As for your invitation for the summer, I'm still thinking about it. Although I've barely had time to do that. There is just so much going on right now. For one thing, Tika's wedding in just two weeks, which means she wouldn't be available until after her honeymoon.

So you see, Professor, it isn't as simple as you may have assumed.

Nat

~⌒~

FROM: Alexander P. Elbert, Ph.D., medievalman@JMU.edu
DATE: Wednesday, April 13, 11:42 P.M.
TO: Natalie St. John, pleasantinn@vanet.com
SUBJECT: An Apology

Forgive me, Natalie, for adding one more thing to your very full plate. But I will leave you with this one thought before seeing you tomorrow night . . .

Pray!

A.

~⌒~

FROM: Alexander P. Elbert, Ph.D., medievalman@JMU.edu
DATE: Saturday, April 16, 10:35 P.M.
TO: James Elbert, huggerboy@mountaincom.net
SUBJECT: Happy Easter

Just thought I'd wish you a happy day tomorrow, big brother. I'm sure you and Neve will find some unique way to celebrate the holiday.

Life has taken a decided upswing for me in the form of a woman named Natalie St. John. How glad I am that the relationship with Felicia didn't work out.

Nat is everything I ever wanted in a woman. You'd like her. She's a bigger computer geek than you are! Quit her job at an ISP in D.C. before she bought the inn. But you should see her set-up in her office here. A PC and laptop, laser printer, and some stuff I've never seen before. You'd know. She even designed the Web site for her place. Fantastic.

If you're interested, you can find it at www.pleasantvalleyinn.com.

Alex

FROM: Natalie St. John, pleasantinn@vanet.com
DATE: Monday, April 18, 1:47 P.M.
  TO: Alexander P. Elbert, Ph.D., medievalman@JMU.edu
SUBJECT: "In God's Time"

Easter weekend was another memory to tuck away. Tyler's sermon about God's timing really hit home. How God loves us, His forgiveness through the death of His son, and in the fullness of time, His soon return.

It just made me think again of the geologist . . . and I wonder if it really is time. Is it mere coincidence that you're planning a trip to England just as I'm beginning to weaken? Somehow, I don't think so. For if "the heart of the king is in the Lord's hands," who am I to doubt that He can also deal with me. Now don't go thinking I'm committing myself for the summer—but I am willing to pray about it.

          N.

FROM: James Elbert, huggerboy@mountaincom.net
DATE: Monday, April 18, 3:59 P.M.
  TO: Alexander P. Elbert, medievalman@JMU.edu
SUBJECT: You've got to be kidding me!

Natalie St. John? Did you actually say Natalie St. John?

Oh, Alex, this is rich. Obviously I never told you that Natalie St. John was the owner of PluraNet. The woman you suggested I drop the asking price for! I'm laughing so hard right now I can barely key this in!

No wonder she has an office full of electronic gizmos. She's worth almost as much as I am! (Well, that may be overstating it a little, but you do the math, and any way you calculate it, Natalie St. John is a very wealthy woman.)

She's an innkeeper now, you say? Interesting. Not the mousy little academics that have been your standard fare for the past few years, right? Congrats, kid. Looks like you've hit the jackpot. So ... when are you going to tell her you're part owner of her old business? And what do you think she'll say when you drop that little bombshell?

I've finally decided to take the bull by the horns and send you a little equipment. A laptop, PC, printer. It's time to junk that old Royal, little brother. Let's face it, this is a new day, and not the mossy past. It shouldn't be too big a leap for you. We cyber junkies are something like the knights of old.

By the way, I actually did have some pretty interesting Easter plans. I finally made an honest woman of Neve....

⁓

FROM: Alexander P. Elbert, Ph.D., medievalman@JMU.edu
DATE: Tuesday, April 19, 7:30 A.M.
TO: James Elbert, huggerboy@mountaincom.net
SUBJECT: RE: You've got to be kidding me!

I can't believe it! Are you sure it's my Natalie? Yes, I know you are. I'll try to keep from breaking the news as long as possible. Although, the fact that she hid the true nature of her "retirement" from me would give me just the ammunition I need to counter any barrage she might fling my way.

Glad to hear about the wedding. But then, you knew I would be. Have you told Mum, or should I forward the good news?

Hopefully you'll be receiving similar news from me in the not too distant future—that is ... if I have any success breaking the news to Natalie about our PluraNet connection. She's already gun-shy of men who keep secrets. But that's another story.

⁓

FROM: Natalie St. John, pleasantinn@vanet.com
DATE: Thursday, April 21, 3:20 P.M.
TO: Alexander P. Elbert, Ph.D., medievalman@JMU.edu
SUBJECT: Four Lunatics and a Wedding

You won't be hearing much from me in the next few days, for obvious reasons. Oren is already as brown as a berry from all the garden work he's been doing for the wedding. Lu keeps vowing she's going to lose ten pounds so she can fit into her new dress ... though, just between you and me, I think she's put on at least that much with all the tasting she's doing. Tika walks around muttering to herself about last-minute details. As for me ... if I ever do get married, I'm going to use that balcony scene from *Romeo and Juliet*—and jump!

The ceremony will take place in the garden, of course, with the reception following. In addition, we'll be putting up all Tika's and Jonah's out-of-town guests, so the inn and the new courtyard cottages are all booked to capacity. I've saved you a room ... just in case you can get away. I know this is final exam time, so if you can't make it, I'm sure Tika will understand.

FROM: Alexander P. Elbert, Ph.D., medievalman@JMU.edu
DATE: Thursday, April 21, 10:42 P.M.
TO: Natalie St. John, pleasantinn@vanet.com
SUBJECT: RE: Four Lunatics and a Wedding

I wouldn't miss it for the world!

Twenty-Three

The road-weary old Chevette limped onto the parking pad of the inn, exhaling a throaty cough as the driver turned off the engine. As if by way of protest, two loud pops resounded, and everyone rocking on the porch of Pleasant Valley Inn stood up to see what all the commotion was about.

Lori Chester-Gatto emerged from under the wheel and took a bow, to the applause that erupted from the audience consisting of Tika's and Jonah's family and friends, here early for the pre-wedding festivities.

The out-of-town guests had been assembling for the past two days. Tika's Grandmom and Grandpop, who would give her away; Jonah's father, who would stand up with him as his best man. Even the old couple from Paris whose attic room Tika had rented while she was studying at the Cordon Bleu had shown up on Friday afternoon, speaking no English, but enjoying the food, drink, and scenery as only Europeans know how to do.

"You're here!" Natalie ran down the steps to greet her friend, Andy's new wife.

"Barely." Lori patted the boot of the car. "Just can't seem to get rid of the old girl. She's been my sidekick since law school, and she was an antique back then."

"Well, you made it, so come on in. I've put you and Andy in my room, and I'm taking the sunporch."

"I would protest, but from all he's told me about you, it probably wouldn't do any good."

"Smart guy. Where is he, anyway?"

"Working on a tough case. He'll be driving down tomorrow."

The women deposited Lori's luggage in Natalie's room, had a quiet cup of tea in the gazebo, and that was the last peaceful moment they spent together.

After that, they operated at a dead run and, with Lu's and Oren's help, tended to the needs of other guests, ran last-minute errands, and supervised the meals Tika had planned, but not cooked. To feed all the guests for the various functions—a barbecue on Friday night, brunch on Saturday, the rehearsal dinner on Saturday evening—she had brought in several of her friends from cooking school. The staff was busy, but it was a labor of love on behalf of the couple who were savoring every moment of the weekend, yet longing for Sunday when they would make a lifelong commitment to one another, giving their love a solid foundation upon which to rest.

Alex joined them on Saturday morning, sleeves rolled up and ready to help. Oren was cutting flowers for the bouquets Renee would put together overnight. Lu would arrange some of the cut stems in giant baskets Natalie had bought at the Wacamaw pottery several weeks earlier.

"So, Oren, what do you think of all this?" Alex asked as he slid on a pair of gardening gloves and reached for the snippers the old man was holding out to him.

"I should be askin' *you* that question." Oren gave him a searching glance on his way over to a large bed behind the greenhouse where he had planted several strains of tulips just for the occasion.

"Well, I'm delighted, of course. Tika and Jonah finding each other so unexpectedly. . . ."

Oren rolled that one eye and got down on his knees in front of the flowers. "You're not gettin' my point, lad."

Alex joined him, snipping flowers at the base of the stem. "Oh, I believe I understand, sir."

"Some flowers are rarer than others, ya know. While all of 'em are beautiful in their own right—foliage, blossom, scent—there are some as have somethin' special—somethin' God Himself put in 'em."

"Like the rose?"

"Like the rose. You've found yourself a rose, son. A rose above roses. You might want to think about transplantin' that rose a little closer to home."

⌒

Tika's wedding day dawned cloudless and bright, the sky as clear as the Waterford crystal from her Aunt Marva in Mississippi, the sun as bright as the halogen desklamp sent by her cousin Ralph. An answer to prayer, since the ceremony would take place outdoors. With no humidity or haze, Oren's lawn and gardens at the inn—pruned and manicured—were a spectacular event in themselves. The specimen daffodils, tulips, and a few steadfast crocus waved in the spring zephyr that stirred the gardens. Climbing roses, not yet in bloom, clung to the latticed sides of the gazebo to act as a screen for the wedding party.

It was a feast for the eyes.

Inside, another feast was being prepared to accompany all the hors d'oeuvres Tika had been making and freezing for weeks. Despite Natalie's insistence on hiring a caterer to coordinate the reception, at least, it was all she could do to keep the bride out of the kitchen!

With all the scurrying around, Natalie barely had time to pick up her own dress at the boutique on Main, where it had been ordered and delivered from her mother's old shop in D.C. Yellow organza. Off-the-shoulder. Perfect for a garden wedding. The hat was straight out of an English storybook. A leghorn wreathed in yellow flowers, that framed her face.

When Lu had been asked to serve as matron of honor, she'd laughed right out loud. "Mama Cass in an off-the-shoulder number? Thanks just the same, darlin', but I'd be more comfortable fannin' flies off the weddin' cake!"

Tika herself had been adamant about not letting even her best friends see her before the wedding. And knowing the woman's aversion to feminine frou-frou, Natalie had expected anything *but* this vision in white that greeted her on the side porch leading to the wedding bower.

Tika was wearing her grandmother's wedding gown—ivory satin and lace. Her dozens of tiny braids had been woven with stephanotis, then wound—coronet-style—on top of her head. From this unique crown trailed a long gauzy veil. "Tika, you're gorgeous! Jonah won't be able to take his eyes off you!" Natalie said, but had to giggle when her gaze came to rest on the young woman's brown feet—bare beneath the lush folds of the dress.

"You're not so bad yourself, Boss. Watch out, Mister Professor-Man!"

Lu flew up just then, practically colliding with them as she hurried out to take her seat. "The powder room in the hall was out of TP," she whispered.

Tika laughed. A self-conscious laugh that women make when they know they are at their most beautiful, then pulled Lu into a hug. "You should be joining me and Nattie up there, you know."

"Forget it, darlin'. I like to do my cryin' without an audience." She gave Tika a squeeze. "Now go for it. Go get your man!"

And she waddled off to her seat near the back.

Tika's little grandfather walked up just then, and Tika—towering over him—turned her dazzling smile in his direction, Natalie and the rest of the world forgotten.

Hearing the string quartet cuing Erin Higgenbotham for one of the special numbers Tika had requested—"Endless Love"—Natalie stepped outside, behind the clusters of chairs. Erin looked svelte and slender again after the birth of her first baby, and her voice, if anything, was better than ever.

As Erin's lush contralto trailed off on the final note, Natalie could see Jonah fiddling with his bow tie, and Tyler, looking anything but preacherly as he chuckled under his breath and gave Jonah some last-minute instructions on their way to the arched opening of the gazebo. Pausing at the front, Tyler greeted the guests and called them to an unusual celebration of love.

Then the musicians were striking up the first chord of Lohengrin's "Wedding March." For a non-traditionalist, Tika had surprised Natalie more than once today.

"Nattie, that's your cue," Tika whispered from behind her, dark eyes dancing.

Feeling unusually apprehensive—and not exactly sure why—Natalie took the single, long-stemmed white rose Tika plucked from her wedding bouquet, and marched slowly down the improvised aisle. It was only when she turned, taking her place at the front, that that her gaze came to rest on the one face she most longed to see. Alex. Looking familiar and dear. Looking so right.

Here came the bride! Gliding toward her groom, bare feet skimming the white runner laid over the grassy lawn. Eyes for him alone.

Jonah's wide grin split his face, and he sprang forward to meet Tika halfway down the aisle, to the amusement of the onlookers. For a moment, Natalie felt embarrassed for him. Fortunately, the man of few words would not be required to say more than a couple today—the all-important "I do."

But when it was time for the vows, he astonished them all by speaking intimately to his bride, pledging his love and all his worldly possessions in an eloquent—and original—speech. "It is not good for a man to be alone," Jonah began, "and now I've found the other side of me . . . the one perfect woman God made for me. . . ."

For the first time ever, Natalie saw real tears in Tika's eyes.

But Jonah had more to say . . . a lot more. And when he was through, Tyler looked at the bride, wiped his brow, and said, "I declare, Tika. Jonah has just uttered more words than I've heard from him collectively in the five years I've known him."

The outburst of laughter from the guests was the perfect anti-dote to Tika's slight nervousness, and she went on to promise to love her man, honor him, and obey him—everywhere but in the kitchen!

There was another ripple of laughter before Reverend Tyler stepped up to tell the ultimate love story. The story of Christ's love for His own dear bride, the church. "We love because He first loved us and gave Himself for us. Love is like that, Tika and Jonah—looking for ways to help each other, to delight each other in the good times, to forgive each other in the bad times. . . ."

With that, Natalie felt an ominous sting behind her eyelids and was grateful when Erin rose to sing "The Love of God" as a closing prayer. Maybe Alex wouldn't notice.

But it didn't matter. For by the time the happy couple had jumped the broom—a slave custom revived for this special day—with Jonah's handbell choir chiming the recessional, tears of joy were flowing like the wine at Cana. And Tika's family launched a celebration like none the inn had ever seen before.

Three hours later, when the new Mr. and Mrs. Jonah C. Chord drove off in Natalie's Jaguar, with plans to spend two weeks on the islands off South Carolina and Georgia, the party was still in full swing, and it was 4 A.M. before the last light at Pleasant Valley Inn was turned off.

But Alex and Natalie were still too wired to retire for what was left of the night, balmy for mid-May, and sat together on the porch swing, intending to watch the sun rise. "I've never seen a happier couple." Natalie sighed and snuggled close to Alex on the swing.

"Present company excluded, you mean."

She slanted a sidelong look at him through her lashes.

"I love you, you know," he went on. "Loved you from the moment I saw you, rushing in all flushed and lovely, with your hair done up in that towel."

"From the moment you saw me?"

"It happens all the time . . . ."

" . . . in romance novels."

Leaning forward, he tipped her chin and looked earnestly into her eyes. "It's taken a long time to find you . . . but now that I have, I have no intentions of letting you go. You're what has been missing for as long as I can remember."

"But you've written such romantic scenes. And I'm sure a man like you would have had more than his share of female friends in his life." She couldn't help thinking of the picture on his nightstand.

He shook his head in denial. "Those scenes came from a lonely heart, my love. It's you who has filled all the empty spaces. I do love you, Natalie. More than I could have thought possible."

Did she dare make that giant leap into the unknown? Say the words? Would he really be there to catch her? Suddenly the bravado she had felt when walking down the aisle, failed her. She decided to keep it light. "I love you, too, my lord."

He sat forward abruptly and swiveled to meet her gaze. "What did you say?" His tone was sharp, almost angry.

The mood was shattered.

"Oh, nothing really. You just remind me of a character you created in one of your books—*Love in the Rain,* I think it was. You know the one. The young man who's from nobility . . . a younger son who's an artist . . . and then his brother dies, and he suddenly inherits a title he's never wanted."

"I remember him. Lord Alisdair Drummond."

She nodded. "Well, you remind me of him. Could it be that character was slightly autobiographical?" she said, trying to tease him out of this unexplained mood.

"Now what would make you ask such a preposterous question? Do I look like a nobleman?"

"As a matter of fact, you do. But I know better. You're much too nice to be a Lord Something or Other."

"Oh, I've met lots of Lord Something or Others in my time at Oxford, and I can assure that most of them are sorry scoundrels."

"So you're just plain old Alexander P. Elbert?"

"Sorry to disappoint you."

"Believe me, it's no disappointment." They resumed swinging, his arm resting lightly on her shoulders again. "By the way, are you ever going to tell me what the 'P' stands for?"

"Someday." His arm tightened around her and he pulled her close. "When I know you're positively here to stay."

"Oh, I'm here to stay, Alex. Whether you like it or not."

"I like it just fine." To prove it, he kissed her . . . soundly.

———

Sometime later, their objective was achieved. "There comes the sun." Natalie pointed to the great blazing ball, banishing the night and spreading fingers of fire along the eastern horizon.

"I've always loved watching the sun rise." Alex's voice was hushed, taking in the every day miracle. "It's so full of promise—like us." He moved to bury his head in her hair.

She sat without speaking as the golden orb rose higher in the cobalt sky.

"You should see an English sunrise, Natalie. Nothing compares . . . except maybe your smile. . . ."

Alex would be flying to England next week. After that, only God knew what would happen. With their relationship . . . or with the geologist.

"My father called again last night," she told him in a small voice. "And I did it again. I hung up on him."

"Oh, Natalie—" Alex turned to regard her seriously—"I thought you'd decided to talk to him . . . give him a chance to explain."

"I know. I meant to. I just couldn't . . . so I hung up, softly this time."

"It's all right, love." He tugged her to him and nuzzled her neck. "You'll make things right. There will be another time."

Would there?

Over Alex's shoulder, she watched the rising sun on its steady path through the sky. Was the sunrise a promise of happiness . . . or even more pain?

Twenty-Four

*N*atalie peered at the small screen on the airplane seat-back in front of her. Beside her, Alex was doing the same.

"Aren't you glad you decided to come?" He glanced over at her. "These 777's are fabulous. Your own personal telly." He grinned—that crooked grin that melted her heart like butter on a hot scone.

This time, though, she was determined to resist. "Oh, I don't know," she retorted. "You have to squint the whole time you're watching. The first movie I ever saw on one of these was *Batman Forever,* and let me tell you, Val Kilmer—at only an inch tall—was hardly convincing. Now Cary Grant—there's a man no matter how small the screen, but you don't ever see him on one of these things."

The plane took a sudden dive, sending her lurching against her seat belt, and she dug her fingertips into the arms of her seat.

"At least it might help take your mind off the turbulence," Alex said evenly, seemingly unconcerned about the ornery elements.

"I don't know how you can sit there so calmly. We could go down any minute!"

"We could. But it's not likely. And even if it were destined to happen, my love, we'd go down together and it would be a quick finish. Better that than a lingering illness."

Natalie thought of her mother's last month and secretly agreed. "Still, those last moments of pure terror as you're falling out of the sky—"

"Do you *mind?*" interrupted the lady across the aisle. She was wearing sunglasses and a big hat tied under her chin with a scarf.

"Sorry." Natalie smiled in apology, then turned to Alex. "Now that was embarrassing. I didn't realizing I was talking that loudly."

"Scaredy-cats generally turn up the volume. It's part of the paranoia."

"I'm not a scaredy-cat. I'm just brave enough to say what everyone else is thinking." She stole a peek at the fashionable lady, then whispered in Alex's ear, "Do you think she's a movie star? She looks a little like Sharon Stone, don't you think?"

"She's probably just some wannabe."

"Oh, I don't know. Who else would wear a get-up like that off the big screen?"

The lady in the hat glanced over at them and languidly flipped the page of her magazine.

Alex took Natalie's hand. "Are you nervous about next Friday?"

"Terrified is more to the point."

"Don't you think you should have called him first? Warned him you were coming?"

"Maybe, but I still think my decision to surprise the geolo—I mean my *father*, is the right one. I want his true reaction when he sees me for the first time in twenty-three years."

"What if he doesn't recognize you?"

"Oh, he'll recognize me. I'm one of those people who looks just like their baby pictures. This red hair—" she tugged on a curl—"these round eyes."

He grinned. "An adorable baby, no doubt. And you haven't changed a bit."

"And I thought you loved me for my mind."

"That, too."

She swatted at him playfully and put on her headphones to listen to the Big Band music channel. But not before overhearing the in-flight telephone conversation between the lady in the hat and her agent, Natalie assumed.

"Eddie," the woman purred, "I want to do a romantic comedy."

"Eavesdropping, Nats? I'm surprised at you," Alex scolded.

She wrinkled her nose. "Hey, anything to avoid thinking about the storm outside this plane." Or the one inside her heart. Each time she considered the dreaded encounter at the end of the week. . . .

⁓

Half an hour later, the turbulence began to subside. "Are you sure you know how to get to Bath?" Natalie asked for the fifth time.

"Positive, love. It's an easy drive from Oxford."

"He lives on the Crescent. Do you know where that is?"

"Anyone who has ever been to Bath knows the Crescent. Stop worrying, would you? I'll get you there. I promise."

⁓

The plane landed in Heathrow around 6:30 London time.

Alex pulled their luggage off the carousel. "By your body clock, Natalie, it's only 1:30 A.M. Would you like to check into our rooms and get some sleep?"

The idea of seeing the fabled city at last was energizing. "I'm not a bit tired. I'd much rather take in the sights first and sleep later. Although Mom and I traveled extensively, we never made it to England."

"I can imagine why," Alex observed crisply. "We should at least get settled in, shower and perhaps have a bite of breakfast first."

It was eight A.M. by the time they arrived, via the tube—an underground railway system—in the Marylebone district and the quaint little hotel just a block or two down from the Marylebone Cricket Club. They emerged from the station into crisp morning air.

"I've never seen such long escalators," Natalie commented on their stroll to their hotel.

"The 'tube' is quite far down, actually. But it's a handy way to get about—very fast and convenient. Something like the Metro in D.C. Jeanine Beaumont and her ilk would not be caught dead down amongst the common folk, but take it from me, most of her characters come to life beneath the streets of London."

Natalie could never accuse Alex of being a snob, nor could he pin that badge on her. For when he'd asked where she wanted to stay—the Ritz, perhaps—she'd told him she wanted to meet real Londoners. The Four Seasons was just the ticket.

A gentleman of middle-eastern descent checked them into the small, intimate hotel Alex had chosen—"off the beaten path," he'd said—and a younger man loaded up their baggage under his skinny arms and ran up the steps, dropping Natalie's luggage off on the second floor by her room and chatting in a thick Cockney accent.

"I'll just ring you up when I'm done," Alex said, leaving her at the door, "and you can meet me down in the coffee shop."

But when Natalie left her small, very compact quarters half an hour later, she found the breakfast room closed until noon. "We'll have to find something while we're out," Alex explained.

She took in his buttoned-down Oxford cloth shirt and khaki slacks, then eyed her own navy shorts outfit with a skeptical look. "Am I underdressed?"

"The perfect tourist attire for a June morning. Now, where shall we begin?" Alex folded his newspaper. "We're here for only a short time, and I want this to be an experience you'll remember for a lifetime."

Natalie didn't have to think twice. "The Tower of London. I hear it's a castle like no other. I'd like to see the place where Anne Bolyn was beheaded."

"Right. Breakfast first, then the Tower."

They hopped on the tube, while an electronic voice told them to "mind the gap" between the train and the platform, and were whisked off to the station called Tower Hill. Natalie pointed to the words on the sign above the doorway as they emerged from the station and recited in a judicial tone: "'And there shall your head be stricken from your body.'"

Beside her, Alex chuckled. "Ghastly, isn't it? Our history is a bloody one."

"Still, it must have been fascinating for you to have devoted your whole life to its study."

"Well, that particular practice, among other things, does give one a healthy respect for authority," he joked, taking her hand and tucking it into his arm as they walked down the hill, Roman walls to their right. They were now in the most ancient part of the city, and Natalie could feel the change. It was like nothing she had experienced in her homeland.

But even Romans had to eat, didn't they?

Unfortunately, they found not a single restaurant that was still serving breakfast.

"You may laugh at my next suggestion." Alex pointed to a plaza area above which rose the familiar Golden Arches.

Natalie was horrified. "McDonald's? You can't be serious!"

"Have you a better idea?"

"Not really. But I just never imagined my first meal in England would be at McDonald's."

"Supper was hours ago, Natalie. Plane fare at that. Even McDonald's sounds good to me about now. Come along. It'll be a funny story to tell Lu and Tika back home."

"All right. I'm game. I'm sure old Henry VIII would have eaten his fair share of Big Macs if they'd been around in his day."

"That's the spirit, Nats. Let's go. I'm starving!"

⁓

The crenelated walls of the castle jutted high above as the woman positioned her neck on the execution block. An eager crowd of spectators gathered to watch as the man raised his hands and . . . snapped a picture!

Straightening, Natalie laughed so hard her sides ached. "I can't believe I did that!" she gasped, noting the tentative smiles of the onlookers.

Alex's smile was a little forced, as well, she thought. Here in England, Natalie had noticed a subtle change in his attitude. He seemed a bit more distant, reserved. "You just branded yourself an American, you know that, don't you?"

For some reason, she felt defensive. "And proud of it."

"Of course you are. It's my homeland, too, remember." With that mild rebuke, he led her aside to consult a map he'd picked up in the hotel lobby. "Let's see now. The ravens of the White Tower built by William the Conqueror, the chapel where Anne Bolyn was buried, the row of houses where Lady Jane Grey was held captive before she was executed in the very spot where you just had your picture taken—all within easy walking distance." He checked his watch. "But you won't be able to see the crown jewels, I'm afraid, if you want to make it to Westminster Abbey today."

Natalie pouted. "I wish we could spend more than two days in London."

"So do I. But I *am* anxious to see my family."

She was instantly ashamed of herself. "Forgive me, Alex. I was being selfish. Of course, you want to be with your family." And there was that little matter of her own family—the geologist. . . .

He draped his arm across her shoulders. "You weren't being selfish. London weaves her spell over everyone who comes here. But we'd better hurry. The boat to Westminster is due to leave in less than ten minutes. And the captain is an amusing fellow. It's a tour of the riverfront you'll never forget."

And they were off to view London from the Thames, the river on whose broad banks the Romans had founded the city they had called Londonium. The waterfront was chock full of buildings of various periods, one modern edifice reminding everyone of a jukebox, due to the comment made by the garrulous pilot.

Their hurried tour of the Abbey left her yearning for more, and the Houses of Parliament beckoned in the fading afternoon light. But it was only when Big Ben tolled five that she was suddenly reminded of the photograph on Alex's nightstand back at the inn, and felt a prick of curiosity. Just who was that woman?

⌐⌐⌐

The next day passed in a blur of activity—Buckingham Palace, St. James Park, the British Museum, St. Paul's Cathedral, Regent's Park, the Theatre district.

"Too bad we can't take in 'The Phantom of the Opera,'" Alex said when it was clear that their time for sightseeing had run out. "But there will be other times . . . lots of them." He squeezed her hand in promise, and she felt the pure joy of being in love . . . in the enchanting city on the Thames.

And yet even London held its share of heartaches, she thought, as she stared at the plaza in front of Kensington Palace, remembering countless bouquets of flowers and a princess—gone now—who only wanted to find true Love.

⌐⌐⌐

"You've never looked more radiant, Natalie," Alex said as she descended the steps of the hotel on their last night in London.

"Tell Lori," she admitted. "She loaned me this ball gown. Saks Fifth Avenue trunk sale—and it's never been worn." The heavy emerald silk taffeta fell in crisp folds to her ankles, setting off her hair and coloring as only green can do for a redhead, she knew.

Alex lifted her curled tresses and pressed them to his lips, breathing in her scent. "Fire in your hair tonight, Natalie." He spoke with husky emotion, and there was no mistaking the passion in his eyes. Passion for her. Her own pulse quickened in response, yet there was fear, too, knowing how much he wanted her just then.

She stepped back, out of his embrace, and lightened the moment. "You don't look too shabby yourself, Jeanine."

"Please . . . it's plain old Alex Elbert tonight."

"Well, *whoever* you are, you're looking . . . dashing." She really couldn't think of a word that would do justice to the man standing before her. Alex—in a tuxedo—the dark jacket contrasting with his fair hair, his brown eyes smoldering in their intensity.

He crooked an elbow. "Shall we?"

She assumed a fake British accent. "By all means, dahling. Our limousine awaits."

At his wince, she laughed. "Sorry. Just goeth to show I can never be anyone other than who I am."

He opened the door to the waiting vehicle. "Don't even try."

She slid into her seat. "Speak for yourself . . . Jeanine Beaumont."

⟨~⟩

At the Ritz, Alex and Natalie proceeded immediately to the grand ballroom where many of London's elite were gathering to honor those who had made notable contributions to various projects of the Society for Historic Preservation.

Natalie's eyes were wide, filled with wonder at the sumptuous decor. "I always thought my mother and I traveled in style. But I've never seen anything like this."

Before they could look around, their attention was stolen by a summons from across the room. "Alexander!" The female voice, heavily accented, belonged to an older woman in iridescent copper, who was forging a glittering path through the throng of well-dressed Londoners. "What are you doing here tonight?"

"Anita, how very nice to see you."

The deep-dyed black hair, belying her years, was styled in a tight chignon, and her bright red lips pouted as she crossed her very thin arms, several bejeweled gold bangles clashing musically. "Oh, my Lord Stuffed Shirt, don't play coy with Nita. I do not see you for years, and this is the greeting you give? I shall not have it!" She pulled him into a hug and kissed him loudly on both cheeks.

Suddenly noticing Natalie, the woman turned to inspect her from head to toe as Alex wiped the lipstick off his face with a clean handkerchief. "Stunning, dear boy. You must introduce her to your old friend."

The introduction made, Nita seized both of Natalie's hands in hers. Another big hug. Kiss. Kiss. "You're divine, darling. And have you given our Alex any hope?"

"Very little," Alex reported dryly. "She sees me for exactly what I am." Changing the subject—a little too abruptly, Natalie thought—he explained, "Nita is one of Mum's old convent school friends. Her son Richard and I practically grew up together. I'd spend a month in France each summer and—"

"—we corresponded by post for years," Nita interrupted, straightening her bronze silk wrap over her smooth, tanned shoulders. "Until six months ago, that is, when the dear boy mysteriously deserted us for parts unknown." She narrowed her gaze, studying Natalie once more. "Now one understands why."

Alex shrugged, one hand in the pocket of his trousers. "Just busy, Nita, that's all."

"Now *that* I can believe." The woman's brash laughter attracted the attention of others in the crowded room, and Alex deftly maneuvered them to a more secluded spot.

"Don't shush me, Alexander. I must know what brings the two of you here tonight."

"Oh, it's nothing really. Only a small award for some work in historic preservation—thanks to Jeanine Beaumont." His wink was for Natalie.

Nita raised her arched brows, then knit them in genuine concern. "But didn't you know, Alexander? The news was in this morning's *Times*. Jeanine Beaumont is dead!"

Twenty-Five

*W*hat?!" Natalie blurted. "That's impossible!"

Alex calmed her with a steadying hand on the small of her back. "Guess the old girl won't be contributing to historic preservation anymore."

"Alex*ander*!" Nita exclaimed with a theatrical gesture. "How can you be so heartless? The poor woman—doubtless an old friend of yours—has died, and you feel no grief?"

Alex turned to Natalie. "Remember the critic I told you about—the one who read my very first manuscript?"

"Nita?"

The woman gurgled another husky laugh. "But of course, darling! Who else?"

"So there was no article in the *Times* this morning?" Natalie was beginning to feel duped.

"But yes!"

"A publicity stunt," Alex assured her. "More book sales and all that."

"Alexander and I have always enjoyed playing the small jokes on one another," Nita rambled on, "although this is no joke, of course. Still, his secret is safe with me, even if his *nom de plume* has now sadly expired. Come along now, let's be seated at my table before it fills up with ne'er do wells and scalawags. I've a nice place in the corner where no one will spot you, Alexander."

"Has he always been this way—reclusive, I mean?" Natalie asked Nita on the way to their table, Alex trailing behind.

"Ever since he was a little boy, darling—content to hide in the shadow of his older brother."

Natalie's mind whirled with questions, but she merely smiled at Alex as he held out her chair. While Nita engaged others at the table in conversation, Natalie pursued the answers she needed. "What does this mean, Alex? Are you retiring Jeanine Beaumont?"

"I'm afraid so. For some reason, since I finished up the last book, I've not been able to write a word. Although I've tried, believe me."

"But you've always been so prolific. What happened?"

His smile stopped her heart. "All the heroines ended up being . . . you."

Natalie blushed, grateful for the arrival of a liveried waiter who was serving the first course, a minted pea soup. "And is that so bad?" she leaned over to ask Alex as the waiter hurried off.

"Profoundly wonderful for me. Not so for my readers. How would you like to read the same book over and over? Besides, I'll have quite enough to do to keep me occupied."

"Your classroom lectures, of course. But what else?"

He assumed an enigmatic look. "*That,* my love, is still a secret."

She lifted a spoonful of the soup to her lips, finding it delicious, feeling suddenly out of place. "There are a few too many secrets, if you ask me. Are you sure there isn't anything else you've forgotten to tell me?"

"Nothing of importance," he said as the soup bowl was removed from the silver charger, to be replaced with lobster and a champagne dipping sauce.

"I'm not too sure I like the sound of that." She looked up over a tasty morsel of bacon-wrapped filet.

His gaze was level, searching. "Perhaps it's time to trust me, Natalie. You do trust me, don't you?"

She was beginning to wonder. So much had happened in the past few months. So many questions yet to be answered. . . .

It was during dessert that the awards ceremony began.

"I do hope I can finish this before I'm called up," Alex whispered in between bites of a delicately flavored macadamia nut tartlet. "How is yours?"

"Divine!" Natalie raved over the iced lemon mousse. "So much for the myth that English food is inedible."

He waved his fork. "I've just spared you so far. Way back, a Frenchman said that in England there are fifty different religions and only one sauce."

"Obviously he never ate at the Ritz!"

They had finished their desserts and were sipping piping hot coffee when the master of ceremonies summoned the first recipient to the podium. One by one, the others followed as each one's meritorious service to the Society was recounted.

Finally, the president launched into another glowing tribute. "From Scotland to Wales, this gentleman has made a great difference, and our country is all the more beautiful for it. Although the man who will receive the distinguished Carter Award is no longer a resident of his native land, his love for her lives on in her many medieval structures—from Saxon halls to Norman motte and bailey castles, and several fortified houses of later periods. His research and his drawings have proven invaluable to their restoration and preservation. The gentleman to whom I am referring is, of course, Sir Alexander Elbert."

Sir Alexander Elbert! Natalie gasped and turned to ask Alex if she had heard correctly, but his seat was empty and he was halfway to the platform.

There was a great outburst of applause as many stood to their feet. Alex spread his hands, quieting them much as he would a classroom of rowdy students. "Thank you. Thank you very much."

Natalie sat, stunned.

His speech was delivered with an easy grace and style and that dry, self-deprecating wit so typical of Englishmen. Standing there before his countrymen, he seemed somehow larger than life, more British, almost unapproachable. It was clear that the circles in which he moved were far removed from her little world of computer graphics and innkeeping in a sleepy little town.

He'd been knighted by the Queen! Natalie closed her eyes and imagined him, clad in silver mail, banners flying, the sun glinting off his golden hair as he knelt to receive the tap of a broadsword on both shoulders.

Of course, such ceremony had been done away with ages ago . . . but the image was burned into her mind.

She blinked her eyes open in time to see Alex's nod to the Prince of Wales, seated next to the podium, his great toothy grin a reward in itself.

Sir Alexander Elbert, indeed! Knight or no knight, she intended to get to the bottom of this before the evening ended!

As Londontown's hyperactivity subsided with the darkening skies, Alex and Natalie strolled through St. James Park, eager to make the most of their final hours in the tireless city beside the Thames. Tomorrow Oxfordshire would receive them into her gentle, flowering bosom.

Natalie wasted no time. "So, tell me all about it, Sir Alexander."

He chuckled, draping his arm across her shoulders. "It's no big deal, Nats."

But she would not be put off so easily. "Don't you think you should have told me about your title? I can hardly believe it's something you would just happen to forget."

"Oh, I didn't forget. I was knighted eight years ago for my work with historic preservation, but I dropped the title when I moved to the States. It simply hasn't come up."

She still wasn't satisfied. "But can't you understand what a shock it was for me to hear it from a perfect stranger? Why didn't you tell me yourself?"

They paused along the riverbank. "That title has nothing to do with my everyday life, Natalie, with the man I am on the inside. I really didn't think it was a matter of much importance. When I think of knighthood, I think of chivalry and gallantry and heroic deeds. It seems to me a lowly professor would be the last candidate to be considered for such an honor."

She slanted him an assessing glance. He was either the most genuinely humble man she'd ever met, or a bigger con artist than her father!

Natalie sighed. "I never took you for the secretive type, Alex. You seemed so straightforward."

"I never lied to you, Natalie. Even when we had that conversation about nobility, I never lied."

"No. You just conveniently left out some things." They walked on, the taffeta gown swishing about her ankles. "When were you going to tell me?"

"Would it have made a difference if I had?"

She turned to give him a look of total disbelief. "It certainly would have! I probably would never have allowed myself to fall in love with you. A computer professional from Virginia—and a knight?"

He leaned over to kiss her lightly. "That's exactly why I never mentioned it. All these other parts of my life—I left them behind. What you thought me to be is what I am—a professor of medieval history, the man who loves you. That's all I ever want to be, Natalie."

"Well," she said, relenting, "at least this surprise was a pleasant one. And it does put you in rather an elite circle—Alec Guiness, Laurence Olivier . . ."

He chuckled, that deep rumbling sound she loved. "And Paul McCartney."

"Hmmm."

"You see? The honor isn't all that illustrious, is it? Don't misunderstand me. The man has accomplished a great deal in his lifetime, but not the stuff of which knighthood is made."

"Back in medieval times?"

"Exactly. I can't imagine a rock musician—or a professor, for that matter—searching for the Holy Grail."

Natalie gazed up at the stars, wishing she could talk to God face to face. He was the only One who really knew Alexander Elbert.

Still, maybe she ought to give the man the benefit of the doubt. "I'm sure you're more than worthy of the title. You just don't give yourself enough credit." Was this humility his true nature—or a well calculated ploy to earn her love?

"I appreciate your compliments, but I'd rather hear you say you love me." He took her hand. "Let's sit down over there by the river—near the weeping willows. There's something I have to ask you."

It was a scene straight out of a painting. The splendor of Buckingham Palace behind them, the moonlight filtering through the willow branches, the swans swimming on the glassy surface of the water, the ever-present pelican.

He led her to a stone bench, and she sank down gratefully, her full skirt fanning out around her.

"Do you remember the scene from *Love's Harmony?* It took place right here. I wrote it sitting on this very bench."

In spite of her reservations, she was captivated by the magic of the moment, the memory of that powerful scene inspired by this setting. "How could I forget? Lord Pembroke, sitting here with Alice Brown, the laundress, their love defying all tradition, but stronger than any social boundaries. He asked her to run away with him. Told her that he would forsake his title and his lands if she would only say yes."

"And then he took her to a little chapel not far out in the country where they were secretly married. And off they sailed on the river Thames," he finished softly.

"It was a lovely scene, Alex. . . ."

"But before she answered him, he gave her something. Do you remember what it was, love?"

Natalie closed her eyes, trying hard to recreate the scene in her mind. "I think . . . no, I'm sure it was a ring belonging to his mother."

Alex slipped his hand into his pocket. "His *grand*mother." He opened the velvet-covered box he'd removed from his tuxedo jacket. "It looked something like this."

She drew in her breath sharply at the sight of the ring winking up at her from the jeweler's box. A magnificent emerald, surrounded by diamonds.

"It's the color of your eyes, love. I was hoping you'd accept it—and me. You know I love you, Natalie. Now I'm asking you to marry me."

She was unable to say a single word. Wasn't this what she had longed for all her life? Someone to love her, to value her? A real home? A family? Why, then, could she not say yes and sail away with him?

Alex waited, then spoke into the heavy silence. "For the first time since I was knighted, I can truly say I'm happy about it. Because, you see, I can offer you a title—of Lady Natalie. An elegant name. It suits you."

She looked again at the ring. He would slip it on her finger, then kiss the finger—a replay of the love scene with Lord Pembroke and Alice Brown.

But that story had ended happily ever after. Happy endings were for books of fiction—not fact. Not for the cold, hard world of reality. And never for the St. John women.

The cruel thought gave her courage.

"Alex, I love you . . . but I can't accept your ring."

Twenty-six

"ou were quite brave to look us up on your own, my dear. Quite brave indeed." Daisy Elbert leaned forward across the table and took Natalie's hand. She was a petite woman with faded blond hair and merry blue eyes that reminded Natalie of dew-sweetened blueberries. She wore sensible shoes. "I can't fault you at all for wanting to know us better before giving Alex your answer. He's always been something of a loner—that lad of mine. I suspect you'd be good for him."

Natalie let out a sigh. It had not been easy finding Rosemeade Hall, the palatial estate of Lady Bettina Gladstone and her daughter, the former Lady Elbert. Alex had told her only that he had lived near the university during his Oxford days, and she'd figured on finding a quaint thatched cottage. But certainly not a castle! Just another small oversight, she thought darkly.

It had been worse than she thought. Alex was not only a knight; he was true nobility. And if an untimely demise ever claimed his brother, Alex would be the next Lord Gladstone. Could she assume such a role? And what of their children someday? Wealth? Nobility? It was all too much. Her head ached beneath the weight of such thoughts.

At least, Alex had understood Natalie's need to get away, to "sort things out," as she'd told him before they left London to go their separate ways. Her room at a bed and breakfast in the village of Broadway was giving her the peace and quiet she needed. Needless to say, she hadn't been reading any Jeanine Beaumont.

"You must have a look 'round while Mum is resting," Daisy suggested. "I moved back in after my father died, but it's always been her home, and she rules with an iron hand—even from her bed."

Natalie followed as Mrs. Elbert gave her the grand tour. Natalie insisted on that. Lavishly carved antiques filled the massive rooms—ornate chandeliers swinging from vaulted ceilings, great ancestral portraits hanging in the vast corridors—and canopied beds that had once held the various "George Washingtons" of England could be found in every wing.

The Gladstone estate had indeed evolved from an old castle. The curtain walls had crumbled to ruin centuries before, and the interior of the large Norman keep and medieval hall, in which the family resided, had been completely modernized. But the thick walls, the deep-set mullioned windows, were distinct reminders of just how long this ancient dwelling had thrust upward from the fields of Oxfordshire.

"Alex has spoken of castles—rather authoritatively—but I supposed it was because of his studies, not from actual experience!" Natalie told his mother, her mouth dropping more than once on the walk-through.

"Oh, Alexander never lived here," Daisy said. "I was estranged from my family until well after my husband died. Alexander grew up in a little flat in Oxford, above a café, actually."

"How did you find your way back into your family's good graces?" Natalie positively had to know. So much hinged on the woman's answer.

"Come out into the gardens, dear. We can talk there. Mum's gardener has allowed me a bit of earth all for myself, and I do so love lilies. My day lilies are perfectly lovely at this time of year."

She led the way into an area that had been meticulously groomed, cleared of all weeds. Natalie thought of Oren and felt a pang of homesickness. Wouldn't he just love to see a real English garden?

They settled on a bench in the shade of a poplar tree. "You were asking about my return to Rosemeade," Daisy began. "Regrettably, that only occurred after the death of my father."

"So he was the one who opposed your marriage?"

"Oh, no more than my mother. The English caste system—such a silly thing it is. But that generation . . . " She waved away whatever it was she was about to say. "Mum needed me and she didn't hesitate to ring me up and ask me to move back in. Alexander must have told you something of his grandmother. She's a dictator, that one, and she rarely gets along with anyone—not even my father when he was living, poor man. But we all put up with her in spite of it."

Natalie was mystified. "And you can forgive her—even after disowning you for all those years?"

The blue eyes crinkled, revealing the tiny laugh lines that many women spend a fortune to remove. "She's my mum, isn't she? And I'm an old woman myself. Caring for her keeps me young—that, and my flowers." She rose to pluck a stray weed. "I'd like to say I do my duty by her because the Lord instructs us to love and forgive, but I'm afraid I'm not as noble as all that." She gave Natalie a conspiratorial smile. "Do you want to know the truth?"

That's exactly what Natalie wanted. And not only from Alex's mother.

"The truth is that Mum provides me a life of luxury which, I must say, I missed all the years I was away." Her gaze focused on some happy moment in the past. "Oh, the parties we had here at the Hall . . . before the war. . . ." Then she shook off the thought and looked at Natalie again. "More to the point, I was lonely. Now that the children are grown, with lives of their own, I'd rather live with a crotchety old person than by myself. So you see, my dear, there's nothing to commend me at all."

"Oh, I disagree," Natalie said. "But what about now? Who runs things?" Her gesture encompassed the huge mansion, the sprawling grounds.

"Well, my son James has done his best to forsake his title—though not the money—so Mum runs the estate herself. Loves doing it, too. It's what's kept her alive so long. In America, I expect she'd make a first-rate CPO . . . or whatever they call it over there." Natalie suppressed a smile. "By the by, I shouldn't be running on like this when you're grieving your own mum. Alex told me she passed away last year. I'm so sorry. You must miss her greatly."

"It was much more difficult . . . before I met Alex."

"Were you and your mum close?"

"We should have been. And in a way, I suppose we were, since I was all she had." She wondered if Alex had also told his mother about her estranged father. "Somehow I always got the feeling that if I wasn't her daughter, she wouldn't have chosen me to be her friend—if that makes any sense."

"Indeed it does. Mothers and daughters should be friends above all—though that's quite a 'modern' concept for a Britisher, I'm told. I'm happy to say that my daughter and I have such jolly times when she's here. But I see her so seldom. Still, I've always tried to be someone she'd want to—as you Americans say—hang out with."

Natalie laughed at the irony of it. This still lovely lady, very proper—yet warm, sitting in her English garden, and using the street slang of Natalie's homeland. She loved her for it.

Daisy rose to show Natalie the formal gardens, then returned to the house for tea—an elaborate affair that consisted of many more courses than a simple cup of Darjeeling and some lemon scones! She'd have to remember to give Tika the scoop—in case they ever entertained the Royals at the inn.

While they were nibbling on finger sandwiches, Daisy brought up the subject of her son. "And what else may I do to set your mind at ease about this mysterious man who's come into your life? I can assure you, Alex is a good boy, quite honorable. But then, of course, that's a mother's opinion."

Natalie blushed, convinced the woman had been able to read her mind. There were a few gray areas. But she doubted if even Lady Daisy would be able to settle the matter today.

"It's so much to take in all at once," Natalie said. "I thought your son was just a professor—like my father—and . . . " and her story poured out. Her childhood . . . her yearning for a father when she was becoming a woman . . . then Alex. "He had just convinced me that he wasn't anything like my father . . . that he was honest and open." She shrugged. "Now all this."

Daisy put an affectionate arm around Natalie's shoulders. "Alexander would have never hidden anything from you maliciously, my dear. You see, Joe's death affected him as deeply as your father's desertion affected you." The woman's eyes sparkled at the mention of her late husband. "Joe was a man above men. He loved his children with an intensity you don't often see in a father . . . always telling them they could conquer the world, though he himself was only a diesel mechanic. Alex has always modeled himself after his dad, has wanted to be just like him."

Natalie was puzzled. "But he's a professor. . . ."

"It's the attitude, my dear, not the profession. My son has always wanted a simple life. No castles or titles. And when he tells you that the grand life means nothing to him—he's telling the truth." She allowed her words to sink in, then added, "Alex never planned to stay here at Rosemeade Hall on this trip. Oh, he would have come to visit his grandmother and me, of course, but he was coming here only for you. He's back at our old flat over the High Street . . . in Oxford. It's where he stays when he's in England, Natalie. You see, Alexander will always view himself as the son of a mechanic and a bookkeeper—nothing more."

Natalie didn't know what to say. She believed Daisy—without question.

But there was more. They sipped their tea in silence until Daisy spoke again. "I suppose you and I have the same problem—in reverse. As Alexander may have told you, I defied my family's wishes when I married my American soldier. But I never regretted a moment of the life we shared—brief though it was. He died much too young, but he left such lovely memories."

She rose abruptly and left the sitting area, returning with a photograph in a gilded frame. "This is my Joseph. That photo was taken on our weekend honeymoon. Alexander is the image of his father at that age, don't you think?"

Natalie took the picture to examine it more closely. A slender young woman laughing up into the face of a handsome young man—light-haired, with dark eyes glinting in the sunlight reflecting off a famous London landmark—Big Ben! She'd seen a duplicate of that picture—in the bedroom Alex had occupied at the inn.

The "other woman" in Alex's life was his own mother!

~⌒⌒~

There was but one thing on Natalie's mind. Finding Alex.

The day was beginning to wane, and she could only pray that during their separation, Alex's feelings hadn't begun to do the same.

At Daisy's insistence, she was driven to Oxford in the family Bentley. But once they reached the city, she asked Jack to let her find her own way to the apartment. There was still so much to think through, that she would welcome some time to herself.

Oxford was a magical place, as much because Alex grew to manhood there because of its antiquity, its ivy-covered buildings, its tall spires, its sense of history. Passing some side streets, she could hear the music from the pubs, spilling out into the street. Somewhere on one of those venerable byways was the Eagle and Child, the place where Alex had met with his friends to discuss politics, literature, the issues of the day. Might even be renewing old ties at this very moment. The thought sent her heart racing.

Renewing old ties . . . it's what she wanted more than anything else. To find Alex and recapture the love they had shared . . . if she hadn't lost him with her stubborn insistence on "sorting things out."

She recalled what Alex had laughingly said on the flight over. "When you visit Oxford, don't let those hallowed halls, the lofty atmosphere of academia intimidate you. We have our fair share of learned idiots on this side of the Atlantic as well. Just remember, love, you're a smart gal."

"A techno-geek," she'd replied, putting herself down. "Hardly in your league."

He'd squeezed her hand. "That's why we're so good together, love. The arts—and the sciences—a perfect complement."

Down Banbury Road she walked, past Wycliffe Hall and a large park with early-summer fields in bloom. Almost in the center of town, she came upon the Gothic stone monument to Latimer and Ridley, England's martyrs of the faith.

Ten minutes later, she turned onto the High Street. There it was—the building Daisy had described. Natalie would have recognized it anywhere. The darling little restaurant already a-bustle with the evening supper rush. The planters spilling their bright blooms. The hanging baskets.

A blond-haired man was just coming out of a small door to the side . . . the one obviously leading to an upstairs flat.

She opened her mouth to speak . . . and closed it.

Alex was in a hurry. She picked up her pace and followed him. Ten steps behind.

He turned off the sidewalk and entered Christ's Church College, one of Oxford's most illustrious institutions, through the arched opening. Around the great courtyard he marched, purpose weighing each heavy footstep. It was all Natalie could do to keep up with him.

Before long, he disappeared into the darkness of a portico leading to the college chapel. It was more than a chapel really, she learned. It was a small cathedral, once a see for the Bishopric of Oxford.

By the time she entered the hushed building, Alex was already seated in the choir loft of the church. The stained glass window winked softly in the dying light of day, catching the glow of the candles lit near the altar. Indeed, in the glint of the flames, his bowed head shone, and she wondered, had he been born centuries earlier, if he might not have looked much like this—a young knight spending the night in prayer before the dubbing ceremony.

All women prayed for a knight in shining armor. . . .

And though Sir Alex wore no armor, his honor was untarnished, his commitment strong, and his love for her deep and true. He was her knight. Her knight in tweed and striped ties.

The thought brought a chuckle that echoed against the polished wood and stone walls.

He stood and turned in one fluid motion. "Natalie? Is that you?"

She flew down the aisle to meet him, arms outstretched. "Can you forgive me? For doubting you? For thinking the worst?"

"I wasn't sure you'd come . . . I was asking—" he choked out, holding her tightly to him.

"I've been asking Him, too, the whole way over here . . . asking God to let me find you—let me love you. Asking Him to let *you* still love *me*. . . ."

"I can't believe you've come. It was wrong of me to hide myself from you—so many things. . . ."

"It's all right," she shushed him. "I understand . . . everything. I love you, Alex . . . or Sir Alex . . . or whatever you're called. It doesn't really matter because I know who you *are*."

"I'm the man who loves you desperately, Natalie St. John. Believe that if you believe nothing else."

"I won't doubt you again. Never again."

"And I'll hide nothing else." He led her to a pew, took her hands in his, and began to pray. For guidance . . . for direction . . . but most of all, Alex thanked God for giving them to each other.

In this man, Natalie knew she was supremely blessed.

⌒

Lost in their love and their plans for the future, Alex and Natalie were oblivious to the other lovers who littered the Cherwell in their own punts—the small, narrow boats that dated back to another civilization. They passed a young man serenading his ladylove with a flute, the plaintive music calling up visions of medieval couples.

Finding a more remote section of the river where their boat could drift aimlessly, Alex pulled the pole into the punt and dropped down beside Natalie.

"Let's not have a long engagement, Nats." His caress on her cheek was sure, but tender.

She placed her hand over his. "We're both a little too old for the traditional one-year betrothal, aren't we?"

"I don't think I could wait that long to make you mine."

Natalie blushed, grateful for the cover of darkness. "Have you . . . I mean, are you . . . ?"

"A virgin? Though my chums might laugh, I must admit I am, though I've been tempted." There was a pause. "And you?"

She nodded. "Can you believe the two of us? In this day? To be honest, I'd given up hope of finding a pure man."

Alex gave a wry look. "At my age, it isn't something one publicizes." He leaned over and dropped a kiss on her nose.

"Personally, I think it's wonderful. Obviously, it was a decision you made, and you stuck with it."

"I like to give God the credit . . . and my parents. They waited, as well, and that legacy was handed down to me and my sister. Their sterling example never gave me permission to live for the moment."

"I've somehow felt God's hand on me in that area, too, protecting me, sheltering me."

"Sheltering, yes. That's it. But not for long," he said, anticipation in his tone. "'Marriage is honorable'. . . ." The remainder of the quotation from the Bible drifted on the light breeze.

Natalie squeezed his hand, unaccustomed to the feelings of passion he aroused in her. The thought of Alex someday sharing her bed, loving her as only a devoted husband can. A pure love— their bodies following in the union their hearts and souls had already made.

Though the thought of it was a little overwhelming, she'd done her share of daydreaming. And now, the deeper her love grew for Alex, the more she desired its ultimate fulfillment.

"Have you thought when and where the wedding should be?" he asked.

She gazed up into the star-strewn sky at the moon—the same moon that was shining over Pleasant Valley. "Well, it seems that those we care about most are neatly divided by the Atlantic Ocean."

"But our parents—at least my mum and your father—are over here. And we're not getting any younger."

"Are you saying we should get married here—in England?"

"The sooner—the better, in my opinion."

The moon hovered—full-blown—tracing silvery paths of light across the water. "A large affair or a small one?"

"Small, I think. Do you agree? Although I know how much you women love all the pomp and pageantry of a wedding. . . ."

"Not after Tika's." Natalie laughed softly. "I think I'd much prefer to be married as simply as possible . . . in your mother's garden—among her lilies."

"She'd like that."

There was a long pause as Natalie trailed her hand in the water. "Do you think my father will come?" she asked in a small voice.

Alex turned an adoring look on her. "We'll have to wait and see, of course. But unless I miss my guess, he'll be pleased to give his daughter's hand in marriage . . . to a fellow professor—" he blinked, taking the plunge—"and part owner of PluraNet!"

"What?!" Natalie exclaimed.

Five minutes later, upon hearing Alex's explanation, Natalie's laugh rang out over the river.

"Better you than me, sweetheart." She kissed his cheek. "Better you than me."

FROM: Daisy Elbert, daylily@ukonline.com
DATE: Monday, June 12
TO: Lucinda Luckadoo
SUBJECT: This is really from Nat!

Your fondest prayers have been answered, Lu! No, I haven't met my father yet, but after a false start—about which I'll tell you when I get home—Alex popped the question.

And I said yes! Right there in the middle of Stonehenge—at sunrise. Jeanine Beaumont never wrote a scene like that in one of her books!

You should see the emerald Alex gave me. Even Tika would be impressed with this little bauble. We're getting married—here—in two weeks. Wish you guys could all be with us to celebrate, but I can see your approving nod, Lu. "No use waitin' around, I always say."

Oh, Lu, as much fun as I'm having, I do miss you, but you can understand that my trip home will have to be delayed. So . . . could you take care of the inn until summer's end, and Alex and I can come home together? I know . . . you ran things long before I ever got there! <g>

I have so much to tell you. We always speculated that Alex wasn't all he seemed, but never in our wildest dreams could we have guessed the real truth. You're wanting to know what he's been up to? Well, I'm going to play the brat and keep you and the others guessing for just a while longer. Promise to write again in a few days with all the gory details.

Tomorrow I go to see my father. Would you all be praying? As you might imagine, my stomach is in knots. But God is faithful. I keep having to learn that lesson over and over, it seems.

Much love to you and Oren—Jonah and Tika, too. And tell Oren I'm taking lots of pictures of gardens over here.

Nat

Twenty-Seven

*L*ady Bettina's chauffeur dropped Alex off at Worchester College the next morning, and then drove Natalie on to Bath. "It will be all right, love. I'll be praying all morning as I teach," Alex had said before taking his leave.

The drive seemed to go on forever, the lush English country-side lost on Natalie, who sat cocooned in the back seat of the Bentley, her hands trembling in her lap. Jack, a middle-aged man who still fought the battle of the blemishes, chatted amiably. Natalie responded automatically to his questions, but her nerves were like steel bands, slicing into her raw spirit. She had spent over two decades dreading this day, and small talk from a well meaning chauffeur couldn't possibly tackle her mounting apprehension.

The town of Bath appeared at last, and Natalie sat up straighter to view it rising from the river mist. Jack negotiated the car up the hilly, narrow lane, the stone walls of the city holding back the earth upon which kings had trod to bathe in the healing springs. He parked near the cathedral.

"I'll wait here, Miss." He climbed out and helped her from the car.

"Thanks, Jack. But I'm not sure how long I'll be."

He shrugged. "Oh, do take your time, Miss. Chauffeurs are even better at waiting than they are at driving!"

With a wave of her hand, she left him, her booted heels thudding against the pavement as she hurried across the street to buy a tourist map at a nearby kiosk. Needing a little whimsy in her life at that moment, Natalie chose the pop-up variety.

Crescent Circle was not a far walk at all. Not far enough. Natalie had been hoping for more time to clear her head. More time to plan what she was going to say.

More time . . .

Just a little more time.

"Take it easy, Nat," she muttered to herself. "A journey of a thousand miles starts with one step. First, the Circle. If you can just locate the house, you'll have accomplished something."

Twenty-one years since she'd seen his face.

She'd given herself three weeks to go through with the reunion, and if she had to make the trip to Bath every day until then, so be it. But she'd come this far today. She might as well see where he lived.

Idly looking in the shop windows as she passed, she promised herself lunch at one of the pubs afterward. Armed with that small reward, she forced herself on toward Crescent Circle.

Her stomach felt queasy, and her head was achy. It was the same feeling she'd experienced in high school as she stood by the bulletin board waiting for the faculty advisor to post the list of those who had made the cheerleading squad. But this time, she wasn't part of a hopeful herd. She was alone, and remembering what it had been like to be left off the list, she wondered if she could ever bring herself to ring the doorbell.

Trying to appear nonchalant, Natalie walked around the Circle until she found her father's address. Then she planted herself in front of the tall, white townhouse, admiring the flowers cascading from freshly painted window boxes, running her hand along the wrought iron rail that flanked the steps leading up to the front door.

She bit her lip, determined not to cry.

The late June breeze brushed her cheek—like a kiss— reminding her of Alex's promise earlier this morning. He was probably praying for her at this very moment.

She crossed the lane to a public park directly across from George St. John's house, and sank down on a bench. It was a lovely little area, but spare. Some trees and green grass. No flowers. Just a spot of nature, unadorned, in a circle of asphalt. The only roses she found were upon the cheeks of those nearby. It was the people she noticed around her—rosy-cheeked and blessed with the creamy complexion she'd only read about.

There was a couple, kissing a bit too heartily for a public place. An older woman crooning to an infant in a pram—her grandchild perhaps. A vagrant, smoking an old cigarette butt. Two kids kicking around a very grimy soccer ball.

No longer able to avoid thinking of the encounter, she stared at the house across the street. Tried some far-fetched mental exercise to draw her father out of doors. Thought of the happy times they'd shared. The way he called her his guardian angel. " 'Cause you're always looking out for the old man." No use.

A shadow slanted across her legs.

"Hello there!" called out a rich, warm voice. It was a yellow voice. The kind of voice the sun would use if the sun could talk.

Natalie shielded her eyes against the glaring daylight, but he was still little more than a silhouette. "Hi," she answered, a little wary of this stranger, and grateful for the townspeople nearby.

"American, are you?"

"It's that obvious?"

"Lived in the States for a while myself. Can always spot you Yanks."

His broad mouth twisted into a smile. His skin, tanned from some tropical holiday, no doubt, was bronzed, and his blue eyes twinkled into hers. On his head was a patch of white hair, cropped close, almost Nero-style. He resembled a slightly paunchy Roman senator. She let out a little sigh. Harmless.

Natalie's stomach did a somersault. Could this be . . . ? She had to know. "Is Bath your birthplace?"

"Not a'tall. Moved here from Leeds. Mind if I have a seat next to you there on the grass? Greta, my wife—always telling me I ought to get my exercise, but I believe a friendly chat does as much for the heart as a brisk walk!"

Natalie patted the ground next to her. "I can't argue with that." She wanted—badly—to ask his name.

"You're from . . . ?"

"Virginia. And where did you live while you were there?"

"Maryland. Don't miss the place so much as the people. But England is my home, and England is where I belong."

Natalie felt a stab of disappointment. George St. John had never lived in Maryland. "This is my first visit, but I hope it won't be my last. I love it here."

"Your father lives in Bath, you say?"

She gestured toward the townhouse. "He lives there."

"So *you're* George St. John's daughter."

"Yes." It was the toughest, most heart-wrenching confession she'd ever made.

"George's neighbor at your service. Shared many a pint together in the good old days. The old boy's been away in Scotland for a fortnight, but when he hears you're in town, he'll be thrilled."

"Would you have any idea when he's expected back?"

"Not sure. But Greta knows. Taking care of the dog, she is. Let's walk over and ask. By the way, Clive McSlarrow here."

"Natalie St. John." She risked a smile, not at all sure about the turn this whole episode was taking. But since her father wasn't home, she didn't see any harm in meeting his neighbors.

"Oh, you're the spittin' image of old George!" Greta cackled when she saw Natalie, and gathered her into a neck lock that left her breathless. "'E'll be tickled pink when 'e finds out you've come to see 'im. All those phone calls. . . . " she clucked. "There were times I thought 'is 'eart would break."

"Always looking at the bright side of things, though." Clive was doing his best to keep the conversation on a positive note, Natalie concluded. "Many's the time he's said, 'Someday, Clive, someday she'll let me explain.'"

"Explain?" Natalie was instantly on the alert. "Explain what?"

Clive and Greta looked at each other, and the dumpling of a woman shook her head. "Why, that it wasn't 'is fault you lost touch for so long."

"It wasn't his fault?" Natalie echoed dully.

"Not a'tall. Your mother kidnapped you, dearie."

⌒⌒∽

Natalie couldn't wait to get back to Rosemeade Hall. Finding Jack where he'd parked the Bentley, she woke him with a startling, "Let's get going!"

He jumped to his feet, got out and opened her door, straightening his cap and clearing his throat, evidently embarrassed to have been caught napping on the job.

Ninety minutes later, she burst into the drawing room where Daisy and Alex were having afternoon tea.

"Oh, there you are. You made it back in time for your daily sugar high, love." Alex drew her into his arms and gave her a quick kiss. "I've only just gotten home myself."

Without waiting to be served, Natalie launched into a recital of the incredible events of the day, ending with, "I still can't believe what Mrs. McSlarrow said!" She ran her fingers through her mass of curls in a nervous gesture. "When I asked her to tell me more, all she could say was that two years after the divorce, my mother moved us off without any forwarding address. She said my father rarely mentions it. But I recall it was around that time that we moved in with my grandfather—Mom's dad. He bought her a house a few months later, and all our bills were in his name. I just assumed that was normal under the circumstances."

"You must be completely thrown by all this, my dear," Daisy Elbert spoke with true compassion.

"There are still so many questions. . . . When I think that all these years . . . all the bitterness and resentment I've held against the geologist . . . my *father*. . . ." Unable to say more, she fled into the garden. But even the fragrance of the lilies and the soft moonglow were little comfort. In fact, they were mute reminders of a funeral.

Alex joined her shortly afterward.

She was weak with relief. He always seemed to know when she needed him most.

"Let's drive up to Scotland this weekend." His hand, finding hers, was so real, so warm. "Enough water has passed under the bridge, Natalie."

She sighed. "I suppose so. No more stalling. No more waiting for the phone to ring."

"Good, then. I'll make all the arrangements. Mrs. McSlarrow said your father's in Edinburgh?"

"Lecturing at the University." She leaned into him, drawing strength from his solidity. "What would I do without you?"

He let her cry . . . until all her tears were spent.

The next four days were pure torment.

Usually low-key and laid-back, Natalie was stunned by the maelstrom of emotion churning inside—disbelief, indignation, then mounting rage . . . only to be followed by guilt. Had her mother been alive, Natalie would have been tempted to tell her off for blasting so many lives to bits.

What had her parents been thinking all those years ago?

"Things aren't always as they seem, Nats." Alex did his best to encourage her on the long drive to Edinburgh. "Your mother must have had her reasons. Unfortunately, you'll probably never know what they were."

Natalie wasn't convinced. "But I *have* to know . . . at least, I have to try to find out." She puffed out a sigh. "Granddad died when I was seventeen, so I won't find any help there. . . ."

"You father may have some answers. He's been trying to communicate with you for years, you know."

She didn't need *that* reminder right now. But she knew Alex was only attempting to distract her when he steered the conversation to another topic. "What does he look like?"

"Dad?" She shrugged. "I don't really know any more. As a young man, he had my coloring. The red hair, the fair skin. And he smiled a lot." She turned to look out the window at the passing countryside—sheep grazing contentedly between the hedgerows. "I thought he was the handsomest man alive. And according to my mother, so did the women. They were always falling at his feet . . . and he was right there to catch them."

"Some men have all the luck," Alex observed dryly.

Natalie glanced over at him, her suspicions aroused, and hating herself for it. "And what is that supposed to mean?"

He turned a dazzling smile in her direction. "Nothing to worry your pretty head about. I've never once been bothered by a student infatuation."

She didn't believe it for a minute. "Maybe because you were just too unassuming to notice."

"Remember me when I first came to the inn?"

Natalie couldn't help but laugh. "You *were* a tad tightly laced, weren't you?"

"I still am . . . in the classroom."

"But I was attracted to you, tight laces and all." She leaned over to rest her head on his shoulder. "It's kind of funny, really—my mother and I both falling for college professors."

"Must be a genetic sort of thing," he observed.

"Must be. But I must admit I'm happy to hear your female students aren't fainting away at the sight of you." She frowned. "I couldn't live through that again."

There was a lull in the conversation, and Natalie watched the landscape change as they neared Edinburgh. The gentle roll of the hills were now craggy cliffs, looming above the barren moors.

"You know, Nats," Alex said at last, reaching for her hand, "you do understand that I'm in your life to stay. I like the idea of growing old with you."

"My head says yes, but my heart. . . ."

"Never fear, love. We have the rest of our lives to show you that forever is the only thing I ever had in mind."

Twenty-Eight

T he formidable castle, its iron-gray walls flooded by rays of afternoon sunlight, seemed to hover above the old city of Edinburgh like a dream. Castle Rock, the massive stone hill upon which the town first grew, loomed above the newer part of the city, a brooding watchman, reminding the modern inhabitants of the glory that once was Scotland. Arthur's Seat, another large hill, looked on from a short distance away, calling hikers to conquer its heights. Old and new, cultured and commoner merged easily in this "Athens of the North."

Walking hand in hand with Alex up "the Royal Mile," Natalie momentarily abandoned her troubles. Houses and buildings alike towered over the street that had been the site of many demonstrations throughout history. Its stones had both soaked up the blood of the Covenanters and felt the godly footsteps of John Knox on his daily walk from his home to St. Giles Cathedral.

Narrow lanes snaked off the main thoroughfare, and down these small alleyways, houses peeped over each other's shoulders like old men squinting in the darkness. Natalie could imagine what it must have been like in times past when the stench of squalor and filth—not flowers in bloom—filled the air.

"Have you been to Edinburgh before?" she asked Alex.

"Several times during my Oxford years," he reported. "For the Fringe Festival. Troupes from all over would come and put on plays in every sort of venue. They vied for audiences, handing out bulletins on the streets and causing a general ruckus. Great fun, actually. Something we'll have to do together someday." He squeezed her hand.

A clock hanging above a pub door announced the time, and Natalie sighed. "It will be at least an hour before my father's lecture is over, and my feet are killing me. Could we stop for tea somewhere?"

"Let's try that little place across the street." Alex cradled her elbow and led her to a charming tearoom, done in vibrant shades of red that reminded Natalie of a gypsy wagon. Tasseled shades perched whimsically upon old-fashioned lamps, and the floor was made of old wood, scarred and polished to a high sheen. The Victorian haphazardness was both cozy and welcoming.

When they'd placed their order with the waitress, a dark-haired beauty wearing at least twelve earrings of assorted shapes and sizes, Alex sat back in his chair and shot Natalie a level look. "And have you decided what you'll say when you see your father again?"

"I've been thinking about what you told me. I don't think I'll have to say anything. I'm simply going to walk up to him and wait for him to speak first."

The waitress returned with their tea, and Natalie took a sip. "But what if he's had it with me? When I think of all the times he's tried to reach me . . . and I hung up on him. . . ."

"He's your father, Nats."

"I know. But even fathers have their limits. . . ."

Alex waited outside in the corridor while Natalie peered inside the lecture hall. She returned a minute later, beaming.

"Oh, Alex, you should see him! He's a lot taller than I remember, and he has this mane of white hair." She splayed her fingers. "Magnificent white hair."

He smiled at her enthusiasm. "I heard the audience laughing. They're receiving him well."

"He's making his closing remarks now. I'll wait at the back of the room until he's through talking to the stragglers. Then I'll go up and—"

"And?" He waited, wanting to be sure how she felt, how he could best support and comfort her.

"I guess I don't really know," she admitted. "I suppose I'll just let things take their natural course." Standing on tiptoe, she brushed a kiss across his cheek. "Thanks for understanding that I need to do this alone. But I'll be right back to introduce him to you."

Alex could see the anticipation in the spring of her step as she turned to go, the way her hair bounced around her shoulders.

Then, noticing the lingering apprehension in her eyes, he detained her with a hand on her arm. "It will be all right, Natalie. How could he help but love you?"

Natalie felt as if she'd been slapped in the face.

He didn't recognize her at all. She stood there for several seconds, smiling like an idiot, until he finally said condescendingly, "May I help you, young lady?"

"Well, yes, Professor," she stammered, having not a clue as to what to say next. "I . . . ."

Several agonizing seconds passed.

He inspected his pocket watch and frowned. "If you'll excuse me, I have a supper engagement." A definite air of annoyance edged the once mellow tones of his voice. "If you've a question for me, or a comment on the lecture, Miss—"

"Natalie. My name is Natalie!" The words came out in a frantic rush. He *must* recognize her. . . .

Not even a blink. "I'm sorry, but I must be running along now."

Stunned, Natalie's mouth dropped open as he stepped around her. Then, in desperation, she grabbed the lapels of his jacket.

"For heaven's sake, Daddy, it's me—Natalie! Natalie St. John! Your daughter!"

Then, cool professional that she was, woman of the nineties, fiancée of a titled Englishman, she gave way to the little lost child within and buried her face in her hands.

"Did you say Natalie St. John?"

Her head snapped up. And although his voice seemed to come from a great distance, and she could see little through her tears, she nodded.

"Oh, dear, I do believe we've a case of mistaken identity here."

"Mistaken identity?" Natalie could hardly believe her ears.

"I'm not George St. John. He left town this morning—rather abruptly, as a matter of fact. Asked me to fill in for him."

Swiping at her wet cheeks with a tissue, she gathered what was left of her dignity. "Could you tell me where he might have gone?"

"Back to Bath, I believe. Said he wasn't feeling well . . . and that someone from America had come rather unexpectedly. Someone he hadn't seen in quite a long time."

Peering at her intently, he was about to say more when Natalie thanked him and hurried down the aisle of the great lecture hall and out into the hallway, her heels clicking a frenzied tatoo on the tiled floor. "Alex!" she cried, looking for him. "That man wasn't my father. He's not here. We have to find him!"

"But who . . . what . . . "

"Come on." She put her arm through his and dragged him down the corridor. "I'll tell you about it on the way back to Bath."

"Now? It's a good ten or twelve hours drive, love."

"I don't care how long it takes, Alex. I've got to find my father . . . before it's too late."

～⌒〜

The sturdy oak door barely shivered in its frame as Natalie rapped on the surface. At this hour, the breeze was chilly, and she pulled her jacket more snugly around her shoulders. But it wasn't the cold alone that caused her to pace the landing while she waited, as nervous as her cat Delilah.

A light went on in one of the upstairs windows.

This was it.

He should be coming any minute now. Even at seventy, he should still be in good condition if he were still traveling the lecture circuit. She took a moment to wonder if her father ever explored any volcanoes anymore, or climbed mountains as he had when he was younger.

The hall light went on. Then the outside light. Natalie shivered.

Soon. He'd be coming soon.

The geologist.

The man who'd left them.

Her father . . . *Daddy,* she could call him now . . . after all this time.

But when the door swung open, it was a woman who met Natalie's questioning gaze. A handsome woman, blinking out of slitted lids at this stranger on her doorstep.

"I'm so sorry to barge in on you like this—" Natalie began, wondering if she had the correct address, after all. Maybe this whole episode was a wild goose chase.

"Natalie?"

How had the woman known her name? "Yes . . . I—Is my father here?"

"I'm Charlotte St. John, George's wife. Quick!" The woman led her into the foyer. "The upstairs bedroom. He's very ill . . . and he's calling for you."

Natalie was not prepared for the sight that greeted her when she stepped into the bedroom. She hadn't expected the auburn-haired hero of her childhood dreams, of course. Time would have taken its toll. But this old man? Pale, gaunt, lying so still?

He was hooked up to some kind of machine beside the bed, and Natalie was immediately transported to her mother's sick-bed. The hospital room where she had died. . . .

Natalie sat down in the chair Charlotte pulled up for her. "Daddy, it's me . . . Natalie. Please don't leave me again."

The eyelids fluttered, and when her father opened his eyes, she could see that they were the same as she remembered. Blue as the skies over England on a clear day.

"Angel?" he said, his voice raspy and choked. "Is it really you?"

⁓

FROM: Daisy Elbert, daylily@ukonline.com
DATE: Friday, June 17
TO: Lucinda Luckadoo, pleasantinn@vanet.com
SUBJECT: The Grand Reunion

There's so much to tell you that I don't know where to begin. I've seen him. I've seen my father, and I'll never call him "the geologist" again! God is so kind to have given my father back to me, and just in time. For although the reunion was a happy one, I've sad news to report. Daddy doesn't have much longer to live. He's suffering from a terminal illness—polycystic kidney disease—and unless he receives a transplant soon, he'll be dead in several months. The doctors have already done all they can do short of surgery—dialysis, medications—and now they're waiting for a donor.

Charlotte, his wife for the past ten years and a great gal, says Daddy has had to drag himself from place to place, and when he started feeling dizzy and nauseous in Edinburgh recently, he was forced to cut his lecture circuit short. Now, he's in the hospital, fighting for his life.

Pray, Lu, and please ask everyone else to pray—Andy and Lori, Erin and Tyler. Call Renee, too. Although she never mentions it, I know she's a woman of prayer.

I couldn't bear to lose Daddy now. On the other hand, he knows the Lord—became a Christian about the time he met Charlotte—so I know that if he doesn't make it, we'll be together in heaven. No more separation. No more tears. Just worshipping the Father together forever!

In the meantime, there's Alex to consider, too. He's being so sweet and understanding about postponing the wedding and is willing to wait until . . .

But I can't think about that now. Please . . . just pray!

Nat

~◠

Natalie never expected to be back in London under such circumstances. But here she was, roaming the sterile halls of St. Bart's Hospital while her father slept, finding herself again and again in London's oldest church, St. Bartholomew the Great. Praying all the while.

Despite his illness, the connecting link between father and daughter had been sutured together as if by a fine surgeon's hands. Actually, it had been the Great Physician Himself who had done the job, Natalie thought, cutting away the bitterness and regret of a lifetime and grafting in forgiveness and love.

But would a donor be found before it was too late? People on both sides of the Atlantic were praying. Lu's return E-mail had been encouraging. The prayer chain at Trinity had been notified, not only on behalf of Natalie's father, but for Natalie herself. She could feel new strength as God answered those prayers.

~◠

It was a rainy Saturday morning near the end of July, but George St. John held on to life with the tenacity of a toddler about to lose his brand new bouncing ball to the neighborhood bully. Natalie, now renting out a furnished flat near Regent's park, sat with him each day—along with Charlotte, who never left his side—reading to him, watching television. And playing "Go Fish."

"To make up for all the times we missed, Angel." His smile was weak, but ever present.

"We'll have a long time to make up for that, Daddy." Natalie said with an optimism she didn't feel. "After all, you'll have to be around for the wedding. I need you there . . . to give me away."

His blue eyes misted over. "Give you away? How can I possibly do that, when I've only just found you again?"

⟨⟩

```
FROM:    Natalie St. John, natjohn@ukonline.com
DATE:    Monday, August 4
  TO:    Lucinda Luckadoo, pleasantinn@vanet.com
SUBJECT: Our prayers have been answered!
```

We've found a donor! All the tests have been run and I am a compatible match for my father's transplant. He refused at first, naturally. And Alex had a few reservations. But we know now that it's the right thing to do, and as soon as Daddy is strong enough for the surgery, I'll be minus one kidney.

How can I thank all my prayer partners—especially you, Lu?! God used you to start working on my shriveled-up heart long before I ever found my father again. That—and old Elva Jacks's letters.

So . . . it looks as if Daddy will be able to give me away, after all—a Christmas wedding—in Pleasant Valley? That is, if the surgery is successful.

Alex has decided not to go back to JMU this semester, after all. He's staying here in England—to look after Daddy and me. And, get this, Lu, he's landed another writing contract. But not for a romance series—for a thriller/adventure, with the pen name of Jack Ramsey!

By the way, give Tika and Jonah our congratulations! Lady Daisy is already knitting booties. She says babies are her weakness. . . .

Much love to you all,

Nat

**Christmas Night
Pleasant Valley Inn**

Snow was falling heavily outside, frosting the gardens in white.

Lu pulled out a hankie. No flies to swat at this wedding. Might as well use it brush away the tears.

"I, Natalie, take you, Alex, to be my wedded husband. . . ."

The traditional vows always made Lu cry. "To have and to hold, to love and to cherish . . . in sickness and in health . . . forsaking all others as long as we both shall live. . . ."

It was all so *sweet*. And to think how far this young woman—all decked out like English royalty in her wedding finery—had come. She'd been so lonely. Now she was surrounded by a whole parlor-full of people who loved her.

Lu squeezed Oren's hand and glanced around at the others assembled here—all dressed up for a Christmas wedding in front of a merry fire.

There was George St. John—Lu still thought of him as "the geologist"—looking a little green around the gills from his surgery. When he'd kissed his daughter after giving her away, he'd tucked a tiny silver angel in her hand, then dabbed at her tears with a handkerchief her soon-to-be mother-in-law slipped him on the sly. A man who'd do somethin' like that couldn't be all bad.

There was that nice young man, Andy Gatto, and his new wife—standin' as close as a pair of bookends. Andy had told Lu he was tickled to death with the way things had turned out for his old friend Natalie. Said she deserved true happiness—same as he'd found with Lori.

Renee and Tommy Alcott looked like they might be considerin' honeymoon number three—she'd have to encourage them to book a cottage early—before the summer rush.

Tika, actually plump for the first time ever with her advancing pregnancy, was standing near the piano where Jonah was softly playing, ready to cue Erin Higgenbotham for her solo.

Erin Higgenbotham had had a little trouble gettin' through her number, but she'd made it, and Reverend Tyler had gotten on with the ceremony without another hitch.

Old Silas—from his wicker rocker, pulled into the parlor for the occasion—was grinning like a Cheshire cat, no doubt believin' he had personally engineered this whole affair.

And speaking of cats, Delilah and Merriwether were curled up together like old friends beneath the rainbow of lights on the Christmas tree where the staff had gathered last night to open presents and eat Tika's hazelnut torte.

When Natalie had presented her gift to them—the keys to the inn itself and a deed made out in all four names—Lu and Oren Luckadoo, Tamika and Jonah Chord—you could have knocked Lu over with a feather. So the inn would still be home for the rest of her life!

Somehow Nattie had changed all of them, as only Nattie could. They'd learned to love a little stronger, laugh a little longer, give a little more. And maybe they'd taught her a thing or two—about forgivin' and letting bygones be bygones.

As the rush of memories flew through her head, Lu, feeling younger than she had in years, beamed through her tears.

"And now may I present Mr. and Mrs. Alexander Phineas Elbert—Sir Alex and Lady Natalie," proclaimed Tyler.

Sir Alex? *Lady* Natalie?

Well, lah-de-dah!

Epilogue

FROM: Natalie Elbert, nselbert@ukonline.com
DATE: February 2, 11:21 A.M.
TO: Andrew Gatto, sosueme@aol.com
SUBJECT: You're never going to believe this!

The honeymoon was a dream come true! When we got to the airport, and Alex told me we were going to Egypt and Israel, I thought he was joking. But when we climbed to the top of the pyramid of Cheops and he gave me my wedding present, I knew I'd married a real card.

PluraNet!

He gave me back PluraNet!

Can you believe that man? So I'm stuck with it again. Care to help me find a buyer?

Nat

FROM: Andrew Gatto, sosueme@aol.com
DATE: February 3, 1:09 P.M.
TO: Natalie Elbert, nselbert@ukonline.com
SUBJECT: RE: You're never going to believe this!

You're on your own, kid!

Andy

Dear Reader,

We would appreciate hearing from you regarding this Harvest House fiction book. It will enable us to continue to give you the best in Christian publishing.

1. What most influenced you to purchase *The Moment I Saw You?*
   - ❏ Author
   - ❏ Subject matter
   - ❏ Backcover copy
   - ❏ Recommendations
   - ❏ Cover/Title
   - ❏ Other_____

2. Where did you purchase this book?
   - ❏ Christian bookstore
   - ❏ General bookstore
   - ❏ Department store
   - ❏ Grocery store
   - ❏ Other_____

3. Your overall rating of this book?
   - ❏ Excellent ❏ Very good ❏ Good ❏ Fair ❏ Poor

4. How likely would you be to purchase other books by this author?
   - ❏ Very likely ❏ Not very likely ❏ Somewhat likely ❏ Not at all

5. What types of books most interest you? (Check all that apply.)
   - ❏ Women's Books
   - ❏ Marriage Books
   - ❏ Current Issues
   - ❏ Christian Living
   - ❏ Bible Studies
   - ❏ Fiction
   - ❏ Biographies
   - ❏ Children's Books
   - ❏ Youth Books
   - ❏ Other_____

6. Please check the box next to your age group.
   - ❏ Under 18 ❏ 18-24 ❏ 25-34 ❏ 35-44 ❏ 45-54 ❏ 55 and over

Mail to: Editorial Director
Harvest House Publishers
1075 Arrowsmith
Eugene, OR 97402

Name _____

Address _____

State _____ Zip _____

Thank you for helping us to help you in future publications!